the negotiator

AVERY FLYNN

Entangled Publishing, LLC
2614 South Timberline Road
Suite 109
Fort Collins, CO 80525
Visit our website at www.entangledpublishing.com.

AMARA is an imprint of Entangled Publishing, LLC.

Edited by Liz Pelletier
Cover design by Erin Dameron-Hill
Cover art from Shutterstock

ebook ISBN 978-1-63375-958-9
MMP ISBN 978-1-64063-331-5

Manufactured in the United States of America

First Edition April 2017

To my mom, Carol, because we all become our mothers in the end. Also, because I've looked at her in that tone of voice too many times to still be alive and yet here I am—proof that a mother's love can be infinite, even if her patience is not.

Chapter One

"**I**'m going to kill you, Hudson. Slowly. With a spoon."

Sawyer Carlyle paced the five feet between his desk and the seating area in his office at the top floor of Carlyle Tower. Usually his office was his sanctuary with its cool, crisp, modern furniture and floor-to-ceiling windows that overlooked Harbor City, but today it was his hiding place.

When his executive secretary Amara Grant had buzzed him about the first mystery job candidate, he'd been confused. By the time the tenth had arrived, he knew his brother had set him up.

"You can't kill me. And you'd better stop quoting shit movies or I'll tell the world you enjoy chick flicks," Hudson said, his laughter coming through loud and clear on the speaker phone. "Anyway, you need me. I'm the only person who can distract Mom from her mission."

Oh yes. Operation Marry Sawyer Off. Helene Carlyle had come out of a three-year mourning period for their father with one thing—and *only* one thing—on her mind: finding the perfect wife for her eldest son. How Hudson had managed to miss out on all the fun was beyond Sawyer, but Mom had doubled down on her firstborn. So far all of the candidates had been slightly different versions of the same person. Old money. No personality. Always said the right things and played the Harbor City high society game. Plus, each of them had that strained, slightly pained look of someone forever holding in a fart. It was all the fake shit that Sawyer really didn't have time for if he was going to keep Carlyle Enterprises growing while the international construction boom imploded.

He stopped in front of his desk, the ridiculous ad Hudson had sent out everywhere was open on his computer screen.

WANTED: PERSONAL BUFFER

Often snarly, workaholic, demanding executive seeks short-term "buffer" from annoying outside distractions AKA people. Free spirits with personal boundary issues, excessive quirks, or general squeamishness need not apply. 24/7 avail req'd. Salary negotiable. Confidentiality required.

Snarly. Workaholic. Demanding. So what? He was who he was and he wasn't about to apologize for it.

Sawyer drummed his fingers on the top of his desk, empty of a single item except his computer monitor, wireless mouse, and the phone. "This damn ad is a joke."

"Still, you have an entire anteroom full of candidates I've already pre-screened to not cry at your first snarl, so stop your bitching."

Sawyer wasn't "grumpy." He was *busy*. Did no one understand the difference?

He pivoted and stared out the windows at the expansive view. He could point out the Carlyle Enterprises' high-rises with barely a glance. It was the same in cities all over the globe. Their father, Michael, had made his mark, and now it was up to Sawyer not to tarnish the old man's memory. In today's market that was no easy feat, and it hadn't been one he'd expected to take on quite so soon.

At thirty-two, he was the youngest Carlyle to ever head the family business founded four generations before. He'd trade that distinction for having his dad back in a heartbeat. "I never asked for this."

"Actually, you did," Hudson said, misunderstanding

Sawyer's declaration. "I believe it was after Mom cornered you with three potential wives at the museum fundraiser. And as all good little brothers should do in such a situation, I helped you escape, got you drunk, and then let you pour out your soul to me. *You're* the one who told me you needed a buffer from Mom."

The joke about a personal buffer had been funnier when Sawyer had been holding a half-empty bottle of Scotch.

"So after years of ignoring everything your big brother has ever told you in your entire life, you picked *this* as the one thing to pay attention to?" Sawyer shoved his fingers through his thick hair and turned back to face the phone as if Hudson could see his scowl. "All I wanted was for you to run interference and steer some of the candidates away from me and into your bed."

"Since ninety-nine percent of everything that comes out of your mouth is all about the company, the fact that I ignore most of what you say shouldn't be a shock. Anyway, I thought the ad was pretty damn funny."

"You would." His brother, the comedian.

"So what are you going to do?"

Sawyer glanced up at the closed double doors, beyond which lay Amara's domain of the outer office. "Send them home."

"Without even considering the idea of having your own buffer?" Hudson asked. "Come on. You and I both know what you'd really like is to not have to do anything but focus on the love of your life: Carlyle Enterprises."

A buffer. It was idiotic. He scared off most people just fine on his own. Well, everyone but their mother. She wasn't about to get mowed over by him or thrown off her game by his surly attitude. Helene Carlyle was every bit as used to getting her way as he was. It made for some interesting Thanksgiving dinners.

"I should make you be the one to tell the people out there that there's no job. It would serve you right."

"No such luck, big brother. I'm at the cabin."

Sawyer should have known. Hudson preferred his private cabin—which no one had ever been invited to visit— over everything. He may have an office in Carlyle Towers, but that didn't mean he used it any more than he had to. "It's a Thursday."

"Unlike you," Hudson said with a lazy drawl, "I know when to take a break and enjoy all the beauty the world has to offer."

"What's her name this time?"

"Who says there's only one?"

Sawyer laughed despite himself. His brother was set in his ways just as much as Sawyer was. "You're hopeless."

"No, I just know how to take time to smell the roses."

"That's a bad habit you'll have to give up one of these days."

"Spoken like a man who can't see the trees for the forest."

"That's supposed to go the other way around."

"Not in your case."

So what if he was a big-picture man? That big picture wasn't just the best view, it was the only view that mattered. "Hudson, you're a pain in my ass."

"Right back at you. Good luck tonight."

An itchy dread about something he almost remembered scratched the back of his neck. He swiped right on his monitor and his calendar popped up. Below the notes about the Singapore deal he was in negotiation about was a notation that the Harbor City General Gala was at eight. They were naming the hospital's new heart center after his dad. The cardiologists and surgeons had done everything they could to help save Michael Carlyle, but they hadn't been able to. They were amazing physicians and nurses, and they deserved the state-of-the-art equipment and space.

"Damn," he said, ignoring the tightness that squeezed his chest whenever he thought about his dad. "I'd blocked it out of my mind."

"Don't worry about bringing a date," Hudson teased. "I'm sure Mom will have two or three all lined up for you there."

With that final dig, his brother hung up and the sound of the dial tone filled Sawyer's office, bouncing off the unadorned metal and glass surfaces. He hit the end call button and took another look out at the city at his feet before crossing over to the door to do what needed to be done—tell everyone to go home because there was no job.

• • •

Clover Lee was in the wrong place. She had to be.

The office at the top of Carlyle Tower was filled with the kind of huge guys in dark suits who either protected you from the bad guy's muscle men or actually *were* the bad guy's muscle men. Their gazes had slid toward her as soon as she'd stepped off the elevator, completed a quick up and down threat assessment, and then turned away, letting identical blank looks slide into place.

Remember why you're here, girl.

Because every day was an adventure and most poor suckers were stuck on the couch with a bag of plain chips—but not her. Adventure. Romance. New places. Interesting people. Fun. Thrills. Chills. Beauty. Agony. Ecstasy. Lust. Love… Well, not that last one—because who wants to settle down?—but give her a big old double order of the rest with extra-large fries on the side. So when she'd spotted that weird ad for a personal buffer, it was just the thing to catch her attention—and fund her next adventure.

Yes. That was *exactly* why she was here. Lifting her chin, she pressed forward into the sea of testosterone and intimidation to an African-American woman in a conservative black suit sitting at the only desk in the room. She didn't even bother to look up when Clover stopped in front of her desk. The nameplate on the desk read Amara Grant, Executive Assistant.

"Good morning, Ms. Grant. I'm here for the buffer interview."

"Another one?" The woman sighed, but her long fingers never missed a beat as they flew across her keyboard. "Okay, take a seat if you can find one." She motioned with her chin toward the general area of the crowded office.

Someone must have brought in extra chairs to accommodate all the warm bodies. It was the best explanation Clover could come up with for the mishmash of sturdy leather club seats and ordinary rolling office chairs lining the walls. The only available option for Clover was a chair with a purple seat squeezed between two men who each looked like they could bench press a bus.

In for a penny, in for a squashed seat.

She crossed over to the empty chair. "Excuse me," she said to the two men.

The men made noncommittal grunts but shifted over.

Quickly sitting down, she clutched her purse to her lap and took in a deep breath, while she scoped out the competition. The suits and hair color may vary from man to man, but there was a sense of sameness radiating from them—a uniform toughness. If she was trying to sneak her way past any of them to annoy Sawyer Carlyle, they'd beat her back like a fly.

While that was an awesome talent to have, it wasn't in Clover's arsenal. The initial interview with Hudson Carlyle had assured her the position was not one requiring brawn. In fact, he'd suggested a clever mind was best suited for this job. Keeping that in mind, she tried to come up with something that would make her stand out for more than just being a five-foot-five chick with a Hello Kitty tattoo on her ass. God knew her resume wasn't going to do it.

She'd done time as a snake milker—don't ask; smiled for pictures as a paid bridesmaid—bridezillas, she'd known a few; bellied up to the table as a dog food taster—think stale crackers with a funky aftertaste; learned the true benefit of good arch support as a professional line stander—always in the rain or the cold or the blazing heat; and distilled the mysteries of the universe as a fortune cookie writer. Clover had done it all to pay the bills, have some excellent adventures, and stay as far away from the small town of Sparksville as possible. However, up until a few days ago, she'd never even *heard* of a personal buffer.

Ideas swarmed to the forefront. She could play up her adventures as being international experiences in non-familiar surroundings. She worked well with others. She was loyal, determined and—she took a look around at the men in black, the executive secretary who looked like she pitied the fool who'd even try to fuck up her day, and the huge double doors opposite the elevator that were shut tight—totally out of her depth.

Anxiety unleashed an invisible hand that squeezed her lungs and made it hard to take in a full breath. Shit. Nothing good ever happened when she got nervous. That's when her mouth went into verbal vomit mode. She closed her eyes and took in another deep breath.

If anyone is out there listening, please let me just get through this interview. I really need this job. The clock is ticking on Australia.

The click of a door opening snapped Clover out of her mini-panic attack, and she opened her eyes.

Sawyer Carlyle stood in the middle of the open doorway to his office. Her Google image search hadn't done the man justice.

The whole package was...wow. He was over six feet tall

and muscular, enough so that the other men in the room didn't look quite as intimidating. Or maybe it was the way he held himself—so sure and borderline cocky—that made everyone else fade a little bit into the background. The sexy package was completed by a dark pair of designer glasses, slightly overly long brown hair that he brushed to the side, and a dimple right in the middle of his chin. He looked over the room, his gaze went past her and then jerked to a stop before rewinding and dropping down the necessary foot from the mountains sitting on either side to her face. One of his dark eyebrows went up over the black frame of his glasses. The corner of his full mouth curled up for a fraction of a second before melting back into a firm, straight line. His focus moved on to the man on her left and kept going.

The heat coiling in her stomach lingered long enough to practically shout: you're in danger girl! before cooling off once the intensity of his gaze had passed her by.

"Gentlemen." Sawyer paused, his attention zipping back to her. "And lady. It seems there's been some confusion—"

The elevator *whooshed* open at that moment, and a tall woman in her late fifties walked out as regal as any queen flanked by two women perfect enough to be on the cover of a fashion magazine. Suddenly, the elastic hair tie looped around the button of Clover's borrowed interview pants, giving them an extra inch of breathing room, became even more pathetic. One of the tall, lithe model-types stood inside the open doors, blocking them from closing. The other sashayed out into the office with the older woman.

"Sawyer, you're not putting me off again," the obvious ring leader said, her cultured tone sounding of exclusive clubs and vacations in the Hamptons. "We have lunch scheduled at Filipe's. I'm sure whatever you have planned can wait. You can't take over the world on an empty stomach, after all."

He sighed. "Lunch is not in my schedule."

The woman didn't give an inch. "I won't take no for an answer."

Sawyer tapped his middle finger against his thumb as he dipped his chin and rolled his head from one shoulder to the other. It was obvious he didn't want to go but for whatever reason couldn't come right out and say it.

No one moved. The other buffer candidates didn't do anything.

This was it.

If Clover was going to stand out in a good way, she needed to do it now. She stood and took several steps toward the trio of women and pasted on her best don't-fuck-with-me-and-I-won't-fuck-with-you smile.

"Excuse me, ma'am, but it's obvious Mr. Carlyle is too much of a gentleman to say outright he's not interested in a foursome with you guys and"—she dropped her voice to a stage whisper—"to be totally honest, you seem a little too old for him."

The man in question let out something that sounded like an elephant snorting while giving birth. Not that she knew what that sound was like, but it was the best her brain came up with for translating the half-pained, half-surprised noise with a little bit of laughter mixed in. Pushing back the thought, she kept her attention on the older woman who'd turned her ice-cold glare toward Clover.

"So please let me be clear," Clover continued. "You don't build a company of Carlyle Enterprise's prestige by spending your days dallying with women more likely to cry over the loss of a nail than flooding in the Yangtze River, so shoo before I call security. Mr. Carlyle's schedule is jam-packed today, but do call ahead next time you want to 'do lunch.'"

"And who *exactly* do you think you are?" the other woman asked, each word enunciated with crisp, clinical disapproval.

"Just exactly who I am." She smiled with as much warmth as the other woman's voice. "Clover Lee."

The woman blinked, looked at Sawyer, and then turned her focus back to Clover. "Are you saying," the woman started, each word coming out slow and distinct as if she was pissed as hell but too classy to yell, "that my son would rather work than go have lunch with his mother?"

Son? *Son?* SON?!?

Oh shit.

This was why Clover shouldn't get anxious. Only bad things happened when she let her nerves get the best of her. She needed to say something. She needed to apologize. She needed to find a hole big enough to swallow her completely.

She couldn't get a single word out.

The woman's mouth—*Sawyer Carlyle's mother's mouth*—twisted up and her eyes narrowed, but her freezer-burn level stare moved away from Clover and onto her son. "Sawyer, this is not over."

Without another word, one of the most powerful women in Harbor City high society whirled around and joined the woman still holding open the elevator doors.

"Analisa, let's leave Sawyer and his...*person* to their 'jam-packed' schedule," she said.

The woman who'd walked into the office with Mrs. Carlyle gave Sawyer a sexy wink and then joined the other two. Maybe it was the woman's sky-high heels. Maybe it was just her natural gait. Whatever it was, the slow roll of her hips as she strolled back onto the elevator snagged the attention of everyone in the office, even Amara stopped typing long enough to look up and shake her head.

The quiet hum of panic-tinged white noise buzzed in Clover's ears as the elevator doors closed and took the trio of women down the sixty-three floors to the lobby. Heat beat at her cheeks. The agony of oh-hell-what-did-I-do-now was a brick in her stomach.

She turned to face Sawyer, who still stood in the middle of his open doors, staring at her as though she were an alien and he wasn't sure what to do with her. She really hoped he chose to send ET home instead of dissection or worse. "That was your mother?"

Wow. Ah-mazing conversational skills there, Clover.

Sawyer nodded and started toward her, his long legs eating up the space between them. "Uh-huh." His gaze was still firmly fixed on her, and his expression said it all. Dissection or worse.

She swallowed hard, the sound echoing in the office Clover now realized was intensely quiet. Even Amara had stopped typing and was staring at Clover like she was a bunny trapped in the corner and about to die.

"So I'm totally fired before I even start, right?" She offered a wobbly grin, but he didn't seem to get the joke. Who needed Australia? Surely the endangered Rock Wallabies that she would have been helping could save themselves. "Okay then, have a great life and good luck with the whole pissed-off-mom thing."

He stopped just out of arm's reach, his hazel eyes seemed softer up close and held a hint of curiosity behind his glasses as if she were a puzzle he was determined to solve. "Well, that's a new one."

"What? Gotten fired before they were hired?" She let out a strangled laugh. "Oh yeah. It's happened to me a bunch. There was this one time when I was applying at a weight loss call center when I told the woman on the phone that she was perfect just the way she was and the supervisor lost his—"

"No." He shook his head. "No one's ever gotten my mom to retreat."

"I'm sure you're exaggerating." She gulped and tightened her grip on her purse strap as she scurried backward, slapping her hand behind her in an effort to hit the elevator call button. "I'll be off then. Have fun picking out a much less mouthy buffer."

Finally, she made contact and pressed the heel of her hand against the button. Now was when she should have turned around, faced the closed elevator doors, and pretended that no one was behind her while she waited *for-ev-er* for the elevator to make its way back up to the top floor. But she couldn't. It wasn't that it would be rude—God knew she'd just proved her ability to fly right past rude and sail into verboten territory. It was because of *him*.

Sawyer Carlyle might be dressed in a suit, the cost of which would finance her adventure in Australia and about a dozen others, but that didn't mean he was civilized. Nope. Something in his intense hazel gaze promised other things, dangerous things, too-bad-to-be-good-but-I-don't-care things.

He reached her side in a few determined strides, but this time he didn't stop outside of touching distance. Instead, he slid his hand across the small of her back, sending a meteor shower of sparks across her skin, lighting her up from the inside out.

"Amara, please clear my calendar for the next hour." He marched forward, the force of his hand taking her with him, as he strode toward his office. "Gentlemen, thank you for your time, but I'm afraid the position has been filled."

Filled? Oh God, what had she done?

Chapter Two

Sawyer didn't know what to do next. It was an unusual feeling. Normally, he always had a plan—that was the benefit of being a big-picture kind of guy. If one approach didn't work, it didn't matter because as long as he reached his goal, how he got there didn't matter.

He flexed his hand as he walked around his desk and sat down, needing something to do with the hand that had rested on the small of her back so he wouldn't be tempted to touch her again. He wasn't a stranger to beautiful women, but the woman sitting in the guest chair scoping out his office wasn't someone he'd put in that category—at least not in that suit.

The jacket was boxy and ill-fitting. The pants pooled at her ankles as if they were meant to be worn with much less sensible shoes than the nip of a heel attached to her dull black pair. Her hair was a soft, golden blond that was straight and styled parted down the middle. Her makeup was minimal, a light pink lipstick and maybe a little something around the eyes. Those eyes, though. Big, brown, and laughing. At him? Maybe. Definitely at the situation. It was unusual to say the least.

He'd just hired a woman for a job that hadn't existed until a few minutes ago, and he didn't even know her name.

He grabbed ahold of that fact like it was a cold beer on a hot August night—the solution to all of life's uncertainty. "Let's start with your name."

She stood up from the guest chair and extended a hand over his desk. "Clover Lee."

On automatic pilot, he reached out and shook her hand.

There it was, that little zap of something extra again, and he promptly let go. "Clover?"

"Legally, it's Jane," she grimaced and sat back down, flexing her fingers as if she'd felt the shock, too. "But no one calls me that. My mom is very stuck in her boring small-town ways out in Sparksville. I mean our dog is named Spot, for God's sake—and not ironically. So I guess I should be glad to be just plain Jane and not—"

"Do you have any experience as a personal buffer… Miss Lee?" he broke in, sensing she could continue for days with tales of "boring" Sparksville.

"No, but I am a fast learner and have an extensive international background." She reached into her purse and pulled out a single sheet of paper and handed it to him.

Scanning the sheet, things began to fall into place. Not-a-plain-Jane Clover Lee had an obvious aversion to consistent employment.

She jumped from one temporary job to another almost as if each one was just an excuse to get to the next. She'd gone from weird odd jobs stateside to teaching English in Thailand or helping organize small business cooperatives in Ghana and then bounced back to the U.S. for another round of jobs he'd had no idea existed. Her resume couldn't be more unlike what was expected of the well-heeled Harbor City elite if she'd tried. That's what had thrown off his mom and probably him as well—she personified the unexpected. It might just be what he needed for something as ridiculous as a "personal buffer."

He set the resume aside, the single sheet breaking up the clean lines of his otherwise spotless desk. "What are your salary requirements?"

Her cheeks turned a soft shade of pink, but she didn't drop eye contact. "The other Mr. Carlyle spoke of a range, and I believe I'd be at the high end of that number. Ten thousand for six weeks of work, after that I'm gone."

He laughed—a rusty bark of a sound that made her eyes go wide. That he, by himself, was worth almost a billion and the company worth a hundred times that didn't factor into this. He had started out his life at Carlyle Enterprises negotiating with union bosses who were little more than mob henchmen before eventually moving on to brokering deals worth the GDP of small countries. Ten grand? It wasn't much, but that was never the point of talking money when putting together an agreement. Winning was. If he didn't have that, then that grand "big picture" vision started to waver, and he wasn't about to let that happen.

Relaxing against the back of his chair, he let his lips curl into a patronizing smile. "That's a lot of money."

"It's Harbor City." Her pointed chin went up an inch. "It's an expensive place, and this is a twenty-four hour, seven days a week demanding job—your ad said so."

Mark that as another reason to smack Hudson upside the head. "Why a month and a half?"

"I have a prior commitment," she said.

"Looking at your resume, it could be anything from a golf ball diver to a mattress tester." His cock gave a happy twitch at the mental image of her out of that hideous suit and spread out on his king-size bed. Why had his brain gone there? *Because it wasn't your brain thinking, dumbass.*

Her smile grew until she practically radiated sunshine. "I'm leaving for Australia."

"What's in Australia?" And why the hell did he want to know? If he kept getting distracted and couldn't come up with a plan to submarine his mom's marriage schemes, then he needed to reevaluate his negotiating abilities.

"Endangered Rock Wallabies," she responded as if that answered anything.

A thousand more questions popped to the forefront, but becoming fascinated by his personal buffer was not on the agenda. "Five thousand."

Her smile changed. It didn't dim with disappointment, it developed an unexpected mercenary edge. "Nine point five."

Silence was a negotiator's best weapon and he unsheathed it, wielding it with the ease of years of practice. Most people broke only a minute or two in. The soundlessness made most nervous, it made the doubts in their heads louder. But once again, Clover proved she wasn't most people. She sat straight in the steel-gray club chair across from his desk, her hands folded in her lap and her legs crossed at the ankle. Put her in different clothes and she'd look like a debutante sitting for her portrait, confident she was about to take over the world.

Clover leaned forward as though about to speak, and Sawyer knew he had her. She'd probably counter at seven and they'd end at $5,500. Not too bad a price to pay for someone capable of keeping his mom at bay.

"I can see working with you is going to be very demanding and, after meeting your mother, a serious challenge. Twelve." One side of her mouth lifted, and he had the gut-sinking suspicion that he'd just walked into a trap. "Final offer."

What the…?

Sawyer couldn't remember the last time someone had surprised him in a negotiation. Or won. Doubling down, he leaned forward and placed his elbows on the desk. No way was he going to lose. She had to be bluffing. "Six thousand. Final offer."

She let out a lengthy sigh and stood up. "And now you're showing that you're just as difficult to work with as your mother. Fifteen thousand or you'd better get used to boring lunches discussing the latest fashions."

Sawyer blinked. And for the first time ever, *he* had no idea how to respond in a negotiation. Maybe she actually *would* be worth the money if she maneuvered his mother as expertly as she bargained. She started to reach for her purse as though to leave, and he knew he'd lost. "Sit down, Ms. Lee. I believe we have a deal."

"Agreed." A self-satisfied smile tipped her lips upward as she sat back down. "One last thing, I'll need to be an independent contractor not an employee."

"Why?" he asked before he could stop himself, still trying to catch up to the fact that he'd just been out-negotiated by a woman who'd earned a living bouncing from one ridiculous job to another.

Her steady gaze skittered away to the left before snapping back to him. "I don't like being tied down."

A lie or too much of the truth? It shouldn't matter, but for some reason it did. "That explains your resume."

Up went her stubborn chin. "Is there a document outlining my job duties?"

"There will be." With a few taps and swipes on his monitor, he opened up a new document and then pulled out the shelf hidden into the frame of his desk where he kept his wireless keyboard. "Obviously you'll need to be available 24/7." He typed it out in bullet points. Fast. Efficient. Concise. "When you're not acting as my buffer, you can help Amara with overflow work."

"Why do you need a buffer?" she asked, grabbing the heavy chair by its arms and scooting it closer while she was still sitting in it. "Is your mom really that bad?"

His fingers faltered for a second and his mind went blank before the ingrained training fell into place. The first lesson in growing up as one of Harbor City's elite was that no one talked openly about anything that could even tangentially be considered unpleasant.

"No." He resumed typing out office tasks such as data backups and scheduling. "She's wonderful. She's just a little obsessed with marrying me off."

Why did he say that? What was going to come out next? That his first crush had been his brother's math tutor?

Clover leaned in close, as if exchanging this kind of personal information was the same as asking about the weather. "And you're not the marrying kind?"

He pulled at his tie, his collar suddenly tighter than it had been a few minutes ago. "No. I'm the working kind." Glancing down at her resume, her international experience caught his attention. "Do you speak other languages?"

She nodded, gliding her fingers across his bare desk as if she was unconsciously searching for something to fidget with. "I can speak Spanish, French, passable Mandarin, passable Thai, and Malay."

A lightbulb went off. "As in the Malay spoken in Singapore?"

"Yep, I just got back a week ago from six months there teaching English."

Negotiations for the deal in Pulau Ujong, Singapore's largest island and the home to most of its population, had stalled with Mr. Lim. Bringing in someone more familiar with the culture and the language might just be what he needed to get to an agreement.

"I'm working to close a deal right now to build a trio of high-rises in Singapore," he said. "Your insight may be valuable, but mostly I'll need you for social events and at the office as backup for Amara."

"She can't send away your mom?" Clover asked.

He snorted. "Amara can do just about anything, but my mom mows her over. Mom convinced my dad to hire Amara years ago even though she had zero training or experience, and so Amara has a soft spot for her."

"Why can't *you* tell your mom to leave you alone?" she pressed.

God. How many times had he asked himself that same question since she'd started her Marry Off Sawyer campaign? More than he had dollars in the bank. But facing down Helene Carlyle wasn't about being louder or more stubborn or blowing her off. Like mother like son, that approach just made both of them dig in deeper. Working around the force of will that was his mother took charm and finesse, something Sawyer had in very limited supply, if any at all. Plus, she was his mom, and you didn't have to be Catholic to have the guilt that came along with disappointing your own mother.

"You met her for about two minutes." He hit print on the document. The list of job tasks would be waiting for Clover in the outer office as soon as she walked out the doors. "I've known her my whole life. When the woman has the bit between her teeth, it takes a helluva lot to dissuade her. I just need some time to come up with a way to do that. Six weeks sounds just about right." He stood, needing movement to shove back the uncomfortable questions Clover raised. "Amara will show you to HR so you can fill out all the necessary forms and sign the nondisclosure agreement." A discreet beep sounded from his monitor's speaker, and a reminder for tonight's gala popped up on the screen. "Damn."

"Problem?" Clover asked, peeking around the edge of his monitor as if that wasn't intrusive at all.

"I'll need you to attend the Harbor City General Charity Gala with me tonight." There was no way he was facing his mom alone after what had gone down today.

Clover jerked upright, her eyes wide. "Tonight?"

"I'll pick you up at seven." Gut tightening, he strode to his office door and opened it. "Be sure to leave your home address with Amara."

Clover walked past him, muttering something he couldn't quite make out. He should have shut the door as soon as she passed through, but he didn't. Instead, he watched her turn that bright smile on Amara and wondered what in the hell Hudson had just gotten him into.

Chapter Three

Hands on her hips, head cocked to one side and chewing her bottom lip to the point of pain, Clover stared into the open doors of her small closet and tried to imagine anything inside as being appropriate for a big deal event like the Harbor City General Hospital Gala. Build a house for Habitat for Humanity? She had something to wear for that. A week in the desert working on an oral history of a native tribe? Yep, she had it covered. A party with Harbor City's richest and snobbiest? *That* was going to take some creativity.

For that, she needed Daphne. Clover did a quick mental calculation. Her best friend was an airline attendant and in Portland tonight. So that meant it was still early. What the hell, it was worth a try. Clover grabbed her phone.

Clover: *BFF SOS*

Daphne: *What up?*

Clover: *Have to go to a charity fundraiser ball thing. What to wear?*

Daphne: *1. Awesome! 2. Ummmmmmm… diamonds?*

Clover: *Funny, you hag.*

Daphne: *It's why you love me. My closet is yours.*

Clover: *You're the best.*

Daphne: *LOL. Tell me in person tom morn when I get back to HC*

Clover: *xoxo*

Daphne: *:)*

After a quick check at the clock, Clover hustled into Daphne's room in the apartment they'd shared since graduating college. She slid over the bright and patterned hangers to the dark and rarely worn section in the back and pulled out a pair of wine-colored cigarette pants. Okay, she had at least ten pounds on Daphne, but as long as she could still button them then they were something she could build off of. She pivoted and held them out in front of her. One look at her reflection was all the nope she needed.

It shouldn't matter. It wasn't like she cared what other people thought about her, but it was hard to remember that she was a different person from that awkward small-town girl who years ago had walked into Harbor City University for the first time overwhelmed, scared, and beyond out of her depth. Thank God her dorm roommate turned out to be Daphne. If it hadn't been for her, Clover might have tucked tail and run back home where it was safe, and that would've been the worst thing ever. Daphne had helped her become Clover in more than nickname only.

She went back to Daphne's closet and started flipping through the hangers again. If only she could call her mom for a little mother/daughter advice chat. She even went so far as to reach for her phone before drawing back her hand without ever touching her cell. Nope. Her mom would have too many questions.

Have you met someone you like?

When are you going to settle down?

What about that one boy from that one trip? He seemed nice.

It would be a why-do-you-make-such-poor-life-choices and why-don't-I-have-grandbabies-yet guilt fest from the get-go, just like every time they talked. She was so not in the mood for that. Anyway, her mom would probably tell her to do some tired Audrey Hepburn pearls and a little black dress thing—nothing imaginative, nothing fun. If Clover was anything, it was the total opposite of that, which is why she'd left Sparksville in the first place. It was also *exactly* why she and her mom rarely got along anymore. All her mom wanted was a mini-me Stepford wife clone. All Clover wanted was to forge her own adventurous way.

Having reached the end of the line when it came to Daphne's closet, Clover started shoving hangers back down the way she'd already come, hopeful she'd missed something fabulous.

An hour later Clover's bed was covered in piles of black, gold, hot pink, white, and red full-length dresses and long skirts that had been pulled from hers and Daphne's closets. She'd tried them all on. Some were too small. Others were just laughably wrong on her. Sawyer was going to be here any minute and Clover stood in the middle of her room in bare feet, a sports bra, hair in a high ponytail, and Daphne's floor-length, simple black chiffon skirt.

Clover did a quick spin in front of the mirror to watch the skirt twirl. After spending the last hour changing clothes with the seriousness of a woman facing the guillotine, she had to do something just for fun. She was halfway through the turn—her reflection a blur in the mirror—when the idea hit.

She sprinted over to her dresser, yanked open the top drawer and pulled out a sequined black racerback crop top. After nearly dislocating her shoulder wriggling out of the sports bra from hell, she put on an equally uncomfortable strapless bra and slipped on the top. It came to rest at the bottom of her rib cage, showing off the three inches of pale skin above the skirt's waistband. A pair of strappy designer-knockoff black stilettos and a pair of chandelier earrings with sparkling fake emeralds completed the look.

One look in the mirror and Clover's nerves evaporated into mist. The outfit wasn't Harbor City socialite material, but neither was she—and thank God for that. She grabbed her phone, snapped a selfie, and sent it to Daphne.

Daphne: *OMG yes!!!*

Clover: *You really think?*

Daphne: *Fuck yes. You slay! Hate missing this.*

Clover: *Miss you, too. Catch up tomorrow?*

Daphne: *Hells yes. Croissants and coffee on me.*

Clover's phone vibrated in her hand.

The number that flashed on the screen was the one Amara had given her for Sawyer. The text read: *Now.*

Clover: *Gotta go.*

Daphne: *Kill 'em with hotness!*

Clover: *xoxo*

Hustling as quick as she could in the steep heels, Clover dropped her phone and her lipstick into a little purse as she quick-stepped it to the door. She paused at the front door long enough to take in a deep breath, steel her spine, and give herself a ten-second pep talk.

You're there to do your job. Don't let all the rich bitches scare you.

With that, she opened the door and hurried out into the evening and toward the ebony Town Car double parked in front of her building.

• • •

Sawyer scrolled through email on his phone while he cooled his heels in the backseat of his chauffeured car. Still no response from Mr. Lim about the tweaked proposal he'd sent last week. Something was wrong—that Sawyer couldn't pinpoint the problem made him twitch. Deals like this one didn't come along every day, and Sawyer wasn't about to miss out on it. Whatever it took, he was going to land it.

"Sir," his driver said. "I believe your date has arrived."

"She's not my date, Linus. She's—" He looked out the window and the next words died on his tongue.

Clover stood at the top of the steps leading to the door of the brownstone, looking very much like a very not plain Jane. The sequins on her black top that molded itself against her high curves sparkled in the setting sun's light, showering the bare slash of toned skin above her waistband in dots of light. The sight drew his attention like a tractor beam. The filmy skirt that fell from her waist to the ground teased at what was underneath as she sailed down the stairs, all smooth sex appeal and tempting promise. Even her hair tantalized—a long, golden silk rope of a ponytail that his fingers itched to either take down or wrap around his fist as he—

Fuck, Carlyle. Get your shit together. You do not get to go there. She may not be technically an employee, but she's still off-limits. Very. Off. Limits.

"Yeah, tell that to my cock," he muttered to himself as he pushed open the car door and stepped out onto the sidewalk just as Linus was rounding the front of the Town Car to hold open the door. The driver arched an eyebrow at Sawyer's break in a long-established protocol but kept the rest of his face bland and unreadable.

It was enough though. Sawyer ground his teeth together, determined to pull back from whatever brink he was toeing.

"Jane…"

Her smile lost some of its wattage as she crossed her arms and popped out one hip, the move emphasizing the fullness of her tits and the soft curve of her waist. His brain fizzled—a condition he was beginning to worry wouldn't fix itself as long as he kept wondering what the exposed bare expanse of her stomach would feel like under his fingers.

"Clover," she said.

"Yes, Clover," he said, trying to restart the synapses in his brain, which was a lot easier said than done when he was this close to her. "Did you need some more time to finish getting ready?"

The words—obviously a desperate plea from his subconscious—were out before he could stop them and hung in the air like a half-deflated balloon.

"I *am* ready," she replied, her tone a few degrees warmer than ice cream. "Why? Is there something *wrong* with what I'm wearing?"

"Yes. No. It's…" Sexy as hell. "Different."

There went her chin. "So am I."

"This isn't exactly an event for different." *Shut up, Carlyle. Shut the fuck up.*

Her brown eyes narrowed, and she let out an angry little hurumph. "Then I guess you don't need me."

With that declaration, she spun around, giving him a perfect view of the skirt clinging to her ass—which he shouldn't be noticing—as she marched back toward the stairs leading to her door. He'd already fucked this up enough as it was. Everyone knew he wasn't the charming Carlyle, that was Hudson. Sawyer was the asshole Carlyle, and he'd just proven it by letting his prick do the thinking and then *acting* like one when he was talking.

He hustled a few steps forward and caught her elbow before she got any farther away, trying his best to ignore the jolt of electricity that went straight to his cock. "Please don't."

Yanking her arm out of his loose grasp, she rounded on him—fire in her eyes and something that looked a lot like hurt shimmering underneath. "On one condition."

"What's that?" As long as it wasn't him making a public ass of himself, he was totally on board.

"Don't complain about what I wear," she said, her voice tight and a little higher than normal. "It's not like most people who specialize in temp jobs have closets full of ball gowns and formal dresses."

You are a privileged douchebag, Carlyle. All those details he'd missed before came into focus. The anxious thrum of her pulse in her neck. The way her bottom lip was slightly swollen, no doubt from nervous nibbling. The way she fiddled with the skirt as if she wasn't used to wearing it or it didn't feel quite like her. The whole mind-blowing look he had taken in at first glance, but per usual he missed the details and the little tics that clued him in about the emotions simmering underneath.

After his dad's unexpected death, he'd compensated for this massive shortcoming by being extra careful with his mom, never rocking the boat when it came to her. That's what had gotten him into this mess where he needed a personal buffer. There had to be some middle ground between the forest and the trees, but damned if he knew— or had ever known—where it was.

"You're right," he said, meaning every word. "I'm sorry."

Accepting his apology with a stiff nod, she strode past him to where Linus held the car door open. "Shall we go?"

Without waiting for his answer, she slid into the backseat of the Town Car. He followed behind, ignoring the clear look of disappointment in Linus's eyes that even Sawyer couldn't miss. The driver had known him since he was a kid and had watched him grow up in the backseat of his dad's car as often as he could persuade the old man into taking him into the office. His dad used to say that there was no better sounding board than Linus. For his part, Linus said he just knew how to "uh-huh" at the right times.

The door clicked shut behind Sawyer, and he found himself sitting almost knee to knee with Clover. He needed to say something—anything—but once again the Carlyle charm fizzled out when it came to Sawyer, so he clamped his mouth shut and kept it that way the entire trip to The Grand Hotel.

Somewhere out there, Hudson was laughing his ass off. And his mom? God, he couldn't wait to see what her reaction would be to seeing Clover on his arm.

Chapter Four

To be honest, Clover's first high-society gala was kind of a disappointment. None of the women were dripping in diamonds or draped in fur—too gauche no doubt. The men in tuxedos were more balding-banker types than spies-who-liked-their-martinis-shaken-not-stirred. Everyone was very polite and *very* not interested in talking to her once it made the rounds that she wasn't one of the East Upton Lees who counted most of the country's oil refineries in their portfolio, but just a regular Lee from little ol' Sparksville.

Even Helene had kept her distance, holding court on the opposite end of the enormous ballroom surrounded by a trio of obvious bride candidates who couldn't keep their eyes off Sawyer. Not that he seemed to notice. Nope. He'd spent the last hour looking to-die-for hot in his tux while either sexy-glowering at her (it's apparently a thing) or on his phone as he talked business. It wasn't fair. No one should be that hot and that annoying at the same time. Not that it mattered. She was here as Sawyer's buffer not his date. It was best—if not particularly easy—to remember that when he was looking all 007.

Even worse? At the moment, she was about as useful and necessary as a bike to a fish, which meant she was thoroughly and completely bored. Plus, her feet hurt in the kill-me-now heels she'd borrowed. Shifting her weight, she snuck one foot out of her heel and stretched her toes under the cover of the floor-length skirt. Her foot did everything but sing the Hallelujah Chorus in gratitude at being set free from its narrow prison.

Of course, that's when a man appeared out of nowhere

by her side, startling her and sending her awkwardly wobbling on her one foot that was still in a shoe.

His hand shot out to steady her, releasing her almost as fast as he'd saved her from tumbling over. "You don't have to confirm it, but I can tell," he said, leaning in conspiratorially. "Your date's a dud."

"It's not a date." The truth came out before she could think better. *Sigh.* When would she learn to just keep her mouth shut? Sawyer had been so tight-lipped in the car, she didn't know what cover story—if any—he wanted her to use.

"Really? Then let me introduce myself. Tyler Jacobson," he said. "And since it appears your date is not a date, that must mean you're free to dance."

Not a good idea when she was on the job. "I'm allergic."

"To dancing or to handsome men?"

She chuckled. He was definitely handsome. Tall, dark hair, blue eyes, and enough charm to get a starving man to offer up his last bite of bread. "A little of both."

He swiped a champagne flute from the tray of a passing waiter and handed it to her. "Luckily for you, I happen to know that this is the cure."

She took a sip, smiling for the first time since she'd walked out her front door. A little harmless flirting at a gala—now that was an adventure she hadn't had before. The night was beginning to look up.

"You don't give up, do you?" she teased.

Tyler's smile was for her, but his gaze slid sideways to Sawyer as he talked on his phone to someone about Singapore. "Not once I've set my mind to something."

Clover's spider sense tingled as she looked between Sawyer and the other man in his equally well-fitting tux. "And what *exactly* do you have in mind?"

"One dance, that's all. Then I'll bring you right back to your dreadfully boring not-date."

"He's not boring." Infuriating? Stuffy? Devastating to

her panties? She'd give a hell yes to all the above, but not boring.

"Whatever you say." He took the champagne from her hand and set it on a passing waiter's tray, then tucked her hand into the crook of his elbow and led her out onto the dance floor.

One dance. One fantasy moment with a man who looked straight out of central casting. A little adventure to put in her memory bank. Nothing in her job duties said no dancing. She'd just be sure to keep an eye on Sawyer, and if Helene — or anyone else — approached, she'd slip away from her partner. Until then, it was Cinderella time.

Like every other song the band had played tonight, it was a slow one. So here she was in the arms of a handsome stranger in a tux in the middle of The Grand Hotel, which totally stayed true to its name with the amount of columns and marble and sparkling brilliance, and danced. It was a scene right out of a princess movie — and about as sexy. There was no zing from his fingertips on her waist. No languorous desire sliding across her skin. No anticipation pushing her to close the very socially-acceptable gap between their bodies.

"So how did you and Sawyer meet?" Tyler asked, his tone light but the look in his much more serious eyes told another story.

She had no frickin' clue what was going on between the men, but for once she wasn't going to step smack dab in the middle of it. Nope. She was going to keep her motor mouth out of trouble.

"Underground fight club," she said with all the seriousness she could muster. "He bet against me. And lost."

Tyler laughed. "Now *that* I wouldn't doubt. Never bet against a woman in black."

"How do you know Sawyer?" *Diam*! The mental Malay order came too late — the words already out of her mouth.

All the teasing charm died away. "What makes you

think I do?"

"Women's intuition." And the fact that he couldn't stop talking about Sawyer.

"He was the best man at my wedding, well, almost wedding."

That threw her enough that she lost a step and hastened to pick up the rhythm again. "*Almost* wedding?"

He shrugged and spun her around on the dance floor. "My fiancée liked my best man more than me."

"Ouch." She couldn't keep the horror off her face. "They didn't…"

"Not that I know of, but who knows."

Wow. She needed to stop talking. Now. Too bad her mouth had other ideas. "You're very blasé about it all."

"It was years ago, and anyway"—he paused and turned a devastatingly sexy and completely disingenuous smile on her—"now I have you to distract me from my deep, dark wound and repair the hole in my heart from the loss of the woman I loved and the man who'd been my best friend since prep school."

Someone had spent too much time in the melodrama category on Netflix. Either that or he was used to dealing with socialites who'd take him at his word. And here she'd thought growing up in Sparksville that the Harbor City rich were so much more sophisticated than that.

"You're laying it on a little thick there."

His smile didn't falter, but some actual fun seeped into it. "Too much?"

"Oh yeah." She nodded, matching his mock serious tone.

"Then I suppose I'll have to find another way to steal you away from him. Good thing I'm a helluva lot more adventurous. How about breakfast in Paris, lunch in Milan, and dinner Barcelona?"

A large hand clapped down on her dance partner's

shoulder—not hard enough to cause a scene but definitely serious enough to make a point—and brought their dancing to a jarring halt. Sawyer stood behind Tyler, all predatory determination and sizzling heat. Her belly did that flip-flop thing that released all the stupid kamikaze butterflies in her stomach and her breath caught.

"Leave her dining choices to me, Jacobson," Sawyer said to her dance partner, but the smoldering look in his eyes was all for her.

And for once, her mouth stayed blessedly shut.

The other man stiffened, all the teasing drained out in an instant. "I'm just entertaining the lady while you're busy."

"I'll take over from here," Sawyer said.

"Of course." Tyler released her and executed a deep, mocking bow. "Until next time… you know, I didn't ask your name…"

Brain catching up to the fact that she'd ended up in the middle of a pissing contest that she highly doubted had anything to do with her, she ignored Sawyer's scowling, caveman presence and reached out to shake the other man's hand. "Clover Lee."

Instead of shaking her hand, he brought it up to his mouth and brushed a kiss across her knuckles. "An unforgettable name for an unforgettable woman."

It was sweet, but there wasn't any heat behind it—from either of them—and he walked off the dance floor without a parting shot directed toward Sawyer. Whatever the story was behind this little bit of dick wagging, it had the feel of a long-running feud, and Clover promised herself to play it smart and stay the hell out of it.

She took a step toward the spot where she and Sawyer had been standing before, but his hand slid across her hip and he turned her into his arms in one fluid, confident move. It only took a few beats of the music for that socially-acceptable space between their bodies that had been so easy to maintain with Tyler to disappear between her and Sawyer as if it had never existed. His long fingers splayed across the small of her back, the tips of two fingers warm against the strip of bare skin above the skirt's waistband and set off sparks that tightened her nipples and weakened her knees. Suddenly, her Cinderella-at-the-ball fantasy dance didn't feel so kid-appropriate anymore.

"What were you doing with Tyler?" Sawyer asked, his palm pressing more firmly against the small of her back at the other man's name.

"Dancing." True story. Also, it was about the extent of her conversational skills at the moment, since she was fighting against a determined tide of desire from the touch of only two of his fingers on her skin. Pitiful. She really needed to get laid more often, if this was all it took to knock her brain loose.

"He's trouble," Sawyer said with disgust as if the words tasted like day-old radiation. "Stay away from him. That's an order."

Clover craned her neck to get a look at Sawyer's face from this close angle. His jaw was concrete and his dark eyebrows were pinched together in an angry *V*.

Holy shit. He was serious—and he expected his "order" to be followed.

That. Was. It.

Her feet froze, jerking them to a stop in the middle of the dance floor. Other couples whirled around them as indignation bubbled up inside her to the surface, sizzled along her skin, and decimated her very feeble verbal filter.

"I don't know what's going on with you and Tyler, but I am not a fire hydrant." She kept her voice low and her face serene but jabbed a finger into his unyielding chest to bring her point home. "I am not a bone." Jab number two. "I am not a grubby tennis ball covered in dried mud." A third for good measure. "I am not a *thing* for you two dogs to fight over. I am a woman with my own brain, my own will, and my own determination. Sawyer Carlyle, you might be giving me a paycheck, but you sure as hell didn't buy me and you *definitely* don't have the right to tell me who I can and cannot dance with—especially not when you are obviously more interested in your phone than the rest of the world around you." *Shit.* That last part got a little too close to the truth hiding in her soft, caramel center. *Bring it home, Clover.* "My job is to be your personal buffer, and your mom has kept her distance. Was there someone invisible that I couldn't see who was bothering you?"

She sucked in a breath as the rush of adrenaline pounded through her, practically lifting her off her aching feet. Oh, if only it didn't feel so good to let loose like that, she totally would have learned to keep her mouth shut by now. God knew that skill sure would help her keep a job for longer than five minutes.

Job.

"*Goondu,*" the word rushed out. Her former landlady in Singapore was right. She was an idiot.

Her lungs clenched and her stomach dropped into the great unknown abyss. She'd just told the man signing her paycheck to go fuck himself. Well, not exactly in those words, but that was the gist of it and she *needed* this job.

Clover Lee, you are a self-sabotaging asshole.

She didn't want to meet his gaze. All the saints and angels above *knew* she didn't want to, but she forced herself to look up at Sawyer. She'd been in front of the firing squad often enough to know it didn't hurt any less if she closed her eyes and thought of Australia.

But his glower was gone. He was…smiling? Yep. It wasn't a big one, but one side of his mouth was definitely curved upward.

"Uh…" She gulped. "Sawyer…Mr. Carlyle…Umm—"

Before she could get any further in her often tried, and

often failed, begging-for-her-job presentation (she really needed PowerPoint slides at this point), the ding-dong-ding of a xylophone sounded.

"Everyone, if I could have your attention." Helene Carlyle stood on a small dais, looking at ease in that regal way that people who grew up with old money always seemed to have. "My son, Sawyer Carlyle, would like to say a few words in appreciation of Harbor City General's amazing staff and all the great work they do there that you good people are helping to fund by being here tonight. Sawyer…?" She looked around as if she didn't already know where her son was. Clover didn't buy it for a minute. "Please join me on stage and afterward, I know Cecilia Dowers of the Chicago Dowers would like ten minutes with you, dear."

Everyone in their vicinity turned to look at them, but Sawyer was still only looking at Clover.

He dipped his head down so his lips nearly brushed her ear. "We'll finish this later."

Then, he lifted her hand, flipped it over, and placed a searing kiss in the center of her palm before striding to the front of the ballroom while Clover fought tooth and nail not to melt into a puddle in front of Harbor City's elite.

• • •

Walking through the crowd to the raised platform at the other end of the ballroom, Sawyer tried to remember the last time he'd had his ass handed to him on a silver platter that matched the spoon he'd been born with and came up blank. He *definitely* couldn't remember a time when he'd enjoyed it quite that much.

Seeing Clover with righteous fury turning her cheeks pink and making her eyes sparkle as she stood there in that teasing slip of a top had been a clarion call to his cock—so much so that this walk across the room was a little more bowlegged than normal.

She was pissed and she didn't back down from it. Even his mom chose well-meaning, if totally deranged manipulation, over direct attack. It wasn't their way to face things with so much open emotion or derision. Good or bad, they all danced around the topic. He could have a giant glob of mustard on his chin dripping a river down onto his tie and no one would have said anything beyond that he might want to excuse himself for a minute. If they wouldn't be straightforward to help him, they sure as hell wouldn't call him out when he was acting like an ass.

But Clover? There were bulldozers that would have a harder time flattening someone. That woman did not hold back. She was *everything* the women—including tonight's candidate, Cecilia Dowers—that his mother was throwing at him were not.

The idea smacked him right between the eyes and by the time he climbed the three steps to the top of the dais, he knew exactly what he was going to do next. The anticipation of Clover's reaction was almost as enticing as his mother's.

He squeezed past the band leader and took the mic from his mother, ignoring the speculation gleaming in her eyes. Oh yes, she'd been watching him with Clover and had timed this little announcement to perfection.

"Thank you, Mother, and thank you to everyone here. I don't need to tell anyone about the amazing work that Harbor General does. Our family's biggest hope is that, with the addition of the Michael Carlyle Cardiac Wing, they will be able to continue to do what they do best—save lives." He paused as the crowd clapped on cue, most of them probably only listening with half an ear. "But that's not the only announcement I have to make tonight. In addition to celebrating the opening of the new cardiac wing, I have news of another kind of matter of the heart." The silence after that line had a different feel to it. Everyone here might play at polite, but the uber rich loved gossip almost as much as they enjoyed caviar and champagne—and they'd been watching his mother's Marry Off Sawyer campaign like they monitored their stock dividend results. "I'd like to introduce you all to my fiancée, Miss Clover Lee."

As if controlled by an unseeing hand, the crowd turned to look at Clover still standing in the middle of the dance floor, and then everyone started talking at once. Clover stretched a wide smile across her face, clearly as excited as he to everyone in the room, but Sawyer could see the daggers she was shooting him from her eyes. He was going to pay for this later. Why did that bring an answering smile to his face? Out of the corner of his eye he spotted his mother. Unlike the others, she wasn't looking at Clover. She was looking straight at him, shocked disbelief shining in her eyes for a moment before years of training took precedence and a placid look took its place.

She couldn't call him out. She couldn't keep pushing her candidates at him. As long as his new fiancée was in the picture, he was free to attend to the big picture of Carlyle Enterprises and Helene knew it. For her to do anything else wouldn't be the Harbor City elite way. Mission accomplished.

Now all he had to do was manage the minor detail of getting Clover to agree to an adjustment in her job duties.

Chapter Five

Clover was finally going to learn how to fold a fitted sheet. Of course, she was going to gain that skill in the prison laundry after she killed Sawyer. She hadn't agreed to lie to the entire world—and even if she had, the pompous ass should have given her a heads up first that it was coming.

The Prince of Carlyle Enterprises didn't seem to realize that though, judging by his shameless grin as he accepted congratulatory pats on the back while making his way through the crowd. By the time he finally got to her, 90 percent of Harbor City's one percenters had shaken his hand—with one glaring exception. Helene Carlyle had stayed back on the dais, armed with a barely touched glass of champagne and an assessing look directed at Clover. Before she could translate the look in the other woman's eyes, the man they had in common stopped in front of her and the band started up again.

Playing the good fiancée, she sparkled up her smile and hooked her arm through the crook of Sawyer's elbow before raising herself up on the tippy toes of her torture device shoes. "We need to talk. Now."

She had to give him credit, Sawyer didn't hesitate in dancing with her, right out of the ballroom. He took a quick left, followed by a right, and then opened up an unmarked door and pulled her inside. In the dim light filtering under the door, she took stock of shelves, filled with toilet paper, towels, tiny hotel soaps, and mini shampoo bottles, lining the walls of the space barely big enough for the two of them. Considering he'd found his way here as easily as a kid in a fairy tale following a breadcrumb trail, it didn't take a huge leap of logic to realize he'd been in here before.

The fun answer as to why would be this was where Sawyer took his dates for some hot are-we-going-to-get-caught public sex. The real answer was probably more along the lines of him seeking out privacy for another of his never-ending business calls. Mr. Adventure, he was not.

She walked the three-step length of the supply closet before whirling around to face him—arms crossed and unimpressed expression in place—determined not to be the one to crack first. He'd tried that silent negotiating thing with her in his office earlier today. Little did he know that she'd honed her skills in the Turkish bazaars. He was way out of his depth.

"You're pissed." He held up his hands, palms forward. *Ding. Ding. Ding.* "You think?"

He shrugged his broad shoulders. "It's just a minor detail."

"A minor detail? Are you nuts?" He had to be. How else could he talk to her in such a calm tone about an insane idea? "This is not what I signed up for. I'm not lying to everyone I know for you."

"Don't think of it as a lie," he said, leaning back against the door and blocking off the one exit. "Think of it as a temporary truth."

"You're certifiable." He had to be. A fake engagement to one of the most eligible bachelor's in Harbor City so he could avoid his mom's matchmaking attempts? Now *that* was an adventure to write home about. Not that she could because of…*all* the reasons in the world. It was hard to come up with a specific one when he was standing so close, smelling so good, and looking so much better than even the sexiest paparazzi photo. "Anyway, it's not part of my job duties."

"The ad did state that you'd do anything within the law to act as my buffer."

She re-crossed her arms, mimicking his arrogant pose. How typical that he'd think she'd go along with his plan. She wasn't some naive hick he could just lead around. "No one would believe we were engaged. I can't fake attraction, and 'uptight' is just not doing it for me." She was a liar, but that was beside the point.

Sawyer raised one eyebrow as if to say *so that's how you want to play this*. Pushing away from the door, he took a step closer to her, all cocky confidence. "Don't mistake me for one of the small-town boys you're used to." He took another step until they were practically pressed up against each other in the small space "Faking it…" He lowered his head, coming close but not quite touching her and making her breath catch. "Is not going to be an issue."

True story, but she'd pack that admission in her hand basket and take it to hell with her. "Of course it will," she halfheartedly denied. When his gaze narrowed, she rushed on. "And besides, everyone out there saw you ignoring me for two hours then fighting over me like a favorite chew toy with Tyler. Everyone's going to assume it's just a stunt to continue this feud and not real attraction."

"They won't," he said and dipped his hand down, tracing a fingertip across the hem of her crop top. "Not if we play it right."

He never dropped his touch below the material, never made skin-to-skin contact, but he didn't have to. She felt his touch anyway, and it made her entire body crackle with anticipation.

"You just met me." It came out breathy, but she was mostly shocked she was able to get it out at all.

He dropped his hands from her shirt and raised one to lean against the wall behind her head as his gaze slid up, locking on hers and nailing her to the spot with some unspoken command her brain couldn't process but her body understood immediately.

"Everyone knows I'm not a man who waits when I've decided what I want."

And there went her panties—and most of her brain, because instead of reiterating her hell no all that came out was, "You don't know anything about me."

"So I'll learn." He lowered his head, coming close enough that she could feel the brush of his words across her cheek. "I've always caught on fast."

Oh God. This was either so bad it was good or so good it was bad. She couldn't decide and her body didn't fucking care. Her brain, though, wasn't quite ready to give up the fight. "I can't keep a job, my bank account's almost empty, and I live in an apartment with a roommate. Everyone will think I'm a social climber."

"Unimportant details." His fingertips traced across her jawline.

"No one will ever buy that *you're* attracted to *me*." Okay, that argument sounded ridiculous considering what anyone would see if they walked in on them right now, but the thinking part of her *knew* this had crossed the line from fun adventure to bad idea and was desperate.

"If they think that," he said, hooking a finger below her chin and tilting her face up so her mouth was just inches from his. "Then they're idiots."

His lips came down on hers and her brain gave up the ghost. This wasn't about thinking. It was about sinful promises, wild nights, and knee-knocking lust—the kind that had her pulse going from sixty to light speed in the span of two heart beats. Dominant and focused, he teased her with his tongue, playing along the seam of her lips before slipping inside. Desire, hot and slick, settled low in her core as the kiss went from tempting to exploratory to mind blowing—and she gave back as good. What could she say? He might be her stuffy uptight boss, but he was an amazing kisser—the kind that made her want to fall into the moment and never climb back out. And she wasn't the only one. They couldn't get enough of each other, tongues pushing against one another, the occasional nipping when one of them tried to catch a breath, and even frustrated grumbling when clothes got in the way of their needy hands.

With a groan, he released her mouth, leaving her lips kiss-stung and hungry for more, and turned his attention to the line of her throat and that one spot right behind her ear that had a direct lust line to her clit.

"Sawyer," she moaned as soon as he hit it. Her toes curled and her nipples stiffened with the lightest nip and lick from him.

He mumbled something against her skin that she didn't catch as he dropped his hands from her face and let them glide down her curves and around to her back, dropping lower until he cupped her ass and lifted her upward. Thanks to the loose cut of her skirt, she didn't have any trouble wrapping her legs around his lean hips and pressing her most sensitive spot against him. As soon as she did, she rubbed herself against his hardness—*fuck*, Sawyer was packing significant heat.

Sliding her hands through his hair, she arched her back against the wall as she tightened her thigh lock and undulated her hips against his unmistakable bulge.

"So good," she whispered, her voice ragged and needy.

Good didn't even begin to cover it, but it was as descriptive a word as her totally-in-SOS-mode brain could come up with when his lips made their way from the bottom of her earlobe to the place where her neck met her shoulder. He nipped her there and sucked it better as she slid her hands over his hard chest and made fast work of his shirt buttons. One. Two. Three. Enough to let her sneak a hand inside—

The supply closet door flew open.

Light from the hall poured in.

A harsh gasp sounded followed by a hurried, "Excuse me."

The door slammed shut.

Heat beating her cheeks, Clover let the back of her head hit the wall with a solid thunk and unwrapped her legs from around him to slowly slide one foot to the ground. "Oh shit."

"Don't tell me you're embarrassed," he asked with a soft chuckle.

Her other foot hit the floor and reality seeped in. "Of course I am."

He stepped back a few paces and busied himself with re-buttoning his shirt. "And here I thought *you* were the one always up for an adventure."

Which is just what this had been for him—a walk on the wild side for Mr. Upper Crust. The realization would have pissed her off if it hadn't been for the heat still smoldering in his eyes. She was young, free, and having a Cinderella-at-the-ball kind of night—in a twisted sort of way, of course. It's not like any of that makeout meant anything. It was just part of the too-hot-for-a-cartoon-movie fantasy and now it was time to go home before her not-glass slippers resulted in the loss of her toes.

"So are we in agreement?" Sawyer asked as he adjusted his cuffs.

Of course, it was back to business for him. Well, two could play at that game. His negotiation tactics might be unusual—she'd never dry humped anyone at the Turkish bazaar—but she couldn't deny they worked because she was about to say yes.

She was going to agree to be a temporary fiancée to a man she'd just met—or translated to Clover terms, just another job to list on her whack-a-do resume. Of course, that didn't mean he wasn't going to have to make some adjustments to their agreement. If she was in, she was going *all* in and so was he.

"Agreement?" Clover smoothed back a few stray hairs and tried to get her heart rate back down to not-running-a-marathon levels. "About the fake engagement?"

"Yes."

"We'll need to work out the details." There. That sounded all tough and corporate.

He straightened his glasses that she must have sent askew during the kiss. "I usually leave those to other people."

Nice try. "Not this time."

He shrugged those mouthwateringly broad shoulders. "Have it your way."

"Always." Okay, not really, but it made her sound all badass and she had a feeling she was going to need that bit of bravado to keep her head on straight for the next few weeks. She was going to need that edge because Sawyer was about to learn the art of negotiation from a real master. She couldn't wait to see how he'd take it. Now this was gonna be fun.

Chapter Six

Vito's Diner sat on the corner of Hammish and Fifth. The burgers were thick and charbroiled. The shakes were made with full-fat milk and ice-cream. The breakfast was served twenty-four hours a day. Best of all? There wasn't a socialite in sight. It was the only place Sawyer Carlyle wanted to be after they'd run the gauntlet trying to make a quiet exit out of the gala and the last place Clover probably imagined he'd ever go.

She sat across from him in the booth—he'd taken the side with the tear in the blue vinyl seat—and studied the six-page menu that covered everything from colossal pancakes to cheddar melts to mom's chocolate chip cookies. They'd spent the ride over on opposite ends of the Town Car's backseat.

The kiss in the supply closet had been the kind his cock wasn't going to forget anytime soon, but he couldn't let it happen again. One, she may not be his employee but he was still signing her checks. That employer/employee line was there for a reason. Two, he wasn't fooling himself. They were still in the middle of a negotiation. He'd been in the game too long to lose an advantage because his dick had started doing the thinking for both heads.

The waitress stopped at their table, pad and pencil at the ready. "Hey Sawyer, you feeling the burger or the tuna melt tonight?"

Easiest decision of the night. "Cheeseburger, please, Donna."

"Excellent." She nodded, her French fry earrings bobbing. "Everything on it?"

"You bet, and extra bacon."

"Got it. Chocolate shake?"

Just the mental image of the shake loosened some of the tension pinching his shoulders tight. "The biggest you've got."

"That kinda night, huh? I'll add some extra cherries for you." Donna chuckled and gave him a wink before turning to Clover. "How about you, hun?"

"Can I get the same kind of cheeseburger he's having but with jalapeños instead of the extra bacon?"

"You got it," Donna said. "Anything else?"

Clover's gaze traveled down the full menu page devoted to shakes and malts as she worried her bottom lip between her teeth. "I'll take the pineapple shake but a small, please."

A small? That was a sacrilege at Vito's—sort of like turning down a cheesesteak in Philadelphia or a real deep dish pizza in Chicago.

"They're really good," he said. "You're gonna regret that size."

"He's right, hun," Donna said, backing him up.

Clover gnawed on her lip for another three seconds before nodding her head. Decision made. "Okay, I'll give you that win. As big as they come, extra cherries."

"Now that's how you do a night at Vito's." Donna slipped her pencil in with the three others stuck in her steel gray bun. "I'll have it out to you two in a jiffy."

Donna strolled away, humming in that tuneless way of hers, to go drop off their ticket to her husband, Steve, in the kitchen.

"I take it you come here a lot," Clover said, flipping her menu shut and putting it back in its original spot between the half-filled ketchup and totally-full mustard.

"Yeah, Linus pretty much saved my sanity the first time he took me here after one of my mom's never-ending charitable fundraisers."

He was there so often now he'd made it onto the regulars' board. After he'd spent a few meals decompressing from one or another of his mother's events, he'd asked about Vito. Turned out Vito was Donna and Steve's dog, who'd been banned from his own restaurant under threat from the city health inspector.

Clover toyed with the sugar packets. "Fancy parties aren't your thing?"

"Not when she's got five women lined up like she's casting the role of Mrs. Sawyer Carlyle," he grumbled, sounding like an ungrateful ass and not caring one bit.

"Which brings us back to business."

"Yeah, I guess it does."

"Then let's get to it." She pulled a napkin out of the dispenser and smoothed it out on the table before pushing it across to him. "I'm assuming you have a pen in your jacket, my purse barely fits my phone and my lipstick."

"I don't think we need to write anything down." But he reached out to take the napkin anyway, his fingers brushing hers and sending a shot of electricity straight down to his cock before she pulled her hand away.

"Nice try, Big Bucks." She went straight back to fiddling with the sugar packets as if she wanted to touch something— someone—as much as he did right now. "You're writing it down."

He took off his glasses and with deliberate care cleaned them with the napkin she provided. Dick move? Oh yes. Negotiations weren't about being nice. Good thing being an asshole was never a problem for him. "Don't trust me?"

Her snort was about as far from the sound a socialite would make as he was from closing the Singapore deal. "I trust written agreements more."

"Okay, let's start at the beginning then." He smoothed out the napkin on the table and then withdrew a pen from the inside pocket of his jacket. "We need a cover story. No one is going to buy that we met and got engaged in the same day."

Not by a long shot they wouldn't. While she delicately annihilated her bottom lip and fidgeted with the sugar packets, he scanned his memory for RomCom movie plots for something that would work—not that he was about to say that out loud. It was bad enough Hudson knew his guilty pleasure. If Clover had that little tidbit in her pocket, he had no doubts she'd use it against him.

She made a little ah-ha sound and her face lit up; the sugar packets fell onto the table forgotten. "Secret relationship."

He nodded. "We could have met while you were in Singapore on one of my trips over to see Mr. Lim." He'd seen it work, on the big screen at least, but those schemes always required backup. "I'll have to bring my brother Hudson in on it for corroboration, but we can pull it off."

She slumped back against her seat. "Your mom won't buy it."

"She will if we do it right." Socially acceptable PDA, being seen together, family events. His stomach tightened at the possibility of how Clover would wilt under a solo Helene Carlyle interrogation. There was only one way to avoid that. "You'll have to move in to my place."

Her brown eyes went wide and she went right back to playing with the sugar packets. "That's a little extreme."

"Why?" It was, but the more he thought about it the more he liked the idea. His dick fucking loved it. "Most couples move in together once they're engaged, plus it will mean that we'll be together enough that it'll be hard for my mom to corner you when you're by yourself and get the truth out of you."

"I can hold my own with your mom." She grabbed a third sugar packet. The woman should never play poker.

"Scaring her off isn't the same as being caught in her

crosshairs," he said. "We have to make her believe this so I can give the Singapore deal the attention it needs. Once I close that, we can have our break up and by then I'll have a plan to get my mom to give up her ridiculous marriage campaign."

Donna picked that moment to come by with a tray loaded down with food and shakes. It smelled like heaven—all bacon grease and whipped cream. She gave him a wink and took off again without a word. No doubt, she was planning on needling him for information about his date as soon as she could get him alone. Donna was almost as bad as his mom.

The first bite of the burger made him close his eyes in appreciation as he offered up a silent thank you to pigs everywhere. Clover wasn't as quiet. Her delighted moan made his cock thicken against his thigh, then he made the mistake of opening his eyes. It took both hands for her to hold the giant burger, but that wasn't the part that turned his own bite to ash in his mouth. Her gaze was heavenward as her pink tongue darted out and licked up the splattering of mayo on the corner of her mouth and bottom lip. The move gave him all sorts of really good bad ideas. She could have moaned again after that, sang "Jingle Bells," or hollered at him, he wouldn't have heard over the blood rushing in his ears on its way from his brain to parts farther south.

On automatic pilot, he took a second bite of his burger and didn't taste a damn thing.

"If we're going to do this," Clover said, setting the burger back down on her plate. "Then we're going to have to actually act like a couple."

He took a drink of his tasteless shake, ignoring the extra cherries, and managed to get is brain back on track even with its limited blood supply. "That's why you're moving in."

"That's not what I mean," she said, shaking her head. "You need details. Couple activities. Couple inside jokes.

Couple rituals. If you really want to make it believable, then you have to commit to not just talk the talk, but walk the walk."

She put her glossy red lips around the straw of her pineapple shake and sucked, and he could swear he heard the sparks and sizzles of his synapses exploding.

"Like what?" he managed to get out.

"Saturdays at the flea market."

Okay, that horrible idea brought him back from the edge of fantasy. "There has to be something else."

"It's perfect," she said. "I always go in the morning. We can find something to refurbish, and it will be just the kind of couple detail that will make all of this seem more real."

"People actually do that?" It sounded about as fun as his mom's ideas about arranged marriage.

"Haven't you ever seen *Flea Market Flip*?"

He shook his head and took another bite of his burger, which had thankfully gotten its flavor back.

"It's my favorite show," she exclaimed as if that made this insanity any better. "Add it to the list. You can't miss that. We can binge-watch on Friday nights to get pumped up for the flea market the next day."

"I don't like it." He fucking hated it.

Clover narrowed her eyes at him, her sexy mouth pursing with disapproval. "You don't have to like it. You just need to do it so we can find some more details to back up this ridiculous fake engagement."

This is why he was a big-picture man. Details sucked. "I'm afraid to ask, but what else?"

"Post-event late night dinners at Vito's. Picnics in the park. Sunday brunch at your apartment with your family." She tapped a finger on the pen resting across the blank napkin. "Go on, write it all down. It'll be golden, trust me."

"And in six weeks when you leave for Australia, what will we tell them?" The end game was clear as day, but how to get there was muddled.

She took another bite of her burger and mulled over his question. "We're just too different. It wouldn't have worked. It was the whole *The Way We Were* thing."

"The what?"

"You haven't seen it?" She looked at him as if he were an alien. "Robert Redford? Barbara Streisand? Buckets of salty tears?"

"I got nothing."

"Add it to the list," she demanded. "We'll have movie night and can alternate picking. Come on, write it down."

He did, managing to hold the half of his burger that was left in one hand as he did so. Movie nights—he just had to keep it on the down low that he preferred chick flicks. Flea markets—about as fun as shoveling after an ice storm. Dinners out—now that he could get behind. As he was writing she listed more of her requirements. Chocolate syrup in the fridge for her morning oatmeal. Jasmine scented bubble bath. Raw potatoes to snack on. It took him right up until the end to realize she was fucking with him—at least on some of it.

He glanced up from the heavily inked napkin, his suspicions confirmed by the all-too-innocent look on her face. Yep. She was messing with him.

"Is everything just another fun adventure to you?" he asked, realizing too late that he hadn't added a damn thing of his own to the list. Some hotshot negotiator he was.

"What fun would life be if it wasn't?" She winked as she sucked up the last of her shake and then popped the final cherry into her mouth.

Cherry. Mouth. Lips. Tongue. Taste. Clover. It all mixed together in his head with the kind of vivid details he usually never fleshed out—especially not in a jerk-off fantasy that he wasn't about to indulge in. She was a sorta employee and held the fate of this subterfuge in her hot little hand.

Without warning, the mental image of that hand wrapped around one of his favorite body parts nearly undid him.

Fuck. Get in the game, you fucking chump.

"Okay so you can skip the bubble bath and the raw potatoes, but since this job has just jumped fourteen notches on the difficulty scale, I'm going to need additional compensation."

Of course. "Like what?"

"A black card to cover the cost of clothes, shoes, and other incidentals."

The woman was mercenary. He couldn't help but admire it. "I don't think so."

"I obviously don't have the kind of wardrobe that a fiancée of yours would have. I don't want to embarrass you with your friends, after all, and if I happen to get a few items for my trip to Australia, too, well, you should still consider yourself getting off cheap."

Forget mercenary. She was downright brilliant. In three short sentences, she'd managed to put him in his place about his comment when she'd walked out of her apartment building in that sexy little shirt and skirt combo, reminded him of the need to make this whole fake engagement seem real, and managed to make him outfitting her for her next adventure downright sensible. The woman was dangerous.

"As long as you don't end up looking like just another boring socialite, then I can give you that point. Lots of bright colors and a little bit of skin showing." His gaze dropped to the bottom edge of her crop top. "For effect."

"Uh-huh." She raised an eyebrow. "Whatever you say."

He demolished the last bite of his burger, using the time to clear his head of useless fantasies. "I have two conditions of my own."

"Shoot."

"Beyond Hudson, no one can know the engagement is

a fake. Not your girlfriends, not your family."

Her perky smile dimmed. "Why not? It's not like they move in the same circles as your family."

"Because my mom probably already has an investigator looking into your background." More than likely she'd started the process earlier today after Clover had told her to take her lunch invitation and shove it where the sun doesn't shine.

She tugged her bottom lip between her teeth again. "I don't want to lie to them."

"We don't have a choice, not if we're going to carry this off." One slip and the game was up. The fewer people who knew, the more likely it would work.

Clover stacked the plastic creamer cups, her jaw stiff. "Fine. And the second condition?"

"What happened in the closet can't happen again," he said, capping the pen and putting it back in his jacket.

Her head tilted up and her grin was anything but perky. It was sexy, teasing, and exactly what his dick didn't need right now. "Okay, so we avoid closets."

"Clover, you know what I mean." And God did his dick object to him putting that detail into words.

"Got it." She nodded her head solemnly, ignoring the creamer pyramid that had been so fascinating only moments before. "No super-hot, make my toes-tingle kissing in a supply closet or anywhere else."

She was laughing at him. His male ego objected, but that was nothing compared to the official complaints being filed in triplicate by other parts of him. Without glancing down at the napkin, he signed it and slid it across to her for review, realizing too late that he hadn't written down the last requirement.

Paging Dr. Freud.

Clover didn't seem to notice. She just signed it, folded it up, and put it in her purse before closing it with a snap.

So there it was. He'd woken up this morning with a normal life. By noon, he had a personal buffer. By ten o'clock, he had a fake fiancée. He couldn't even imagine what new little adventure tomorrow would bring.

Chapter Seven

The next morning, Clover's phone vibrated on the bedside table, buzzing and bouncing against the glass tabletop. She peeled an eyelid open, holding a hand up against the early morning sun shining through her window like a laser beam. The rest of the apartment she shared with her bestie was silent—except for the *buzz, buzz, buzz* of her phone. Letting her eyelids droop back down, she slapped her hand blindly against her bedside table until she made contact with it, swiped right, and brought it up to her ear.

"Hello," her voice came out sounding like a rusty door in a haunted house.

"Jane, I can't believe you didn't tell me, but I'm just too excited to care," her mom said, obviously already on her second pot of coffee. "Congratulations! When's the big day? Tell me all about Sawyer. I want details now, young lady."

Clover's eyes flew open, and she was suddenly fully and utterly awake with the icy dread only her mom could inspire sliding down her spine. "Hi, Mom."

"Don't you 'hi Mom' me, young lady," her mother said, going Mach Two. "I want details about this engagement, and I want to know when you and Sawyer will be coming home for Sunday dinner. It's bad enough that I only found out because Kelly Osgood posted about the news on Facebook after seeing it on some Harbor City gossip blog. There's no way I'm going down to Heber's Deli for your dad's pastrami without details of my own."

Sapo tonto! Not only was she a stupid toad, she was a naive idiot who'd thought she just might make it through this fake engagement without her family finding out. Why did her mom's oldest friend also have to be a gossip junkie?

"I can hear you breathing, Jane." Her mom gasped. "Oh God, tell me this isn't another one of your silly adventures. It's way past time when you needed to start acting like an adult."

Translation: When was Jane finally going to settle down and start mass producing grandkids like a human rabbit? Okay, her mom hadn't used the words "mass producing" or "human rabbit," but that's basically what she wanted. Thirty was just around the corner, according to her mom. Funny. Last time Clover had checked, it was still four years away. A fake engagement should have lessened some of that pressure to settle into a boring life just like her mom's, instead it had all the markings of adding gas to the fire under her mom's ass.

"I've been acting like an adult for years, Mom," she said through gritted teeth. "I paid my own way through college. I have good friends. I pay my bills on time." Even if this month it had been by the skin of her teeth. "You may not like the life I lead, but it's mine and I like it." And she liked that it was as different from her mom's staid life in Sparksville as possible.

Her mom's sigh was as weary as it was familiar. "I just worry about you, that's all."

And *BAM!* the mom-guilt cannon landed a direct shot.

Deep inhale. Deep exhale. She mentally closed the door on her annoyance. "I know, and I'm sorry I make you worry."

"So help me stop worrying about this engagement that came out of nowhere."

The truth hovered on the tip of Clover's tongue, but she'd promised no one would know. And if her mom knew, so would all of Sparksville—plus the truth wouldn't do any good but make her mom worry even more. They weren't alike in any way and tended to argue more than agree, but they were family and that meant a lot to both of them.

"It happened kind of fast." Not a lie. *And not exactly the truth, either,* Khwāy p̧ayyāx̀xn. *Moronic water buffalo, indeed.* But Clover drew the line at outright lying to her mother.

"I'd say so," her mom said. "How long have you been seeing him?"

"It was kind of a whirlwind thing, you know how much I travel, and we wanted to keep everything hush-hush until we knew for sure it was the real deal." Her palms were sweaty and her mouth dry. God, she really did suck at this. Good thing she'd never listed life of crime as a dream goal.

"And you're ready to get married already?"

There it was, her mom's Jane-why-can't-you-just-do-things-like-a-normal-person sigh. It brought out the reflexive snarl in Clover.

"When you know, you know," she said, her voice as sweet as high fructose corn syrup. "Isn't that what you always said about Dad?"

Her mom let out a surprised chuckle before the natural staidness settled back into her tone. "May you live long enough for your own words to be thrown back at you."

"I know it seems crazy."

"Love often does—especially when it comes at you out of the blue."

That unexpected understanding from a woman whose thinking Clover rarely, if ever, clearly comprehended left her momentarily speechless.

"You still there, Jane?"

"Mom…" The urge to spill it all tightened her throat. She hated lying. Even if she'd been any good at it, she'd have hated it.

"I wouldn't be me if I didn't worry you were rushing, but I'll table it until I can set my own eyes on him and see for myself," her mom said, covering Clover's silence with her own chattiness. "When are you bringing him up for Sunday dinner? We're only two hours away. You could come next

Saturday, spend the night, and head back to the city after lunch. Can I mark the calendar for next weekend?"

That was not going to happen. "I'll have to talk it over with Sawyer. I know his schedule is packed." Or it would be until she got on the plane for Australia in six weeks.

"See that you do, otherwise I'll be forced to show up on your doorstep." It came out like a joke, but only a fool would believe it was one. "Love you, Jane."

"Love you, too, Mom," she said before hanging up.

The truth of it was that she did. For all of their differences—and her bone-deep commitment to never grow up to *be* her mother—there was a lot of love between them. It was just the prickly kind most days.

A shriek sounded outside her door a half second before it flew open, and Daphne rushed into her room.

"You're getting married?!" she cried out in one very loud voice.

Since hiding under the covers wasn't an option, Clover nodded and steeled herself for Lying To The People You Love Sucks: Part Two.

• • •

The fact that Sawyer needed to get to his brother Hudson before their mom did was only one reason why he was in his personal gym on his phone at seven in the morning on a Friday—the one day he blocked out the world and worked from home every week. The more important reason was that Hudson was not a morning person and some things didn't stop being fun the older Sawyer got. Busting his brother's chops by calling before Hudson's surprisingly agile brain had awakened was definitely one of them.

Settling into plank position with the phone turned to speaker mode and placed near his fisted hands, he listened to it ring. And ring. And ring.

It went to voicemail three times before Hudson finally

picked up. "Are you outside the cabin with a spoon?"

Sawyer laughed, the move making his abs hurt more than the second minute of holding a plank normally did. "No."

"Is Mom okay?" his brother asked, concern sharpening his tone.

Sawyer dropped out of his plank, regretting that he'd even put that thought in his brother's head. "Mom's fine."

Two beats of silence followed by a less than cheery, "Then fuck off."

Chuckling at Hudson's obvious misery at being woken up before the crack of noon, Sawyer started in on pushups. "I want you to be the best man at my wedding."

"Who is this and what did you do to my brother—not that I'm complaining, but our mom would be upset."

"He had a spoon," Sawyer said, sweat starting to bead on his forehead. "It was either him or me."

"You're fucking hilarious."

"You're not the first person to tell me that."

"Bullshit." Hudson snorted. "No one *ever* says that about you. What do you really want?"

"I need you to tell Mom that I've been dating Clover on the sly for months ever since I met her in Singapore on one of my trips to see Mr. Lim." He pounded out another set of pushups, then rolled onto his back for a breather while Hudson's brain caught up.

"Who is Clover?"

"My personal buffer." Sawyer downed a gulp from his water bottle while telling himself that the pickup in his pulse was because of the workout, not because of the blonde and her sparkly crop top he'd spent the night thinking about. "But Mom doesn't know that either so keep that to yourself."

"Wait. I thought you refused to hire a personal buffer."

"I did, but then Clover scared off Mom. How could I not hire her after that?" Just the memory of the look on his mom's face before she'd stormed off would be cheering him up for weeks.

"This is Jane Lee we're talking about, right? She was the only female buffer candidate I sent your way." Hudson's voice was thick with disbelief. "Does she have superpowers? Is she suffering from radiation poisoning?"

Sawyer picked up his phone and slid it into the wall mount by his pull up bar. "Not that I know of."

"Then how did she do it?"

"She told Mom off." He gripped the bar and pulled himself up, curling his legs to a ninety-degree angle.

"And she's still alive?"

Sawyer couldn't keep the smile off his face as he began to ease back down, slow and controlled. No one—and he meant no one—ever told Helene Carlyle what to do. "Yep."

"I kinda want to marry her myself."

His grip slipped and he landed with a thunk on his feet, his grin gone. "You can work your charms on her once she gets back from Australia."

"That's mighty…uh…generous of you."

He wiped his palms on his basketball shorts hard enough to make his thighs sting. "It's a fake engagement to keep Mom off my back so I can close the Singapore deal, not an actual real relationship."

"Of course," Hudson said with a sigh. "It's work."

"Exactly." He gripped the bar again and jerked himself up. "In six weeks, Clover leaves to go help walnicks or hallababies or something."

"Wallabies?"

"That's it."

"Are you drunk? None of this sounds like you. Who came up this idiotic plan?"

"I did." His arms burned on the way down and back up. "She told me off at the fundraiser, I announced we were engaged while giving a speech at the event, we made out in the closet, and then we sealed the deal at Vito's."

What in the hell was he doing telling his brother all that? It was just the type of ammo Hudson wouldn't hesitate to use. *Just because you can't stop thinking about that closet doesn't mean you need to talk about it, dickhead.*

"You fucked her at a diner?"

"No, you asshole, we came up with a contract at the diner."

"Now *that* sounds more like you."

"Actually, she insisted." That had surprised him. It was not what he was expecting from someone with Clover's resume.

He knocked out five more quick pull-ups before his brother got in his next question. "So what's she get out of this deal?"

"Fifteen grand."

"That doesn't sound legal."

"It's not for *that*." No matter how much he'd thought about fucking her every which way possible last night. "She's an employee—well, an independent contractor. I'm not going to sleep with her."

"Making out was that bad?" Hudson asked.

Sawyer dropped to the ground, glaring at the phone. "I'm not answering that."

"So it was that *good*." Hudson barked out a laugh before using a fake German accent, "Very interesting."

His brother was a jackass—but one that he needed or this whole plot would implode. Now that was a big picture he didn't like the looks of. "Are you going to back up my story or not?"

"What happens when Mom finds out that the whole thing was a sham?"

"She won't." He'd make sure of that. "Clover and I already discussed it. We'll come up with a believable breakup story and that will be that."

"Uh-huh. Sure it will."

"It's a business arrangement, and I know those inside and out."

"Yeah." His brother chuckled. "But you don't know shit about women."

Ten minutes later they had a workable plan and his brother was back to doing whatever it was he did while at his cabin. He always claimed he was with a date or three, but Hudson was always saying stupid shit to cover up the fact that he had a perfectly good brain behind his pretty-boy face. Things like Sawyer not knowing women. He didn't need to know them. He just had to make sure he and Clover were on the same page, which according to their contract, they were. No need to stress over imaginary details.

Shaking off the doubt creeping across his shoulders, he got on the treadmill, ready to run until even the possibility that his brother was right was gone.

• • •

Sitting at the table in her sunny kitchen, Clover drained the morning concoction in her Keep It Weird oversize mug—four sugar packets, half a cup of milk, and a generous splash of coffee—without spitting it out in laughter at the look of absolute horror on Daphne's face.

"You can't be getting married," she said, her brown eyes were huge, and if she'd been wearing pearls she would have been clutching them. "You barely know him. What if he's a serial killer who only gets away with it because of his money and connections?"

The croissant and coffee had just been a trick. As soon as Clover thought she was safe, Daphne had started in on the best friend version of the Spanish Inquisition before helping her throw the contents of her closet into an oversized vintage suitcase she'd gotten at a flea market and restored—with her own little tweaks, of course.

"He's not a serial killer. He's a businessman. He's…" Clover floundered trying to find the perfect word to describe Sawyer Carlyle, but the information she'd gained through her Google-fu after he'd rushed her out of his office yesterday had been frustratingly limited. Their "date" at the charity fundraiser last night hadn't answered any, either—beyond the fact his kisses melted her brain.

The man may run one of the largest international construction firms in the world, but he wasn't much of a chatter. A few quotes here or there in various business articles, but no Twitter, no Facebook, no Snapchat, no social media at all. She wasn't about to tell Daphne that, though… she loved the woman like the sister she'd never had but saying Daphne was a worrywart was like saying soccer players' legs were a thing of jaw-dropping, panty-melting goodness. It was just a fact of life.

"He's really busy," Clover finished lamely.

"You mean he's really fucking hot," Daphne said, twisting her miles of dark hair up into a knot on top of her head.

There was no doubt about that. The man was all broad shoulders, square jaw, and the kind of big hands that made promises about other parts of his anatomy—ones that she'd confirmed for herself in the closet last night. Sawyer Carlyle may not talk to the press, but they loved him anyway, blasting out photos of one of Harbor City's most eligible bachelors taken at society events, charity fundraisers, and on the street. She couldn't blame them. Even when he was glaring at the camera, the man took a hell of a sexy picture.

"But you gotta remember," Daphne said, "Ted Bundy was hot, too."

"Okay, no more true crime TV for you." Clover warned and cut up the pancake Daphne had shoveled onto her plate.

Clover took a bite to be polite but…yeah, eating the whole thing wasn't going to happen. Daphne was going through a healthy-eating phase and the pancakes were pumpkin and quinoa mixed with little green bits she was pretty sure were kale.

She was saved from having to actually take a second bite by Daphne's own single-minded determination and 100 percent commitment to melodrama. "It's all happening so fast. I can't believe you're moving in with him—let alone marrying him!"

And if her stomach wasn't in rebellion enough from the hipster pancakes, the guilt from lying to her family and friends gave even the air an acidic taste.

"What can I say?" Clover shrugged. "He just wants me near him 24/7. Anyway, what kind of serial killer would ask a potential victim to marry him?"

"Those creepers who are always posting about wanting foot models or bikini babes for calendars on Craigslist," Daphne said around a mouthful of the barely edible pancakes.

Clover shook her head. "And you look like such a normal person."

"I know." Daphne grinned, her dark good looks not even hinting at the snarky personality behind her pretty face. "It fools the boys every time. Don't change the subject. Something about this quickie engagement stinks."

Clover opened her mouth to argue, but managed to close her trap before she reminded Daphne of her last boyfriend who'd turned out to be a serial cheater and general asshole. There. Now that was a good sign. The filter between her brain and her mouth was usually broken as she'd proven over and over again yesterday.

"Look, I know this is unexpected—which you should totally expect from me—but I need you to trust me and just go with the flow on this one." If anything, her friend should be used to Clover always doing the unexpected. "Sawyer has this big deal he's working in Singapore, and well, you know I was there to teach English. I didn't know much about him and he didn't know much about me," she continued, hating every word coming out of her mouth. In a few years, they'd all laugh about the crazy that's-so-Clover prank, but for now, she had to stick with the story she and Sawyer had agreed upon. "We never thought we'd see each other once we got back home, but when I showed up for the job interview and we realized that fate had thrown us together, well…we went with it."

Daphne shut her mouth, but there was no missing the worry lines on her otherwise smooth forehead. You couldn't be friends as long as they had without seeing the hidden signs of trouble.

"I love you, Clover, you know I'm behind you no matter what you do," she said, her forehead still crinkled in concern. "But you've done some crazy shit in the past, and I just want you to be careful. This is even nuttier than that time you started the sidewalk self-tanning booth business, or the time you went to Egypt to volunteer on a camel farm and realized they spit, or when you thought the kebabs and donut cart was the way to finance your trip to Peru to work on jungle conservation."

None of those were things she ever wanted to relive, but this was different. This would work out just as she'd planned. It had to.

"I know, this is more…" Clover floundered for the right word, "unexpected than most of my adventures, but I need you to go with me on this. Right now, Sawyer and I are perfect for each other."

For a long moment, neither of them said anything as the real truth itched its way up Clover's spine. Then, finally, Daphne gave her a guarded smiled and raised her coffee mug in a toast. "What we badasses form…"

"May no man put asunder," she finished the familiar mantra.

Yeah. Shared history. It mattered. And it made her lie even worse. She opened her mouth to say something, anything that would make this less painful, but the doorbell interrupted her.

"Your prince has arrived," Daphne said.

But it wasn't her prince. When Clover opened the apartment's front door, it was Sawyer's driver, Linus, waiting for her on the other side.

Chapter Eight

The back of the Town Car was even bigger without Sawyer inside filing the backseat with pheromones and hotness. Plus, she felt ridiculous sitting in the back by herself while Linus sat by himself up front wearing—not exaggerating—a chauffeur's hat. The whole situation was making her knee jiggle and her motor mouth rev up. Okay, it wasn't just that. It was that she was really doing this.

Having a fake engagement.

Lying to everyone.

Living with a man she barely knew.

But it was for a good cause, right? Fifteen grand, a new wardrobe, and acting as a good Samaritan personal buffer. Could she still be a good Samaritan if she was getting fifteen Gs? What was so different about this? It was an adventure. Her passport had more stamps in it than Daphne had shoes in her closet. This was just one measly trip across town to the land of the rich and home of the snobs. How scary could it be? Her pulse skyrocketed and her thoughts spiraled around her head until all she could focus on was the anxiety making her lungs tight.

"Linus, I can't do this," she said, leaning forward so he could hear her a million miles away in the front seat. "Please pull over."

The chauffeur glanced up into the rearview mirror and gave her a quick once-over. "Is everything okay?"

"I'm not a girl who's made for backseats." Her eyes widened at the double entendre. "Oh God, that sounded totally wrong."

Linus almost laughed. At least the rearview mirror

reflection showed a corner of his mouth twitch. "Yes, ma'am."

Linus double parked in front of the bodega where she bought her weekly lottery tickets. She was out of the backseat and opening the passenger's side door before he even made it around the front of the Town Car. She slid inside. There was a tissue box stuffed between the two front seats and a half empty iced coffee from Ground Out Coffee in the cup holder. It smelled different up here. Less like expensive leather and more like chilled mochaccino, cherry cough drops, and solid working class familiarity.

Whatever the driver thought about her horning in on his space, he didn't say a word as he got back in behind the wheel.

"Thank you," she said when he shut his door. "This is much better."

"Whatever you say, ma'am."

That false honorific went across her conscience like a cheese grater. "Clover."

Linus avoided saying her first name by nodding as he pulled into traffic.

Three blocks closer to their final destination and the nerves were back, making her so jittery she felt like a money-eating vending machine that someone was shaking to get the last bag of Skittles out of. The energy built, needing to go somewhere, anywhere before she exploded—which meant only one thing.

"So I don't usually drive in the city." And her mouth was off and running. "It's usually the subway for me. You wouldn't imagine all the weirdness you see down there. I saw a rat the size of a small dog last week and managed— barely—not to pass out. Don't tell anyone, but rats are my weakness. It's bad. Did you ever see that movie *Ratatouille*? There's a scene where all the rats come pouring out of the ceiling. I can't watch that part—and it's a cartoon."

Linus, looking like he was out of an old movie in his dark suit, hat, and gray hair, kept his hands on ten and two and his eyes on the road. His silence just made her own verbal diarrhea worse.

"One year for Halloween, my brother Bobby hid an army of remote controlled robotic rats he'd built under my bed. I had just gotten up to go to the bathroom when he started them up and they came rolling out, swarming around my feet. I still have nightmares about that. So, as you can imagine, avoiding the pony-sized rats on the subway today was nice." She pivoted in her seat to face him, her grin as tight as her nerves. "Thank you for picking me up."

"Of course," he said.

"Bì zuǐ shǔ xiǎojiě!" Oh yes, of all the Mandarin stuffed into her brain, it came up with "shut up rat lady" when it was too late to keep Linus from thinking she was touched in the head. "Sorry, I talk when I'm nervous."

"You don't have to be nervous around me." Now he did smile. No doubt about it. "In fact, I'll tell you a secret: you're not even supposed to notice me."

The statement was weird enough to cut through the apprehensive fog blinding her. "Why in the world not?"

He shrugged and made a left onto Gramercy Avenue. "Because I'm just the driver."

"Sawyer notices you," she said, jumping to defend her fake fiancé's honor for the second time in less than twenty-four hours. "He said you saved his sanity by taking him to Vito's."

"The Carlyles are different," Linus said.

"How?"

His impossibly stiff back actually straightened another ten degrees. "I'm sure you know."

Oh, someone was suspicious—and he had every right to be. Besides Mama Carlyle, no one had more reason to doubt her and Sawyer's story than the man who spent every day with him. *Time to spin this one out, Clover girl, but not too much.*

"Pretend I just met them all yesterday. What would I learn about them?" she asked, keeping her tone light and friendly.

Linus raised an eyebrow but otherwise kept his neutral expression and his attention on the road. "They're good people. They're a family. Mr. Carlyle's death hit all of them very hard but they leaned on one another. I'd hate to be someone who messed with that bond."

"That sounds like a warning." And a pointed one at that.

"Only an observation."

Uh-huh. She might be from Sparksville, but small towns didn't mean small brains. "It was his idea, getting married so fast."

Another turn, this time onto Thirty-Third Street. "Mr. Carlyle has never been one to let anyone get between him and his grand vision."

"What was he like as a little boy?" she asked, wanting to know the answer more than she expected.

Linus stayed silent and she thought he wasn't going to answer, but then that smile of his broke out again.

"Shorter."

"But otherwise the same?" She could picture it. He'd probably been the only four-year-old in his undoubtedly expensive preschool with a business plan in his backpack.

"Yes, ma'am."

"Clover," she corrected automatically.

He nodded noncommittally and pulled over in front of a high-rise on the corner of Expensive Avenue and Forget-About-It Street. Okay, those weren't the actual street names, but it sure felt like it. Craning her neck as she looked out the passenger window, she could almost make out the name "Carlyle" written across the top of the building in giant sweeping font.

Whip fast, Linus got out of the car, rounded the hood, and opened her door. "Mr. Carlyle is waiting for you in the penthouse. Just have Irving buzz Mr. Carlyle to let him know you're on your way up." He held out his hand to help her out. When she didn't move, he dropped his voice so there was no way anyone heard his words amongst the clatter of Harbor City. "No need to worry, Clover. You'll do just fine."

Were her nerves that obvious? *Only if you're breathing, rat lady.*

She took a deep breath and accepted the driver's help out of the car, even though she'd been stepping out of vehicles unaided for as long as she could remember. Somehow she knew he'd see it as her being rude, and she couldn't do that to him.

"Thank you, Linus."

He nodded and closed the door behind her.

Squaring her shoulders so no one would notice the way they quaked, Clover forced one foot in front of the other toward the opulent glass doors. She'd made it halfway through before she realized she had no frickin' clue who in the hell Irving was.

• • •

It turned out that Irving was the doorman who had a big, shiny name tag—thank you whoever was watching out for her upstairs. He had a huge fluffy black mustache, perceptive eyes, and a Russian accent as fake as her engagement. She liked him immediately.

The exaggerated Bond-villain pronunciation he used when he called up to Sawyer's penthouse and his devotion to smoothing his impressive 'stasche with his fingertips was a thing to behold. In fact, she was so fascinated watching Irving that she didn't have any time to double think her life choices. No. Her stupid brain saved all the fun, torturous stuff for the looooong elevator ride up to the top floor of a very tall building.

The doors *whooshed* open to reveal…a totally lux open-concept penthouse. It was all grays, blacks, chrome, and cold industrial chic without a living soul in sight. She was afraid to touch anything. Gobsmacked and a little petrified, she must have lingered in the elevator too long because the doors started to close. Leaping forward, she sped through just in time.

"Hello?" Standing in the foyer, she glanced around the empty space. "Mr. Carlyle?" Still nothing. She took a tentative step forward, her high-heeled boots clicking on the slate tile floor. "Sawyer?"

"In here," he called out from somewhere down the hall on her left.

She click-clacked her way down the hall and through the open doorway at the end before jolting to a stop. The room was massive, taking up the entire length of the building with floor-to-ceiling windows covering three walls, giving him a two-hundred-and-seventy degree view of the Harbor City skyline. Opaque glass block half walls divided the huge space into three distinct rooms: office, sitting area, bedroom.

Sawyer was in the first one, sitting behind a glass-and-chrome desk, scowling at his laptop. If he was devastating in a suit and deadly in a tux, the man was scorching in a plain white T-shirt. Because he was sitting down she couldn't see but her fingers were crossed that he'd paired the bicep-baring shirt with a pair of worn jeans that hung low on his hips and clung to his ass. He may have declared that they were hands-off, but he didn't say anything about being eyes-off and a girl had to get her kicks from somewhere—especially when he hadn't even slowed down in typing since she'd taken a step inside his domain.

When he didn't look up or acknowledge her presence, she cleared her throat. "I really hope you pay the cleaning crew extra for all the Windex they have to use," she said, breaking the silence.

Sawyer looked up, took off his glasses, and rubbed the area under his brown-green eyes. Then, he looked around as if he'd never seen the room before.

After a quick perusal that skipped right over her, he pushed his glasses back in place and dropped his gaze back to his screen. "The doorman should be up with your bags soon."

"That's what Irving said." Now this wasn't awkward. Not. At. All.

"Irving?" Sawyer asked, his fingers poised on the keyboard.

"The doorman."

"Huh." One dark eyebrow arched upward above the top of his glasses. "I'd always figured him for something more like Vladimir."

He went back to typing while she lingered in the doorway feeling as guilty and excited as a teenager loitering outside a liquor store.

Instead of taking the hint and going on an exploratory mission, her nerves took ahold of her mouth. "So what's the plan?"

They had backgrounds to plot, stories to come up with, and an entire secret love affair to create before Sawyer's mother got a chance to break them.

He kept typing. "You settle into your suite on the other end of the hall and I figure out what in the hell is sinking this Singapore deal."

"You're working on it from home? On a Friday?" That was…not what she expected.

"Always." A soft ding sounded and his fingers made only the briefest of pauses as they clickity-clacked across the keyboard. "That'll be your bags."

Cheeks burning at the obvious dismissal, Clover spun on the ball of her foot and marched back down the way she'd come. Fine. Let Mr. Work From Home pound his frustration out on the poor defenseless keyboard. She'd do the fake backstory plotting on her own. His mom was just going to love hearing about how they met at a wine and paint class where Sawyer had been the nude model.

• • •

"You crackhead!" Clover railed, her voice not needing to be too loud in the all glass and metal penthouse for it to carry everywhere. "Don't do it. You are waaaaaaaay overspending."

Sawyer glanced up at the empty doorway of his office. The television had gone on about twenty minutes ago after what seemed like an eternity of Clover singing along to Top 40. She'd done it for hours, her alto filling up the otherwise silent penthouse. Of course she'd sing as she unpacked and did whatever else she'd been doing for the past few hours. He'd done his best not to picture it. Especially when he'd heard the shower turn on. Nope. He hadn't imagined her naked and soapy as the water slid down her creamy skin. And he hadn't hummed along with Clover's song, he had just…rhythmically cleared his throat…on key. Thank God she'd moved on from singing to yelling at the people on the TV.

"Ugh. Not pink." She made a melodramatic groan. "Just because the challenge is make a woman's bedroom doesn't mean it has to be pink!"

Calling himself every word for dumbass he could think of as the setting sun's light streamed in from the window behind him, he refocused on the gibberish on his screen. Numbers and ideas were thrown together with all the illogical randomness of a monkey throwing shit at the zoo. So much for his sacred work from home time. For the second time that day, he erased the mess he'd been typing.

The first time he'd hit the delete button had been after

his mom had called. He hadn't picked up. Not the first time. Not the second time. And definitely not the third. If he had, his mom would have known something was up. Fridays were sacrosanct for him and everyone knew it. He worked without interruption from the time he walked out of his post-workout shower to the single glass of single-malt Scotch and the eleven p.m. international business roundup podcast. It was usually his most productive planning and plotting day of the week.

"Ohhhh," Clover crooned. "That is a brilliant idea for retooling that ratty chair."

The six-hotel job in Rio? The pitch had come to him on a Friday. The idea for ten high-rise office complexes in Dubai? Yep, on a Friday. The missing piece of a proposal for a luxury tower in London? Happened on a Friday. But this Friday? He'd come up with exactly shit even as the clock ticked down on the call for proposals on the Singapore trio of high-rises job. Why? Because instead of being able to concentrate, he'd been quietly humming—okay singing— along to whatever pop crap Clover had warbled.

"Fuck this." He pushed back from his desk and strode to the door. This was his house. He could tell her to be silent. Order her, really. He *was* the boss.

He got to the door and…hesitated. He peeked around the doortrame. The hallway was long   the penthouse took up one quarter of the top floor of The Carlyle High-Rise. Each of the four penthouses had a unique glass-and-steel extension on the building's corner that allowed them a two-hundred-and-seventy-degree view of the city skyline. The rest of the penthouse was more typical with an open floor plan that gave him a straight shot visual from his door to the living room. Instead of the market report or the 24/7 business news channel on his big screen, there was a woman in overalls going to town on a chair with a power saw. All he could see of Clover was the back of her head as the screen had her total attention.

"You are going to kick those douchebags' patriarchal asses!" Clover said, raising her fist in the air above the back of the couch.

Leaving his home office on a Friday was the last thing he planned on doing, and yet that's exactly what he did, not stopping until he stood next to the couch. Clover sat with her legs crossed, wearing black yoga pants and—God help him—a thin, oversized "Reduce, Reuse, Recycle" T-shirt that hung off one shoulder and did absolutely nothing to disguise the fact that she wasn't wearing a bra. The hint of nipple brushing against the shirt as she wrote something down in big loopy handwriting into a notebook drew his attention like a tractor beam. He shouldn't look. He didn't want to look. He couldn't look away.

"What are you doing?" "To me" was the obvious ending to that question because whatever it was it had fucked with him greatly.

"Shhhh," Clover hushed him, not even bothering to turn around. "I'll catch you up at the commercial break."

"Catch me up on what?"

"This episode of Flea Market Flip." The show went to commercial then, and she glanced up at him, narrowing her eyes and giving him a naughty little smile that made his cock twitch. "You're totally in violation of the contract, but I'll let it slide since it's our first Friday night."

He was so lost. He'd blame the lack of blood in his brain, but it seemed to be his reality whenever he was around Clover. "What violation?"

"To binge-watch HGTV on Friday nights in preparation for hitting the flea market on Saturday morning." She gave a little cheer and turned her attention back to the TV, which was now showing a commercial for birth control. "We're totally going to find something fabulous to pop your cherry."

The mental movie that started rolling at the phrase

"pop your cherry" had absolutely nothing whatsoever to do with a flea market unless she had a kink for public sex.

"I didn't think you were serious." There were a hundred—a billion—things he'd rather do with her—and to her—than go to some dirty flea market.

She shrugged, the move dragging the thin cotton across her full tits. "Too bad, so sad, buddy, because you signed on the dotted line."

"You'll never get a judge to uphold anything scrawled on a napkin."

"Sure you want to gamble on that?" she asked. "Anyway, I already came up with our backstory. I know how you hate dealing with the details. Your mom was a little shocked when I told her how we met, but she took it better than I'd expected."

There wasn't a single part of those two sentences that didn't make his chest burn. "You talked to my mom? What did you tell her?"

"That we met when you modeled for a wine and paint class I took." She looked up at him, all sweetness and innocence except for the hard glint of trouble in her eyes. "I told her that I was a goner the moment you slipped off your tighty whiteys and were able to hold your pose for so *long*, even though I could see it was *very hard*."

Good thing his family had funded Harbor City General's new cardiac wing because he and his mom were both going to need it. "You did not say that to my mom."

Clover let his words hang in the air for a beat before letting loose with a laugh that bounced off the walls. "No."

"Did you *talk* to my mom?" he asked, too relieved to be pissed—although that would be coming just as soon as he could breathe again.

She rolled her eyes. "Oh my God, relax Mr. Stuffykins. How would she even get my number?"

He opened his mouth to answer, but the show came

back on and Clover shushed him while patting the seat next to her on the couch. If he hadn't been on the verge of a Clover-induced heart attack, he wouldn't have followed her lead. He would have gone back to the office and pounded his head against his desk until the perfect solution to the Singapore problem fell out. Instead of doing that, though, he sat down on the couch—making sure to leave a sanity space of at least a foot between them—and settled in to see what kind of do-it-yourself renovating fresh hell he'd gotten himself into.

Chapter Nine

They were four episodes in and, God help him, Sawyer was actually rooting for a pair of DIY weirdos on his TV screen. Two sisters in their sixties — Eileen and Aurora — were taking on their husbands with the challenge being to pick and redo three pieces that worked into a classic boudoir feel. The husbands, Bob and Larry, were — unexpectedly — kicking ass. Was he rooting for them because they were dudes? No. Bob and Larry understood that people didn't want *delicate* bedroom furniture. The men had put together a plan for a dresser, a bed, and a mirror each with a solid, rough-hewn feel to them. No matter what happened in that room, that furniture was going to take it and stay rock solid. Bob and Larry knew what they were about.

"No one is going to buy that stuff," Clover said, holding out the bowl of popcorn she'd made. "It looks like it belongs in a cabin in the woods where you'd go to write your manifesto."

"Wrong. It's much better than all the flowers and velvet covered crap Eileen and Aurora put together." He grabbed another handful of popcorn, buttery enough to make his trainer have a seizure, and watched as the two teams went into carnival barker mode in their efforts to sell their refinished finds.

"That's called romance and putting people in the mood. It's the vibe you're going for in a boudoir." She sat the bowl on the glass coffee table and, when she settled back against the couch, cut the one-foot sanity zone between them in half. "Not that you would know. Your bedroom is probably all glass and cheerful black."

The fact that she'd thought about his bedroom made that very male part of his brain wake up and take a bow. It wasn't like he was pounding his chest and going all caveman about it, but he couldn't keep the smirk off his face as he stretched out his legs and extended one arm along the back of the couch. The fact that his fingers were now in touching distance of the blond strands that had escaped the messy knot on top of her head was purely coincidental.

Yeah and so is the fact that your cock hasn't gotten below half mast since you realized your fake fiancée wasn't wearing a bra. What are you, fourteen?

"Care to make a bet on the outcome?" he asked.

"What are the stakes?" she countered.

His mind filled with all of the inappropriate possibilities, but managed to clamp his jaw closed and stay in his seat until he forced every pornographic image behind a mental steel door. "Winner gets final say on what we get at the flea market tomorrow."

Shit. That was only marginally better than the first ideas he'd had. Sure, it was more appropriate, but he had no intention of bringing anything home from the damn flea market.

Clover shoved out her hand. "Deal."

She didn't look the least bit doubtful. Why did he think he'd just been suckered? *Because you probably have been, numb nuts.* Still, he shook her hand—even that minor contact sending a jolt straight south. It was just what he needed to jerk him back to reality in a desperate bid for self-preservation. This wasn't just a silly game. It sure as hell wasn't a real relationship. The fake engagement was a month and a half of fun and games for her and six weeks of peace for him so he could settle the largest construction bid they'd ever offered. After that, she'd go to Australia and he'd have figured out a solution to the problem of his matchmaking mama. All he had to do was keep his dick safely behind his zipper and everything would work out fine. Only a complete dumbass drank the toxic cocktail of business mixed with sex when hundreds of millions were on the line.

"Oh look, you're scowling again." Clover shot him a cocky smile and settled back, this time eliminating the sanity zone completely so they were hip to hip. "Looks like somebody just realized he took on more than he could handle."

Instead of confirming the truth, Sawyer turned his attention to the activity on the screen and ignored how good her soft curves felt pressed against him.

Twenty minutes later and Sawyer was left slack-jawed at the outcome. Bob and Larry had had their asses handed to them. Not only did they not win, they took the biggest loss in the show's history.

"This show makes no sense," he grumbled, reaching out for something to soothe his wounded pride—sore loser, party of one. "If people want a table, why don't they just go out and get the one they want instead of wasting their time totally redoing an old table?"

Clover snorted and twisted around to face him, the move bringing her even more firmly against him as she gave him a hey-stupid look. "Well, for one, there's a thing called money and not everyone has as much of it as you do."

"I know that," he said, being difficult just for the sake of it—and because he hadn't stopped thinking about how hot an annoyed Clover was since she'd jabbed him in the chest with her fingernail last night. "But are you seriously telling me you couldn't find something in your budget range?"

Right on cue, the pink rose in her cheeks. "My budget is none of your business—and it's not always about the money." The tip of her tongue darted out and left her full bottom lip glistening. "Sometimes it's the fun of making something new or refinishing a piece to show the beauty that was hiding underneath that no one spotted but you."

"So you're the flea market fairy godmother?"

"Come on, don't tell me you've never experienced a thrill when you've built something."

There wasn't a damn thing he could say to that. He hadn't even liked Legos as a kid.

"Oh my God." She smacked him playfully, square in the middle of his chest. "You've never actually *made* anything, have you?"

He was the CEO of Carlyle Enterprises, he wasn't supposed to be out there in a hard hat and a leather tool belt. "I make deals. I make plans. I make the big picture fit my goals."

"None of which are tangible," she said with just enough blue-collar superiority to hit a vulnerable spot he didn't even realize was there.

"Really?" He turned so they were facing each other, only inches apart. The air crackled around them as the tension built. "You're sitting in one right now. The Carlyle High-Rise was my first build."

She didn't look impressed. "Did you lay the foundation? Put up any of the beams? Paint the walls?"

"No." The single word blasted out of his mouth.

"Then you have no idea the kind of fun you're in for." Her face broke into a huge grin. "To actually take something, transform it, and give it new life? It's a little like magic."

Understanding hit him like a wrecking ball, laying him flat. She'd been winding him up on purpose. Not to knock him down but to blast him out of his own comfort zone and get him to see the adventure ahead of him in the same light she saw it. Damn. For all of his IQ points, he hadn't used any.

"I never would have pictured you as being so philosophical about stripping paint and rolling varnish."

A teasing promise lit her eyes. "And I never would have guessed you didn't have any experience working with your hands."

Now that was just a straight up lie. "I never said that. You know very well that I'm good with my hands." He reached out and tucked a stray blond hair behind her ear, letting his touch linger. "Very good."

Her breath caught, but she didn't move away as his fingers trailed down the soft column of her neck. Her pulse thrummed under his touch and one glance down at the hard peaks pushing against her thin T-shirt confirmed she was skating along the same fault line between sanity and lust that he was.

"Are you flirting with me?" she asked, her voice breathy.

"No." He didn't flirt. That was Hudson. Sawyer was the grumpy brother. He never flirted. Still, his hand didn't drop from where he was touching her and he couldn't tear his gaze away from her perfect pink mouth.

"Of course not." She leaned forward, cutting the distance between them, so close he could feel her soft breath against his skin. "That would violate the contract."

The temptation to dip his head the few inches to kiss her had his entire body hard and wound tight with anticipation. Lust ran through him like a runaway freight train. The little voice in the back of his head screaming that this was a bad idea suffered the same fate as it had in the supply closet last night: death by ignoring. Clover Lee had that effect on him. It was going to be a *very* long month and a half.

"The napkin didn't say anything about flirting," he said.

No, he was totally free to give himself blue balls the size of watermelons every time he came near his personal buffer.

"Ah-ha!" The triumphant sound escaped her lush lips as she straightened, expanding the space between them and dislodging his hand from her soft skin. "You *are* flirting."

Was he? No. He was torturing himself. That was a very different sort of hell. "You take all the fun out of things."

"No way." She shook her head, the movement letting a few more silky strands loose from the knot on the top of her head. "I am the definition of fun. If it wasn't for me, you'd still be in your office banging on your keyboard."

"I don't bang."

"Not me, you don't." She shot him a cocky smirk. "It's in the contract."

The mental image came complete in full color and sound in an instant. Her blond hair spread out across the surface of his desk. The dusky rose of her nipples, wet from his tongue. Her long legs spread wide. The feel of her ass in his hands as he lifted her upward and sank deep within her. *Oh hell.* He was not going to get the image of fucking her on his desk out of his head any time soon, if ever. "Now who's flirting?"

"I'm teasing and teasing is not flirting."

He straightened his glasses and put on his best I'm-just-here-to-learn face. "Oh really?"

Anticipation zinged between them—as tangible as a touch. Every part of him ached to reach out and caress the full curve of her lips, roll her hard nipples, and slide between her slick folds. He fisted his hands on his thighs, fighting the primal urge to take her and put every fantasy of her he'd already had to shame.

"Most definitely not," Clover said in a prim teacher voice. "Their meanings are completely different. Definitions are very important. Like this—" Quick as a blink, she pushed him back against the couch and pivoted so she straddled him, her hands on either side of his face. Her mouth was on his in the next instant, too soft to be what either of them wanted and too real to be a fantasy. Then, as fast as her sneak attack was, she pulled back but remained hovering over his lap, her breath coming in shaky, gasps. "Is not sex so it was most definitely not covered in our contract."

Sawyer had never been so happy for someone to point out a loophole in his entire life.

There were practically angels singing a hallelujah in

three-part harmony. The 0.2 percent of his brain that dealt in details immediately pulled together a list of not-technically-sex things that involved Clover naked.

"It was a bunch of words scrawled on a napkin that wasn't witnessed or notarized, not a contract. But you're right, it did not cover that…or this."

He slipped his hands free from where they were trapped between their legs and grabbed ahold of her hips, yanking her down against his hard cock at the same time as he turned them both so she was beneath him on the couch. Any lingering voice of reason echoing in his head was obliterated the moment she opened her mouth and his tongue swept inside.

Soft and hard they melded together. Touching. Seeking. Getting lost in each other. He hadn't made out fully clothed on a couch since…fuck he couldn't remember right now. He barely recalled his own name. Her T-shirt that had seemed so thin and inconsequential before was like an iron wall between them. Still, he glided one palm up from her glorious ass, over the flare of her hip, and between their bodies so he could cup her breast, flicking his thumb across her hard nipple. She gasped against his mouth and groaned as her body arched beneath him.

The move left the long column of her throat exposed. He kissed and nipped his way down, loving every moan, every soft sigh she made as he did so. Echoing his mouth's direction, he released her nipple and skimmed his fingers across her flat stomach, past the waistband of her yoga pants, and to the juncture of her thighs.

"You are so hot and wet for me that I can feel it through this sorry excuse for a pair of pants," he murmured against the spot where her neck met her shoulder as he fought the urge to give in to his primal side and rip the damn pants in two.

"It was the show," she said, her own hands busy roaming

his chest. "DIY gets my motor all revved up."

Caught between his frustration at the lack of skin-to-skin contact and his refusal to stop touching her any way he could, Sawyer stilled above Clover. She was a hot, seductive mess. Her hair was half out of her bun. Her brown eyes had gone hazy, and her kiss-swollen lips were parted, waiting for more—and he wanted to give her everything she wanted.

"Does that mean you're going to scream out 'paint stripper' when I make you come so hard your toes curl?" He rubbed the heel of his palm against her core, making sure to angle it so he hit just the right spot as he circled.

Her teeth came down on her bottom lip and she made a mewling that sounded like a mix of torture and bliss that he was way too familiar with at the moment.

"You're just going to have to find out for yourself." She took a long, steadying breath, then pushed a hand against his chest. "But not tonight."

If his cock could have cried out in protest at that moment, it would have. Instead, Sawyer raised himself up and off of her, too many questions in his head to verbalize a single one of them.

She rolled up into a sitting position, looking disheveled and way more satisfied than a woman who hadn't had an orgasm should. "We're going to need to adjust the contract."

"Napkin doodles aren't a contract," he said, reason roaring back to the forefront as blood started pumping north again. "And this wasn't a good idea."

"Maybe not, but it was hot," she said, unabashedly. "Look, I'm attracted to you. Unless there's a bazooka in your jean's pocket, I'd say you're attracted to me. So why not have a little fun and enjoy ourselves until I leave for Australia?"

Yes! His cock answered. No! His brain countered. "Things'll get messy."

"Life's messy." She shrugged her shoulders. "That's part of the fun."

"Is everything just one big adventure for you?"

"It beats the alternative."

"And what's that?"

She screwed up her mouth, looking like she'd just swallowed rotten milk. "Living my life trapped in one place and eating apple pie every Sunday even though I hate it because the man I married loves it."

Once again, when it came to Clover, he was at a total fucking loss. "I have no idea what to do with that."

"You're not supposed to." She got up off the couch, looming over where he lay. "Think about my proposition. Six weeks of friendly banging. No one gets hurt. Anyway, it'll be a more authentic lie then, too. A successful fake engagement is *all* about the details." She leaned down and brushed her lips across his in a quick kiss. "Be ready to go at eight tomorrow morning."

His brain was pudding. "Where?"

"The flea market where we're going to get whatever I pick because you lost the bet." She patted him on the cheek and winked. "Good night."

From the couch, Sawyer watched her saunter away to her bedroom, hypnotized by the sway of her hips under that oversize T-shirt. A month and a half of touching and tasting her, taking her up against the wall or anywhere else they wanted. It was nuts. It was bad news. It had him aching and hard enough that a stiff breeze would make him come in his pants. The fact that he was even considering it was a bad sign for his sanity.

Who are you kidding, chump? You were in total agreement the moment she said out loud what you'd been thinking in your fucked-up head.

Who was it who said be careful what you wish for? A fucking genius, that's who. He'd be damned lucky if he made it the whole night through without knocking on her door. The idea of just giving in was almost too tempting to resist.

Chapter Ten

The next morning, Clover was still cursing herself for not shaving during the past three days. She was into not being a slave to the industrial beauty complex as much as the next woman, but getting it on for the first time with Sawyer while her legs resembled a Carolina pine forest was *not* going to happen. She was all for adventure. What she wasn't down for was giving Sawyer leg burn. So that meant she spent the night imagining her fake fiancé buck naked instead of actually getting to see the real thing, because nothing but stubbly legs was strong enough to pull her off his lap last night.

She had a good imagination, but she was beyond tired of using it, especially after feeling him pressed against her on the couch last night. Her heart thundered in her chest. Clover wanted the real thing.

Thanks to the insane shower—four, yes four, shower heads positioned above, behind, beside, and in front of her—she was smooth from her toes to her waist and lotioned up to a state of supreme softness. Catching her reflection in the mirror with her hair, wavy from the water, hanging past her bare shoulders, she jolted to a stop. With her eyelashes darkened by mascara and lightly lined in smoke-gray, she looked more than just a little bit like a younger version of her mother. It was enough to make her reach for the makeup remover in the medicine cabinet, but she stopped her hand halfway to its destination. Not for the first time, she wondered what her mother had been like before she'd gotten married, had kids, and settled into a life of small-town hell. There had been hints—throwaway comments about college trips to London, a summer spent road tripping, and the fact that just the word "Miami" made her mom turn six shades of red—that there was more to Laura Lee than hate-eating apple pie and pretending to be interested in the goings-on at the Moose Lodge.

"What happened to you, Mom?" she asked her reflection. "Whatever it was, it's not going to happen to me."

She swiped on a shade of red lip gloss her mother would *never* wear and strode into the bedroom to throw on her favorite pair of worn-in jeans, pink "Stomp the Patriarchy" tank top, light gray cardigan, and slip-on tennis shoes. She whipped her hair up into a ponytail, grabbed her cross-body bag from where she'd hung it on a hook behind the door, took in a reaffirming deep breath, and strode out into the living room where absolutely no one was waiting.

"Sawyer, you have contractual obligations to meet," she called out.

No response.

She walked to the edge of the hallway leading to his rooms, a flock of butterflies high on meth zooming around her belly. After a quick glance down the still hall, she pulled her phone out of her back pocket and checked the time. Ten after eight…so right on time for her but there was nothing about Sawyer that even hinted at him being late by even a minute. She connected the dots in a heartbeat.

He was trying to welch.

Oh, that was so not going to happen.

Before she'd even made up her mind as to what to do about it, she was down the hall and turning the knob on Sawyer's door. It swung inward without a sound and she stepped inside.

His office was abandoned. Not a note or pen or crumpled piece of paper lay on his desk's clean surface. The morning sunlight streaming through the window walls and making the metal and glass desk sparkle was the only sign of life in the room.

Hiding, huh? Fine. She could be the finder in this little game.

Doing her best impression of a stealthy cat burglar, she tiptoed past the opaque glass brick half wall and into Sawyer's sitting room. A love seat and two oversize chairs— all black, of course—sat facing the window wall. There wasn't a single personal item in view, unless you counted the *Wall Street Journal*, *The Economist*, or *The Singapore Times* arranged on the—glass, of course—coffee table as personal. The rest of the room was as empty as a bar two hours after last call.

She glanced up at the final barrier. A second glass brick wall. Unlike the other, this one went all the way up to the high ceiling and all the way across the width of the room, a blocky opening in place of an actual door. It didn't take three guesses to figure out what was beyond it. Sawyer's bedroom.

There went the fizzy crackle pop in her belly again.

"You're not getting out of this, Mr. Stuffikins, so get your butt out of bed."

She held her breath, waiting for the rustling of sheets, which were probably black, or the telltale sound of bare feet hitting the floor. Neither ever came.

Okay, this was just ridiculous.

She marched through the double-door sized opening and stopped dead in her tracks. A massive bed, big enough for an orgy, dominated the space. The sheets—red, smooth and tangled—were rumpled but tossed to the side revealing…an empty bed. No matter how long she stared— and imagined—Sawyer wasn't there.

The big chicken must have run out while she was in the shower.

Maybe it was the word shower that drew her attention. Maybe it was a sound she'd only heard subconsciously. Whatever it was, she turned to the left and started walking toward the one real door in the entire room. It wasn't closed. It stood half open. So it wasn't like she was exactly spying when she peeked through the opening.

"Mierda," she said, the exclamation a soft sigh of longing.

She *really* should have shaved her legs yesterday morning.

Sawyer stood in a replica of the shower she'd used earlier. Water from the four nozzles rained over his muscular form and splashed onto the glass shower wall as he stood under the spray with his back to her. Clover's imagination hadn't done the man justice. Not even close. He was all tightly bundled muscles, from his thick forearms to the hard curve of his thighs to his high, round ass that could get him a ton of work in gay porn calendars. Seriously.

"Saya boleh mati gembira," she groaned under her breath. Of course, if the fates were kind—or women—she wouldn't be dying happy until she got to touch her fill.

It wasn't just the past six months of her battery-operated boyfriend that had her this tuned up for actual physical touch, it was Sawyer. Temptation didn't even begin to cover it.

He started to turn. Clover had just enough brain power left to dash back so her body was hidden behind the doorframe.

"Fuck, Clover," Sawyer groaned. "That's it. Just like that."

Heat burned her cheeks.

"Yeah, take it all the way."

Oh God. He wasn't.

Sawyer let out a lusty groan.

Oh. My. God. He was.

She needed to walk away. Right the fuck now. Her feet didn't move, but her waist did—it had to be some kind of body possession event—and she twisted until she could get a look inside the bathroom. She drank in the profile view of him. He had one palm planted against the wall and the other hand stroking his hard cock. She knew personally that his hands were big, but they managed to look a little on the small side as he glided it up and down his shaft.

It was wrong to watch, but Clover couldn't tear her gaze away. The way his body tightened with each flick of his wrist excited her, turned her on, and teased every one of her senses. He was close. The fingers on his hand pressed to the shower wall curled as if he could claw his way through the tile. His other hand was a blur of motion. His spine snapped straight.

"Fuck, Clover," he ground out the words as he came hard against the shower wall.

She couldn't breathe. That was—without a doubt—the hottest thing she'd ever seen.

"You know, Clover," Sawyer said as he stepped under the overhead shower spray and let the water run down his chest. "A real fiancée would have joined me instead of just lurking in the doorway and watching."

Embarrassed and surprised, she spun around and jerked back hard enough that she hit the back of her head against the wall. Yay. Maybe that would knock some sense into her.

"Pervert," she muttered to herself, accepting the pronouncement as being completely true about herself at the moment…and really anytime she was around him.

Even from the relative safety of the other side of the bathroom wall where she couldn't see his wet, naked body, the man turned her self-control to lime Jell-O and her body into a hot, horny bundle of nerves and needs. She was pathetic.

What else was she not? Engaged.

"I'm not a real fiancée," she said with all the dignity she could muster at the moment.

"What about your declaration last night to just have

a little fun?"

"I'm not sure that's such a great idea." No, she was *sure* it was not a good idea.

Sawyer made her lose her bearings. If she wasn't careful, she'd wake up and find herself eating apple pie just because it was his favorite and then their time would be up and she'd be brokenheartedly eating apple pie alone in Australia.

"Really? I remember someone telling me not that long ago that letting things get messy was half the fun," he said, throwing her own words back at her as he turned the shower off. "I'll be ready in ten."

An image of his hand stroking himself flashed in her mind. Her core clenched and she forced herself to look at his mess of a bed instead of turning and looking back inside the bathroom. "That fast?"

There were a few beats of silence before Sawyer said with a knowing laugh in his voice, "Unless you've changed your mind about going to the flea market."

Her blood must have been rushing too loudly in her ears because she hadn't heard the shower door open. It was as if Sawyer had just suddenly appeared in the bathroom doorway, water droplets clinging to his shoulders and a black towel slung low across his hips.

Now that she knew *exactly* what was under that towel, she'd have thought it wouldn't be a big deal to see him like that. But it was. *Oh God, it was.*

She locked her focus back on his bed. Bad idea! She dropped her gaze to the floor. "You're just trying to get out of going."

"I just need to get dressed, and then I'll be all ready." He hooked a finger under her chin and tilted her face up so she couldn't help but take in his handsome face and cocky grin. "Unless you want me to stay like this."

Yes! Her body cried. Clover managed to block out that bad advice. "Bailing you out of jail for indecent exposure at the flea market is not my idea of a fun Saturday."

"Then I can't wait to see what is." His hand dropped to the towel, his thumb toying with where he'd tucked one end in to hold it secure. "Now you'd better run along unless you want another show…"

His question hung in the air between them as Clover's whole body went up in flames. Metaphorically, of course—which was a shame. She could do with a little fire and brimstone to get her head back in the game.

"I'll wait for you in the living room." The words came out in a rush as she hurried toward the opening in the glass brick wall before her baser instincts drowned out her better sense.

Who was chickening out now, Clover asked herself as Sawyer's testosterone-infused chuckle chased her out of his bedroom. She mentally clucked her answer as she hustled out to the living room to practice her deep breathing technique until Sawyer came out, hopefully dressed in a full-body snowsuit complete with ski mask.

• • •

The flea market in an up-and-coming Harbor City neighborhood was just as bad as he expected. Loads of crap—some of it dinged up on purpose—and bad artwork being hawked by people wearing ironic T-shirts and bored expressions.

"You aren't even giving it a chance." Clover slipped her hand into his and tugged him down yet another narrow aisle crowded with stalls of bric-a-brac. "You have to really look at a piece and imagine what it could be."

Imagination wasn't something he had trouble with. He was still imagining her naked and pressed up against the tile wall of his shower with her legs spread and her body soft and wet. It's exactly what he'd been thinking about this morning when he spotted her out of the corner of his eye as he was washing his hair. She'd been so distracted? enthralled? horny? that she hadn't even realized he'd known she was there. He'd just meant to give her a shock, he hadn't meant for it to go all the way, but when it came to Clover he seemed to lose all control—and sense.

Just as his dick was starting to get really into it again, Sawyer's fake fiancée jerked to a stop. "Like this." She gestured toward a rusty metal cart that looked like the last good day it had seen was at least five decades ago. "This is perfect. It could be a bar cart or an entry table or a breakfast trolley."

He ran his thumb across one of the handles and white paint crumbled into dust. "Or in the landfill."

Sawyer started forward, but Clover pulled her hand from his and didn't move an inch. She stood beside the cart, her hands planted on her round hips and a challenging fire burning in her brown eyes.

"Oh really?" Clover got a look on her face that anyone with half a brain would know meant trouble. Her full mouth, a cherry red today, curled into a predatory smile that seemed both out of place and a perfect fit for her pixie face. "You don't think this can be brought back and remade into something fabulous?"

He barely glanced back at the cart. Some things were better forgotten about— especially when the woman in front of him was so much better to look at. Anyway, he didn't need to look again in order to give his answer.

"No."

"I pick it," she practically sang out.

"What are you talking about?"

"You lost last night. Remember?"

The only thing he recalled from last night was how damn good she'd felt underneath him. "No."

"The show," she said, pacing her words as if he was drunk. "I picked the winner. Now *you* have to get the cart.

We're going to refinish it together, just like a good little fake couple should."

Crossing back to the rickety cart, he lifted the paper price tag tied with a ribbon around the push handle. "A hundred bucks?"

"Don't tell me you're afraid of a little negotiation. Just because I've kicked your ass in that arena several times already doesn't mean you can't be…competent."

Competent? She was goading him, he knew that, but not rising to the bait wasn't possible. He was a man, a Carlyle. Being competent wasn't an option.

Almost quicker than the impulse hit, he encircled her wrist and whirled her close so that her tight body pressed against his. Desire went from spark to flame as his entire body went hard in anticipation. Oh it wouldn't happen here, maybe not even today or tomorrow, but this was happening, and judging by the way Clover's eyes went all hazy and her lips parted, she knew it, too.

"Gotta say, no woman has ever called me *competent* before."

"Needs improvement, huh?" she asked, but her low and breathy voice outed just how turned on she was.

"Oh Clover, you know better than that." Loosening his hold, he slid his fingers down so they intertwined with hers and began walking into the stall to find the joker who thought he could get a hundred dollars for that pile of junk. "Let's go see just how *competent* I really am."

Twenty minutes and sixty-five dollars later he was the proud owner of a broken down medical utility cart from the 50s. He couldn't be less thrilled. Clover, on the other hand, was practically skipping as they made their way back to Linus and the Town Car in the parking lot.

"I'm thinking red. A bright crimson like your…" Her cheeks turned pink and she let the sentence trail off.

She tried to pull her hand away from his, but he wasn't

having it. There was something about touching her—even just holding hands—that settled him, pulled him down to the here and now.

"Like my sheets?" he asked as he carried the cart. "My bed made an impression, huh? Or was it what you'd like to do to me *in* that bed that has you all hot and bothered?"

The pulse point at the base of her long neck did double time. "I'm not hot and bothered."

He lowered his voice to a growly whisper. "Wet and soft?" Her breath caught, but he kept going. "Slick and ready?" He pulled her to a stop, put the rusty cart down, and pivoted so he stood directly in front of her. "Desperate not to be a voyeur next time?"

Forget pink. Her cheeks were fire engine red. "Your ego is out of control."

Probably, but it didn't change the reality of the situation. "If I'm so off base, then why did you stick around and watch the show?"

"Poor life choices."

"What happened to the woman who proposed a no-strings, six-week fling while we're fake engaged?" he asked and then pressed his advantage. Two could play hardball here. "Don't tell me you've gone all small town conventional on me."

That did the trick.

Her chin jerked up, her face glorious with righteous indignation. "I am not that kind of person."

"It's okay. I always had a little bit of a thing for Mrs. Cleaver in the *Leave It To Beaver* reruns." He traced a fingertip across her collar bone above the edge of her scoop neck tank top. "Maybe we should look for a pearl necklace. Do you think anyone sells one of those here?"

She smacked his hand away. "You are an asshole."

"Pretty much." He laughed and picked the medical utility cart back up again and started walking. "But you'd better keep that to yourself tonight at my mom's cocktail party."

She nearly stumbled, but he grabbed her hand again and kept her upright. "What cocktail party?"

"It's a standing event." God save him from family traditions. "I haven't been in a few months, so it's past time I made an appearance."

"Not so easy to do when your mom is throwing models and socialites at you?"

"Exactly." He nodded, sneaking a glance at her and noting the way she was chewing her bottom lip. "But now I have you."

"You have serious mommy issues," she grumbled.

No. He had don't-make-the-grieving-widow-cry issues. "Stop deflecting because you're nervous."

"Who said I was nervous?"

"You are trying to gnaw your bottom lip off."

Like the delicate flower she was, Clover flipped him off as they strode out of the flea market's front gate and into the parking lot. Linus was waiting beside the Town Car. He gave the *thing* Sawyer was carrying a slow and slightly horrified up and down look but kept his mouth shut as he opened the spacious trunk. They were pulling out onto Eighty-Eighth Street five minutes later, and Clover was still going to town on her lip.

"Don't worry, I know you haven't had time to use the black card yet. I ordered you a dress. It'll be delivered by the time we get home." He'd been planning to make it a surprise but offering up the news now seemed like the better plan.

She crossed her arms over her chest. "No way."

Clover had gone stubborn. What a shock.

"So you already have a cocktail dress?" he asked.

"No."

"Well, you do now."

Her eyes were still narrowed, but not so much that she

could hide the curiosity glittering in their dark depths. "It had better not be totally fugly."

For all he knew, it could be. He'd snapped a surreptitious picture of Clover while they were wandering around the flea market and had sent it to a personal shopper at Dylan's Department Store along with a few notes about what Clover needed. Jaqui had never done him wrong when it came to presents for his mom, so he was confident she'd come through again. Explaining all of that to Clover though would take the fun out of it.

"It's completely hideous," he said with as much seriousness as he could muster.

She rolled her eyes. "The next six weeks are going to last forever."

"Just keep your eye on the fifteen-thousand-dollar prize, Clover, and you'll make it through."

Good advice for himself, too, as long as he remembered to take it—especially tonight. His imagination was already torturing him with images of her in a million sexy dresses. And out of them.

Chapter Eleven

Clover twirled around in front of the mirror one last time and smoothed her already stick-straight hair. Procrastinating? Her? Never. Who *wouldn't* want to brave a cocktail party at the Dragon Lady's den and spend the evening lying her ass off?

Completing her spin, she had to admit the dress Sawyer had bought was not fugly. The multicolored, striped sheath dress was fun, fit like a dream, and guessing by the name of the designer on the label, cost as much as her rent. The new black heels, which matched the dress's black-beaded, sleeveless neckline, were a tad tight on her toes, but not enough to make her take them off. They were gorgeous. She definitely looked put together, but there was no way she was passing for a high-society girl. Thank God, they'd worked that into their cover story during the trip to the flea market.

"Are you going to hide in there all night?" Sawyer asked from the other side of her closed bedroom door. "I didn't take you for a chicken."

Nerves eating away at her stomach lining, she clucked quietly to herself as she crossed the room. She sucked at lying. It made her nervous and when that happened, well…

"Tu es betes comme tes pieds." Yes, she transformed into someone who was as smart as the bottom of her feet. *Deep breaths, Clover. I'm sure Mrs. Carlyle won't be as scary this time. Third time's the charm. Or curse.*

Forcing a confidence into her spine that she sure as hell didn't feel, Clover opened her bedroom door. "Because I'm not a chicken…"

Her voice trailed off as she noticed Sawyer in a

black suit and a patterned pale pink tie that perfectly matched one of the stripes on her dress. That couldn't be a coincidence. Whoever had gone shopping and left the Dylan's Department Store garment bag on her bed had obviously left one for him as well.

"You look nice," she said, voicing the understatement of the year.

The suit did everything possible to highlight Sawyer's broad shoulders, and noticing that did funny things to her stomach—not to mention all points south, making it hard to remember exactly why it was that she shouldn't follow her own advice and have a little adventure climbing Mount Stuffykins.

His focus was only for her and he gave her a slow, heated up and down once-over. "You look ready to unwrap."

She halted in mid-stride on her way out the door. Okay, with the pink, navy, and merlot colored stripes on a white background, the dress looked *a little* like Christmas paper, but that didn't mean he had to say it out loud. An embarrassed heat inched its way up her chest. "If you didn't like it, why did you get it?"

"Who said I didn't like it?" he asked, the lines in his forehead carving a *V* that disappeared behind the top of his black-framed glasses.

Head high and chin pointed up, she strode right past him on her way to the elevator. "You did."

"I was trying to compliment you," he shot back.

"That's not exactly your strong suit." No. Being a pain in her ass was his greatest strength.

"No." Not missing a beat, he was beside her in an instant matching her stride for stride and getting to the elevator down button a half second before she did. He mashed it with more force than necessary. "It's definitely not." Twelve very slow, very silent seconds later, the elevator arrived and the doors parted. "Shall we?"

The doors *whooshed* shut behind them.

She tried to hold on to her annoyance for Sawyer's crack about her dress but the urge to start nervously clucking was too much for her to shut off. "Do you think we can really carry this off?"

Sawyer let out a breath, the tension melting out of his rigid stance. Taking her hand, he slipped it into the crook of his elbow. "We met at a Starbucks in Singapore. You turned too fast, knocked into me, and spilled my drink all over me."

That was not *exactly* what they'd discussed. The man was a wreck when it came to details. Still, the corner of her mouth twitched upward. "You were standing too close to me so there was no way for me to avoid it. You're just lucky it was an iced coffee."

"Didn't matter. After one look at you, nothing would have cooled me down."

The rough gravel in his voice took the cheesy line and turned it into something more. One look at his reflection in the mirrored elevator doors as they descended, and that something became a promise of the hot, dirty, and multi-orgasmic kind.

"*Cavolo,*" she muttered. Holy crap, indeed.

Sawyer raised an eyebrow over the rim of his glasses.

Merida, she'd done it again. She really needed to staple her mouth shut. Talking in another language to herself was weird enough when she was alone. In front of someone else, it was boarding the Weirdo Express. Desperate to cover up her non-English exclamation, she rushed on. "That's a good line. Be sure to use that one."

His forearm tensed underneath her palm. "Told you I was a quick study," he said with a chuckle that held a touch of bitterness.

Determined to get on steadier ground, she pushed ahead. "So we had a whirlwind romance. Of course, I had no idea who you were because I am most definitely *not* a gold digger."

"I kept my identity a secret because I wanted to make sure you were only after me for my hot bod, not my bank account."

"Exactly." She nodded, working her bottom lip over with her teeth as the elevator sped down to the lobby.

"And when I finally told you, you tried to break it off with me with some asinine plan that we'd split up when we came home to the states."

"So of course when you saw me at Carlyle Tower the other day, you begged and pleaded for me to give you a second chance."

He snorted. "No one will believe that."

"Why not?"

His gaze ate her up as he gave her the kind of slow and assessing look that usually ended up with two people getting naked. "I don't beg."

God, was it hot in here? Yes. It was definitely hot in here.

"Too much pride?" There, that almost sounded like her panties weren't on fire.

The bastard gave her a smug grin. "Too much good sense. If something isn't working, making a fool out of yourself sure isn't going to change anything."

The elevator came to a stop and the doors opened, letting in some of the lobby's air-conditioned air. It brushed against her like a cool breeze of sanity. Was she going to get naked with Sawyer? Oh yeah. Come on. He was sexy as sin, unattached, and her fake fiancée. Why not indulge in a little limited-time-offer sex? Of course, that didn't mean she wasn't going to make him work for it.

She sashayed out of the elevator on Sawyer's arm, her heels clicking on the lobby's marble floor. "Well, in our case begging and pleading is exactly what you did."

"Why?" he asked, stopping in the middle of the lobby.

She looked up at him and caught her breath. It wasn't fair. No man should look so good in—and out—of a suit. "Because it was the only way to win me over." Unable to stop herself from touching him, she reached up and straightened his already straight tie. His muscles tensed under her touch as she smoothed her palm down the silk. "And for that you'd do just about anything."

"Would I?" he half asked, half growled.

Judging by the dark and dangerous look in his eyes at the moment? "Absolutely."

His lust-hazy gaze dropped to her mouth; he leaned down and the world stopped. The people walking in and out of the high-rise's plate glass door letting in the horn blares from Harbor City's never-ending traffic disappeared. All she could hear was the blood rushing in her ears as she tilted her face up. Later, she'd worry about how easily he did this to her—made her forget about the rest of the world—but for now all she wanted was for him to follow through on what his body language promised. A long, hard kiss, the kind that steals your breath and fills you with possibility. She parted her lips and raised herself on her toes so that her heels didn't even touch the floor. He dipped his head toward hers but swerved at the last moment and brushed a soft kiss right under her earlobe.

"You really do look amazing," he murmured and straightened, sliding his hand to the small of her back, and led her through the door Irving held open and into the waiting Town Car.

Clover's brain was like one of those old-fashioned cars where the driver had to crank the engine to get it to start. She was turning it over, but nothing was happening. That happened too often around Sawyer and that way lay danger. Having a little fun was one thing, but anything more was totally unacceptable because forgetting the "fake" in fake fiancée for even a minute meant nothing but trouble.

• • •

Sawyer's mom pounced as soon as they walked through her door. Okay, pounced wasn't the right word. More like glided over on her own ice float, sharpening daggers in her socially-acceptable almost-smile. Instinctively, Clover gulped and tightened her grip on Sawyer's arm. Before she could threaten to short sheet his bed if he abandoned her even for a second, Helene Carlyle was smack dab in front of them.

"I'm so glad you two were able to make it with all of the wedding planning you've been doing," Helene said, her voice just loud enough to carry across the room to the two dozen or so relatives and family friends scattered amongst the Tiffany lamps and plush wingback chairs. "I can't wait to hear all about what those plans entail. Sawyer, why don't you go get your lovely bride-to-be a drink."

Clover sank her nails into Sawyer's thick forearm. She had to get through his suit sleeve, crisp shirt, and sinewy muscle, but she just might have hit bone. Thank God, Sawyer got the hint.

He placed his palm over her hand. "I'm not sure that's a good idea."

"Why?" Helene gave Clover a quick, assessing up and down before lowering her voice, fake concern thick in her whisper, "She's not pregnant, is she?"

It took a second for Helene's words to slither through the thick fog of freak-out surrounding Clover and bite her on the ass. Once their meaning pierced her, though, her intimidated hesitation evaporated. It made sense in a weird twisted little way. From Helene's perspective, there couldn't be any other reason why her son would be with someone like Clover unless she'd trapped him with a baby. Ha. More like she would be trapped then, her free-spirited wings clipped to fit the Harbor City high-society mold. That was *never* going to happen.

"No," Clover said, straightening her spine and putting as much fuck-you in her tone as possible. "I'm not."

Helene's smile didn't flicker. "Then I'd say champagne is called for so we can celebrate this pleasant surprise."

The fact that she wasn't pregnant or that Sawyer was supposedly getting married? Honestly, it could go either way.

Okay, so that's how we're going to play it.

That was fine with Clover. She could play chick dirty with the best of them. Of course, she couldn't do that with Sawyer around. Mama Bear here wanted to deliver a message and drive it home with a verbal stiletto and, unless the world had started spinning in the opposite direction, she wouldn't do it with her son around. So be it. She wasn't about to let the Dragon Lady see her sweat.

Pasting on a socially-acceptable fake smile of her own, Clover turned toward Sawyer. "A glass of champagne would be wonderful."

One eyebrow shot above the top of his black-rimmed glasses, but she went up on tiptoe and brushed a kiss across his cheek before he could protest. He looked on the verge of saying something, but after a quick look from his mom to her, he nodded.

"As you wish," he said and crossed over to the bar set up next to a fireplace big enough to walk inside.

Did he... She shook her head. No way was Sawyer Carlyle the kind of guy to quote *The Princess Bride*.

"Let me show you some of my favorite photos of my boys." Helene slipped her arm through Clover's as if they were sisters in some old movie about pioneers and led Clover over to the baby grand piano.

Framed family photos sat on top of its closed lid. On vacation at a ski resort. At a beach. Aboard a yacht. Each one showing off the Carlyles with their big, open smiles and easy togetherness. She picked out Sawyer right away. Even as a little boy in a dirty baseball uniform he had a stubborn set to his chin.

"How about neither of us insults the other's intelligence and you tell me what's going on?" Helene asked, an icy hardness to her voice that didn't match the calm, borderline aloof expression on her patrician face.

Clover glanced around the room filled with men in suits and women in little black dresses. "Looks like a cocktail party to me."

The other woman's gaze narrowed and her pasted on smile faltered. "Is it a matter of money?"

Oh no. She went there. "Excuse me?"

"Disappear and I'll have my financial manager cut a check."

"Wow. How much?" She shouldn't have said it, but there was no way she could let Helene get away without busting her chops for this bullshit.

Helene lifted the photo of young, baseball-playing Sawyer and showed it to Clover. From a distance, it had to look like two people having a friendly chat about how hard it was for the housekeeper to keep Sawyer's white uniform pants clean. "Sign a non-disclosure agreement and a contract saying you'll cut off all contact immediately and I'll make it worth your while."

She threw out the biggest number she could think of that didn't make her sound like a bad Bond villain. "Half a million?"

"Yes," Helene said without blinking.

Damn. If she was another kind of person, that offer would be beyond tempting. "No deal."

"You want more?" The other woman sighed and put down the photo. "How much will it take?"

Clover couldn't resist taking another poke at her. "One point five."

"You learn quickly." Helene nodded. "But not a penny more."

"Is it always just about money for you?" Clover shook her head. "No deal. Honestly, there's no amount of money you can offer me to stop me from marrying your son."

Helene arched an eyebrow in a way that was almost an exact copy of her son. "You're not the first to try this. Everyone has their price."

Ouch. Now that had to have hurt him. If she wasn't so annoyed with Helene's attitude, she'd totally be on the other woman's side. "I'm different."

"I'm sure you like to think so." She turned and flashed a brilliant smile at Sawyer who was only a few steps away, close enough to end the conversation but too far to have caught any of it. "There you are. We were afraid you'd gotten lost, and I have some people I'd like you to meet."

Helene turned and nodded at a pair of women standing near the open door to the balcony. They were tall, blonde, and—Clover's breath hissed out in surprise—the women from the other day at Sawyer's office. Looked like Mommy Dearest here wasn't about to go silently into the good night and give up her Marry Off Sawyer to someone of her choosing campaign.

"Alamak," she muttered one of her Singapore students' favorite expressions of shock under her breath. It fit particularly well here since it translated to: oh, my mother!

Beside her, Sawyer stiffened and let out a quiet—but impressively creative—stream of curses before setting two champagne flutes on the piano. "You've got to be kidding, Mom."

Helene took a delicate sip of her champagne. "I don't know what you mean."

"Those are the wife candidates you wanted me to take to lunch the other day." Sawyer's jaw bulged as he clamped it down tight as if he were afraid of what else would come out.

"Yes," Helene said.

"I." The word came out deceptively even as he whisper-shouted them. "Am. Engaged."

Helene lifted her shoulders in a bored shrug. "I don't see a ring, and until you're in the church…"

The other woman let her words trail off, their meaning as clear as the Waterford crystal in her hand. Helene wasn't about to give up on her original plan. Sawyer growled—literally—and his neck corded. It didn't take an expert to realize that Sawyer was about ten seconds away from going full-on Hulk, all the while the wife to-be twins were bearing down on them.

Shit. She had to do something. This was her job, and she was making a total mess of it. Instead of sitting here gaping like a very entertained fish out of water while Sawyer and his mom quietly fought like rich people did, she needed to do something. Now. The idea was only half formed, but she grabbed ahold of it and blindly jumped.

"Maybe this will do as a reminder until then," she said, drawing both their attention. She grabbed Sawyer by the lapels, yanked him lower, and laid a kiss on him.

At first, he didn't respond and Clover had half a second to think *oh shit!* before Sawyer took her face between his palms and deepened the kiss. She couldn't pinpoint the moment the kiss went from for-the-job to oh-my-God-take-me-now but by the time he pulled away, her hair was messed up, her lips swollen, and her entire body was primed for more. A little punch drunk, she stumbled just a bit as she snuggled into Sawyer's side to face-off with the Dragon Lady and her minions.

All of the icy coolness was gone from Helene's face, replaced by a heated glare and a stubborn set to her jaw—the original to her son's replica. Without waiting for whatever sharpened verbal knife Helene was about to unsheathe, Clover spoke up.

"Sorry, girls, this one's taken," she said, breathless, to the pair of wide-eyed want-to-be wives. "Tell your friends."

After a couple of huffs from the would-be wives and a final chilly glare from Helene, the trio strode off without a glance back at them. Heart hammering against her ribs and the giddy flush of having won another battle against the formidable Helene Carlyle, Clover didn't protest when Sawyer led her through the French doors and out onto the large balcony overlooking the heart of Harbor City.

The last pink rays of the setting sun peeked between the skyscrapers crowding the horizon. They stood next to each other, her hand curled in his, her pulse still jackhammering through her, drinking it in as if they'd been out in the desert for too long. It wasn't the first time she'd seen the city from this vantage point, but it never failed to take her breath away. It was, in a word, magnificent.

"I think you just earned a dinner at Vito's," Sawyer said.

For saving his ass again? Oh yeah. "I would have figured a rich guy like you would have more to offer. Your mom was willing to pony up half a million for me to leave you high and dry."

His head whipped around. "She did not."

"Oh yes, she did," she said with a chuckle. Teasing his mom hadn't been smart, but she hadn't been able to stop herself.

He grinned. "I hope you said no."

"I countered with a million five."

He let out a laugh, low and rumbly, and tugged her over so she stood with her back to his chest. He dropped his hands to the railing on either side of her hips, close enough to almost touch but not quite. "Are you sure you have to go to Australia? Carlyle Enterprises could always use another great negotiator."

"Another?" she scoffed.

"I went easy on you."

"Whatever you say." She gazed out at the city lights beginning to blink on. "It's gorgeous up here."

"Mmm-hmm," he said as he tucked her hair behind her right ear, letting his fingertip glide down the column of her neck. "I used to come out here with my dad and pick out the Carlyle buildings."

Skin tingling from his touch, she tried—and failed—to come up with something witty. "An interesting form of father-son bonding."

"Oh, there were baseball games and the regular stuff, too, but this was always my favorite." He dropped his hand back to the railing.

She could still feel his almost-touching presence, but the lack of actual contact made it easier to think. And breathe. And remember her name. The fact that they weren't looking at each other but at the city skyline made the moment both intimate and anonymous.

"Why was this your favorite?" she asked softly.

"Because from up here you can see the entire city like one big picture. It was my father's favorite view."

And now it was his. Her chest tightened at the thought of him having to have his father-son bonding moment alone. She may have run from Sparksville as soon as she could, but she never felt like she'd left her family—no matter how hard she tried to shake her mom sometimes.

As though suddenly aware of the over-share, Sawyer leaned down and kissed her shoulder. "You know, it's also a great place to impress the ladies."

"Oh yeah? Pick up a lot of women at your mom's house, do you?" she teased, leaning her head to the side to give him better access as he continued to plant soft kisses along her shoulder up to where it met her neck.

"Oh sure, lots and lots," he murmured. "Great pick-up spot."

She rolled her eyes at him over her shoulder, laughing. "Did you seriously just tell me about all the other women you've dated while trying to flirt *with me*? Let me give you some advice. That is *not* a good line to use when flirting with someone."

Sawyer chuckled. "I suck at flirting, but I'm much better at other things."

The laughter stilled in her throat. "So you keep promising."

There. She'd said it. And he said…nothing. Heat beat at her cheeks. Had she overplayed her hand?

Then, Sawyer took one hand from the railing and slid it across her waist, pulling her closer so that every inch of her was aligned with his body. "Have I finally gotten you to concede on a negotiation point?"

"If you'll recall, I was the one who suggested we have a little fun in the first place." There. That sounded cool and flirty, not like she was so hot right now that he could flip up her skirt and fuck her against the balcony railing.

"Now it's my turn to give you advice." He tightened his grip, eliminating any doubt about whether he was as ready for this as she was. "Any time you're talking about having hot, dirty sex that makes you come so hard your whole world turns neon, the last thing you want to bring into the conversation is the word 'little.'"

Unable to stop herself, she rubbed her ass against the very not little length of him and relished his responding hushed groan.

"I'll take that under advisement," she said, her eyes beginning to flutter closed.

"Come on, honey." He dipped his head lower and kissed the sensitive spot where her jaw met her neck. "Let's go have some fun."

Chapter Twelve

Sawyer was holding on to his control by his fingernails. He and Clover had said their hurried good-byes and sat a foot apart from each other in the back of the Town Car—any closer and he was afraid he'd forget that Linus was only a few feet away in the driver's seat. The temptation to strip her down and fuck her in the backseat had him on edge enough that he'd had to practically sit on his hands. Now he was suffering through the longest elevator ride of his life up to his penthouse, staring at her reflection in the mirrored doors as she inched the hem of her dress higher and higher, millimeter by millimeter.

She was toying with him. Sure, it was a private elevator, but the security cameras were obvious. So he stood as still and hard as a statue as she watched him watching her drag her hem a little higher with every floor they passed. Her red-tipped nails played along the bare flesh of her thigh as she teased and tormented him as the floor numbers lit up, one after the other. If he had enough blood in his brain to form a question, it would have been about whether they'd see the penthouse foyer or the silky edge of her panties first. He didn't trust himself to talk. To reach out to her. To do anything more than fist his hands in his pockets to help cover his obvious bulge from the cameras and remember to stand in a certain spot to be sure the eye in the sky wasn't getting the same mesmerizing view that he was.

By the time the ding on the elevator sounded, he'd had all the anticipation he could take. Without giving her time to utter a word of protest, he scooped her up in his arms just as the doors began to slide open. She fit against him, solid and real, unlike the fantasy he'd had this morning in the shower. This was the real Clover—dangerous curves, smart mouth, teasing eyes, and taunting brain able to dismantle him with only the sway of her full hips if he wasn't careful. Primed and pushed to the breaking point, he strode into his penthouse and headed straight for his suite of rooms at a hasty clip.

"In a hurry, Mr. Stuffykins?" Clover asked, her hands busy murdering the knot in his tie as she tugged and pulled the silk free.

Please God, don't let her ever use that name in front of another human being. "Your taste in nicknames sucks."

"It fits you since you need to be taken down a few pegs." One last yank and his tie slipped free.

He chuckled and turned down the hall to his room. "And you said *I* was a bad flirt?"

"Got me there." She shrugged and let go of the tie, letting it drop to the floor just inside his suite.

The desk in the office third of his suite caught his attention. It was a flat, clean, horizontal surface. He slowed his pace, an image of her bent over the glass top, her crazy striped skirt scrunched up around her hips and her legs spread wide as he thrust deep and hard inside her nearly made him stumble. God, it was tempting. So. Tempting. But what he wanted to do took space, time, and possibly a nap in-between sessions.

"And here I thought you weren't bad at anything," he said, picking up his pace and speeding through the sitting room third of his suite.

"Sawyer Carlyle," she said as she went to work on the buttons of his shirt. "Are you trying to flatter your way into my panties?"

"Are you even wearing any?" he asked as they crossed through the door to his bedroom, the king-size bed drawing him like a magnet.

Her fingers went still in the middle of freeing a button

and she looked up at him through her thick eyelashes, wetting her bottom lip with the tip of her tongue. "There's only one way to find out."

Give the woman a cat-o-nine tails and she wouldn't have been able to torture him any more effectively. He'd been joking. She was most definitely not. Pre-come beaded on the tip of his cock at the idea of Clover waltzing around the city without even the skimpiest scrap of lace between her legs. Would she? The possibilities made his cock ache. He stopped at the foot of the bed. There was only one way to find out. Hating to let her out of his arms but knowing if he didn't, there was no way he'd have enough control to take his time the way she deserved, he tossed her onto the bed.

Pillows went flying before she sank down in a sea of brilliant red, her blond hair spread out like a silky curtain. The only thing that could make the vision more perfect was if she was naked.

"You have too many clothes on." If he was the kind of man who begged and pleaded, that's exactly what he'd call the words that had just come out of his mouth.

She smiled up at him and it wasn't shy or coy. She knew exactly what she was doing to him. "Then unwrap me."

"I got in trouble for that line earlier."

"Stop arguing and get me naked," she demanded, a threat of desperate want taking her voice lower.

Now who was teetering on the edge? Time to see just how far he could push her. It was only fair in this kind of negotiation.

"But where to start?" Still standing at the bottom of the bed, he leaned forward and traced a finger down her calf to her ankle before wrapping his hand around the back of her high heels and lifting her leg in the air. "Here?" Her breath stilled as he pretended to focus all his concentration on the black shoe. "No, I think I want you to leave them on. They'll even out the height difference later when I have you naked and pressed up against the window." Keeping her leg aloft, he trailed the fingers of his other hand up from her ankle to the sensitive flesh of her inner thigh and continued north until he hit the hem of her dress. "Here?" He brushed his thumb over the edge of the material. "Nah. You've been teasing me with this for so long that I think it's only fair to torment you back until you're begging me to slide your dress up your hips." He wasn't sure which reaction made him harder, the narrowing of her eyes when she realized there was a negotiation ahead, or the way her sweet mouth opened in surprise when he dropped her leg without fanfare, bent down over her, and grabbed her by the hips. "So where does that lead? Oh, that's right." Fast as a blink, he flipped her over onto her stomach and followed up the move by slowly lowering her zipper a few inches before stopping, loving her frustrated groan. "Yes. I want to unwrap you from behind."

By the time he'd gotten the zipper all the way down, his entire body was hard and demanding attention. A skinny river of her creamy flesh lay exposed to his hungry gaze where the zipper lay open. He caught a flash of her bra's bright blue color and a dusting of pale peach freckles along her spine that led his attention lower to the initial rise of her completely bare and succulent ass.

"Why, Clover Lee." He glided a finger across the swell of one cheek. "I'm shocked at your brazenness."

"Liar," she said, turning her head to look back at him as she wiggled her ass at him like a red flag at a bull. "If anything, you're totally turned on by it. The next time we go out you'll wonder the entire time if I'm wearing any panties."

She was right and, no doubt, she knew it. Fuck, he was already going through every moment he'd seen her before and wondering if she'd been wearing underwear then. It was blissful torment, but nothing compared to having the woman ready, wanting, and half dressed in the middle of his bed.

"Guess that just means I'll always have to check before

we go out."

The white, black, and red lines of a tattoo on her right cheek peeked out from under her dress. He hooked a finger around the material and pulled the unzipped opening wider, revealing an unmistakable cartoon kitten. It stopped him dead in his lusty tracks. He didn't know what he'd been expecting, but this wasn't it.

"Hello Kitty?"

"A youthful indiscretion."

Now *that* he could believe. Probably a spur of the moment adventure, the kind that sounded so good at the time when you didn't think about a lifetime with a cartoon tattoo on your ass. "I can't wait to hear all about it, but there's something else I want to hear first."

"What?"

He slid his hands up the outside of her thighs, catching the hem of her dress and shoving it higher and higher until it was over her ass. Maybe it was on instinct or maybe it was because she wanted to hurry him along, but she spread her legs, giving him a front row seat to one of the wonders of the world. When he moved his hands again—this time cupping the back of her legs, letting his thumbs caress her inner thighs as he moved higher—it wasn't in determination or dominance, but in reverence. Her skin was soft beneath his touch. Silky. Smooth. Addictive. And when he brushed against her swollen folds, they were wet with need—for him, for what they were going to do. Releasing the breath he hadn't realized he was holding, he brushed the pad of his thumb against her core.

Her answering moan nearly undid him.

"I wanted to hear that." He licked the taste of her off his thumb. "Just as sweet as I imagined in the shower. Do you know what I was fantasizing about doing to you while I jerked off?"

Her eyes were closed, her mouth open slightly, and her

words came out breathy, "Tell me."

"No." His hand went to the few still fastened buttons on his shirt. "I'm going to show you."

• • •

Lying on her stomach, her breaths coming in shaky bursts, Clover's world turned electric. Every nerve. Every breath. Every touch. *Everything* was supercharged.

She squeezed her eyes shut. The sensation of Sawyer's fingers as they traced long, lazy patterns across the very farthest outreaches of her wet folds, over the curves of her butt, up and down the sensitive back of her thighs, was almost too much. Adding sight would overwhelm her. Just the glimpse she'd had of him as he'd stripped off his shirt in a determined rush, followed up by kicking off his shoes and stepping out of his pants had her squirming. Her attempt to roll over onto her back and fully enjoy the show had been met with a firm smack on her ass and a practically growled order to stay exactly where she was.

Sawyer was as silent now as the first moment he'd touched her desire-dampened flesh. Was that a minute ago? Five? Eternity? She had no fucking clue. All she knew was that she was lying face down in the middle of his bed—her dress up around her waist and her heels still on—drowning in tormented desire. Even if she wanted to, she didn't think she'd be able to stop the nonsensical pleas and sighs of pleasure with every downward stroke, slow circle, and exploring thrust of his devastatingly talented fingers.

Fisting the red sheets in her hand, another moan escaped as he slipped two fingers, crossed as if making a promise, inside her and slid them forward and back against her most sensitive spots. His thumb never left contact with her clit. He didn't rotate the nub. He didn't rub it. He maintained just the right amount of pressure to keep her strung tight and yearning.

"Sawyer," she cried out, pressing her face into the sheets.

"What do you want?" Calm. Patient. Ready to drag it out forever. He twisted his fingers inside her, turning them enough that they rubbed against the bundle of nerves inside her entrance.

Too far gone to process the words, all she could do was balance on the boundary of pleasure and pain. "More."

In and out, this way and that, he played her desire, propelling it—*propelling her*—toward climax but refusing to do what it took to send her over into oblivion. The bastard. Even without looking at him, she knew he was doing it on purpose. A little payback for teasing him in the elevator? Probably.

"Be specific." He squeezed her ass with his massive hand, each strong finger marking her—not in a way that left bruises, at least not the kind you could see. "What do you want?"

Specific? How could she be that when her world was coming apart in brief flashes of ecstasy? But she dug deep, found the words. "I want to come."

"Already?" He had the balls to laugh while she was reduced to begging. "We just started."

"Please." Shame didn't have a place when she was this close to orgasm.

For the first time, he moved his thumb, a slow, easy circle around her aching clit. "Are you conceding this negotiation?"

The yes was almost past her lips before she clamped her mouth shut. Negotiation. She smiled despite her body's mounting frustration. The man did love to play his games.

Flinging her hair over her shoulder she looked back at him, keeping her gaze on his face, for going any lower would be akin to dancing with the devil. "What do I get for conceding?"

"Everything." Even with his glasses still on, it was impossible to miss the cocky assurance in his eyes.

Her pulse went into overdrive, responding to his confidence, his control. "Big promises."

"I always deliver." Another deliberate turn around her clit.

The urge to close her eyes, sink into the bed, and let wave after wave of sensation flow over her beckoned like a promise. She would drown or she would float—either option would be better than this blissful hell. But she couldn't. It just wasn't in her to give in—not easily and definitely not in the middle of a negotiation.

It took pulling from reserves she didn't know she had, but she did, putting as much strength in her voice as she could muster. "If that's the truth, then an act of good faith to show you're sincere shouldn't be a problem."

The corners of his lips curled into a sexy smirk as he took off his glasses, folding them closed with a distinct click and tossing them on top of the nearby dresser. "What do you have in mind?"

"Make me come." A demand. A plea. A challenge he couldn't resist.

"It's not nice to doubt a lover," he said, hooking his arm under her hips and hoisting her high in the air while her knees were pressed against the mattress so she was completely open and exposed to his view.

Looking over her shoulder, she noted that he didn't look offended. He looked turned on, hungry—her gaze dipped lower—hard and ready. A shiver of want started with her core clenching and worked its way up her spine.

"Who said I did?"

His free hand came down on her ass, caressing it before dipping between her legs. "Challenge accepted."

There was no tease this time. No soft, barely-there touches. He was as sure and commanding with her body as he was with everything else. His fingers filled her, sliding in and out, as he worked his thumb on her clit, rolling and rotating around the bundle of nerves that had become the center of her universe. Every rotation of her hips. Every turn of his wrist as he played with her. Every silent touch that screamed with pleasure. Her flesh was so wet, so ready for him, that every brush of his skin against hers set off waves of sensation so intense she pressed her face into the bedding to muffle the moans she couldn't stop herself from making. The tingling started in her thighs, spreading outward in minutes at first before rushing at light speed. Her entire body contracted as she came, screaming into the sheets.

Blood thundering in her ears, she took a deep breath and sighed as the world fell back into place. The only thing holding her up was Sawyer's arm under her hips. She was deadweight at that moment, but he didn't complain. Glancing back at him, she couldn't help but let out a soft chuckle. The cocky bastard was rolling on a condom and staring at her as if he'd just painted the Mona Lisa, built the Leaning Tower of Pisa, and paddled a one-man canoe down the Amazon. He was incorrigible—and he'd kept his end of the bargain. Now she had to keep hers.

"I concede."

Before she even had a chance to take in a breath, he'd lifted her into the air and set her down on her feet in front of him. She braced a hand on his unyielding chest to steady herself and took her first full look at the breathtaking package that was Sawyer Carlyle. His suits hadn't been lying. Broad shoulders. A wide, muscular chest dusted with light brown hair. Narrow, football player hips with the strong legs to go with them. Unable to deny herself any longer, she let her gaze go to the cock she'd felt all too briefly in the hotel supply closet. Her mouth went dry. Full. Heavy. Long. And oh so happy to see her.

"Like what you see?" he asked before whipping her

dress off over her head and making fast work of her bra.

"Very much," she said, running her fingers across the most unexpected tattoo.

"Good."

His fingers clamped around her wrist and he spun her around before half propelling, half carrying her to the floor-to-ceiling window overlooking the city and pressed her palms flat against it.

"Exhibitionist much?" she asked, her heartbeat racing as she leaned forward and let her hard nipples brush against the cool glass.

"I don't care about who can see us, but I want to see it all while I'm inside you." He stood behind her, the almost overwhelming heat from his body seeping into hers. "I want you to have the whole vast world in your sights when you come again, squeezing my dick and calling my name."

Oh God, his words gave her a bigger rush than any of her previous adventures. If this was what she had to look forward to over the next several weeks, she was going to hold on and enjoy the hell out of the ride before it ended. Watching his reflection in the window, she spread her legs and tilted her ass higher in the air. He didn't need more of an invitation. Hands grasping her hips, holding her steady, he thrust inside her in one long, slow slide that had her gasping for breath even as she undulated against him.

He let out an almost pained groan. "Fuck, Clover."

"My thoughts exactly." Hard. Fast. Slow. Soft. She didn't care. She just wanted it all. Now.

"Oh, don't worry." He withdrew all but the tip of his hard cock. "I will."

• • •

Sawyer clenched his jaw tight and took a deep breath as he fought for control. The way things were going, he wouldn't have any molars left by the end of the night. It was a sacrifice he was willing to make if it meant seeing Clover come apart again. She'd lost herself in the moment and had almost taken him with her, like some kind of teenager with his first girlfriend.

He tried to focus his attention on the high-rises that dotted the skyline so he could calm the urge to surge back into her and let go. The buildings, the big picture of Harbor City, couldn't hold his attention, though, not with Clover here. The smooth lines of her back as she arched her spine fascinated him. The round curve of her hips that seemed to fit perfectly in his grasp was mesmerizing. The welcoming slick warmth of her stole his ability to consider anything else but her—even when he was barely inside her.

She tried to push back against him, but he held her firm.

Letting out a frustrated huff, she let her head drop so her forehead rested against the window. "Don't you *dare* tease me anymore."

"Who me?" As if he had the ability to do that anymore. He was praying for strength not to give in to all she offered, because once he sheathed himself again he knew without a doubt that it was going to be hard, fast, and fucking amazing.

"Yes, you and your go-slow-until-she's-stupid plan."

A bead of sweat ran down his neck as he fought not to thrust into her. Not yet. "It worked."

"Fuck yeah it did," she said with a soft laugh, which made her core squeeze the tip of his cock.

All the color bled out of his world as pleasure shot through him and his balls tightened. Fuck he was close. He ground another few millimeters off his molars and pulled back from the point of no coming back.

"If I go hard, I won't be able to go for as long as I want," he said, his gaze on the reflection of her beautiful face in the window.

She raised an eyebrow. "Are you trying to tell me that your nickname should be Mr. One and Done?"

"Hell no."

"Then fuck me and we'll go slow next time."

She didn't have to ask twice. His control evaporated so thoroughly it was if it had never existed. He drove into her, claiming her as his. The moment he was as deep as he could go something primal woke up in him, recognizing something in Clover that Sawyer couldn't pinpoint but knew was there, intangible and undeniable. After that, it was as if the moment controlled both of them. She met his every thrust, giving as good as she got, rotating her hips and pushing against him to drive him in farther, until they were one unit pursuing and chasing their climaxes together. The sound of their bodies slapping together filled the room along with hard breaths and desperate moans. She was close, he could feel it with every push forward so he slid one hand around her hip and glided it down her soft folds to her clit. She bucked against his touch. So sensitive and responsive.

"Yes, that's it," she panted. "Right there. Please."

Denying her wasn't something he was going to do. Putting one finger on each side of her clit, he rubbed against the bundle of nerves in time with each hard, deep thrust of his cock until she came screaming his name and squeezing him tight inside her. One more thrust and he followed behind her, his orgasm hitting him with the power of a six-ton truck.

When the world slowly came back into focus, he still had an arm tight around Clover's waist, helping her to stand. For his part, two things were holding him upright at the moment: his hand planted against the window and sheer fucking will not to look like a wimp in front of the woman who'd just rocked his world.

"Bed," he managed to get out.

"Yes," she answered in a half-asleep whisper.

Separating them only long enough to roll off the condom and dispose of it in a nearby trash can, he then picked her up in his arms and crossed the room to his bed. It wasn't a place where the women he had sex with spent the night. He wasn't an asshole about it, but the women he dated knew the score going in. So did Clover. This was an arrangement, a little fun. He should take her to her room. It was just down the very long hallway. She had her own bed where the sheets were probably cold, maybe itchy for all he knew. And anyway, they hadn't specifically negotiated sleeping arrangements. In his arms, Clover sighed and snuggled against him, nestling her head against his shoulder.

Fuck it. She was staying with him.

He lowered her to the bed and climbed in behind her, pulling her close to keep her warm. It was the gentlemanly thing to do. Anyway, he wanted to be there when she woke up and wanted round two. Plus, she felt really good—which ran a far second to not getting stuck with the nickname Mr. One and Done. It did. Really. Sure of his reasoning, Sawyer let his eyes fall closed and drifted off to sleep with Clover in his arms.

Chapter Thirteen

A week later, Sawyer sat at his desk in his home office catching up on a morning of missed work, thanks to his second ever trip to the flea market and reread the same email for the third time without comprehending a single word. Too much of his attention was focused on the strange noises coming from the general direction of his living room. By the time the second loud bang sounded—followed by a muffled groan, what had to be a curse in another language, and a shouted promise from Clover that she was all right—he shut the lid of his laptop and got up. He wasn't going to get a damn thing done until he figured out what in the world was going on.

Walking down the hall, he found a pile of deliveries from Dylan's Department Store. Included among the sexy date-night dresses that showed just enough skin to tantalize and work-appropriate dresses in bright colors and patterns that had probably never been seen before in Carlyle Tower was a pair of heavy-duty hiking boots. He stopped and studied the boots. Since Clover wasn't going to any construction sites, they had to be for her Australia trip.

After a quick glance toward the balcony where he could hear her cursing again, he grabbed the boots and carried them to the hall closet and shoved them in the back on the very top shelf next to another pair that had been delivered a few days earlier.

It wasn't like she was going any time soon, and so he'd rather have the big picture showing exactly what he envisioned right now. There was nothing more to it than that. No reason to overthink it. They were just boots.

He found Clover out on the balcony and almost swallowed his tongue, but not before he could offer a quiet thank you to whoever had invented yoga pants and tank tops. Her tight black pants molded perfectly to the curve of the ass he'd worshiped last night and every night for the past week. His cock twitched against his thigh and his brain was already working out if the potted bushes the decorator had placed at strategic positions on the balcony would block the neighbors' view, because all he wanted at the moment was to peel her yoga pants down, spread her legs, and fuck her until they were both blind.

She looked up and spotted him. "Perfect timing," she said as she rolled the heavy, rusted-out wreck of a metal medical tray out onto a newspaper covered section of the balcony.

"For what?" He had ideas. Lots of them.

She held out a white dust mask, the kind that was held in place by a rubber band that went around your head.

Oh no. Not happening. Not in this lifetime.

He crossed the threshold out onto the balcony but stopped well clear of the monstrosity they'd gotten at the flea market the previous week. "I didn't agree to this."

"Of course you did." She leaned forward over the cart and brushed off a piece of flaking paint—the move giving him an eyeful of her hard-on inducing cleavage—and winked at him before straightening back up. "It's totally on the napkin."

He could almost hear the snap and fizz that was his mental synapses short circuiting as the more primal part of his brain took over—the one that concerned itself with fucking or fighting. Scratch that. It was only concerned with fucking which, judging by the knowing little smirk on her face, she knew. Another negotiation tactic? That wasn't fair. Well, if she was going to sink to that level, he really didn't have any other choice but to do the same.

"I remember writing down going to the flea market," he said, reaching behind his neck and pulling off his T-shirt as he strolled over to the chaise lounge. Feeling her gaze on him as sure as a touch, he sat down on the chair, stretched out his legs, and put his hands behind his head. "I never wrote anything down about going to DIY hell."

"What do you think the flea market is all about?" She tossed the dust mask at him and it landed in the middle of his bare chest. "You're going to need this."

He picked up the mask, making sure to flex his biceps as he held up the not heavy item and examined it as if it was even a tenth as interesting as the hungry look on her face right now. "Explain to me again why I would rather refinish that crap cart when we could entertain each other in much better ways?"

With one hand on her cocked out hip, she tried for intimidating but all he saw was hot-chick-he-wanted-naked and soon. She must have noticed that because her eyes narrowed and she got that stubborn tilt to her chin that he'd started looking forward to seeing more than he probably should.

"Don't tell me you're the kind of guy who welches on his promises."

"I believe I did *everything* you wanted last night." The fact that either of them could walk today was damn close to a miracle.

Her blush was immediate and only a shade or two off scarlet. "Enough stalling, Mr. Ego. Put on the mask and help me sand this thing down."

"God, I wish that was a euphemism," he muttered, but he got up and put on the stupid mask and walked over to the cart.

She handed him the steel wool and got to work with a paint scraper. They worked together, she'd scrape off the paint and he'd follow up with the steel wool to sand down the edges between the paint layers. It had been working pretty much the same in his office at Carlyle Tower. She'd claimed his conference table and had gone to work diving into the Singapore project proposal and pointing out areas where a few tweaks here and there in the language or his approach could make a difference. So far, it was working. They had a follow-up dinner meeting with Mr. Lim in a week, which is exactly what he was prepping for when he got suckered into pretending to be someone on one of the HGTV shows Clover loved.

Thirty minutes later, finally finished removing decades of paint, he stood up and stretched his back, barely managing to stop a self-satisfied smirk when he caught her checking him out. "Why are we doing this if you're just going to paint over it?"

"Because if you don't get the little things right in the beginning, it'll just fuck up your results in the end." She laid the paint scraper down on the cart's top shelf, took off her mask, and dropped her fingers to the waistband of her yoga pants.

He went from having a semi just from being in the same breathing space to a full-on steel rod in a heartbeat. She was fucking with him. No doubt about it. Good thing he gave as good as he got—in and out of bed. He yanked off the dust mask and dropped it before circling around the cart until he stood behind her. He didn't touch her. That's what she expected.

"Those are some deep thoughts," he continued on, walking back to the chaise lounge and sitting down, resting his hands on his abs and closing his eyes. "So much so that I'm going on break to think about them."

The sound of steps growing closer, followed by the unmistakable sound of her clothes hitting the floor—at least that's what his lust-soaked imagination said it was—made his breath catch. Keeping his eyes closed and his hands to himself was murder with her so close, but he knew how negotiations like this worked. He gave her an inch and she'd take all seven—shit, what was he thinking because that sounded pretty fucking awesome. But before he could do anything, she straddled him and brought his hands to her—damn—still clothed hips.

She leaned forward, her hair tickling his neck and nipped his earlobe. "Somebody has to show you how the world works at the ground level."

"And you're the woman for the job, huh?" He tightened his grip, hooking his thumbs into the inside of her waistband.

"Exactly," she said as she rocked against him.

Unable to take it anymore, he opened his eyes. Her face was right above his. Her eyes were hazy and her lips parted. *Oh hell.* Forget negotiating, teasing, tormenting, or whatever they were doing right now. He'd had enough.

Adjusting his hold on her hips, he picked her up and swung her over his shoulder as he got up and headed back inside. "Too bad I have another job for you right now."

And he couldn't wait to outline exactly what he wanted from her. After all, turnabout was fair play.

• • •

Sitting in the back of the cab by herself, Clover finished typing up a follow-up email about the boots she'd ordered not being delivered. It was weird. She'd order a few dresses, maybe some lingerie, and the boots. Everything always arrived but the boots. Right about now she could really use those boots as a physical reminder that the date to leave for Australia was getting ever closer, because the more time she spent with Sawyer, the harder it was getting to remember that fact—and she desperately needed to.

Trying her best to ignore the way her gut twisted at the thought, she shoved her phone into her purse, slipped the cab driver a twenty, and bounded out of the cab, eager for a killer Vito's pineapple shake. Okay, and for the company of a certain someone who had been the reason why she hadn't gotten a good night's sleep in two and a half weeks. Not that she was complaining—because she definitely was not, but there was no denying her caffeine intake had dramatically increased.

She pushed open the door and walked into the diner, but instead of the tinkling from the bell attached to the door, the sound of a dozen barking dogs froze her to the spot.

"Don't just stand there, close the door and flip the open sign to closed," Donna said from her usual spot behind the counter, her ever-present gray updo transformed into a high ponytail.

Clover did as asked, despite the fact that she was trying to process the scene in front of her. Sawyer sat in their usual booth looking happy-hour hot with his suit jacket gone, his collar unbuttoned, and his navy-striped tie hanging loose around his neck. However, where Clover usually sat across from him was the biggest poodle she'd ever seen. White, massive, and with the yes-I'm-judging-you look that only standard poodles could really carry off. The dog had a blinged out collar that read: Vito. If one dog in the diner had given the health department a fit, the fact that there were twelve—most of which were wearing party hats and seated at the booths along with their owners—would have made the inspector keel over.

She hustled past the panting dogs and their owners, who were seemingly oblivious to the serious weirdness of the moment as they talked amongst themselves, and slid into the booth beside Sawyer. "What's going on?"

"Vito's having a birthday party."

"We were invited to a dog party?"

"No, I didn't know it was happening, but when I showed up as Donna was closing up she said we could stay," he said, before taking a bite of an extra salty fry. "The thing is, we have to share a booth with Vito."

She stole one of his fries and had it halfway to her mouth when Vito let out a low growl. The dog had its own plate of fries in front of it. *Wait*. She looked closer. Nope. They were fry-shaped dog biscuits. Vito didn't seem interested though as he watched her purloined fry as if she'd snagged it from his dish.

"I've never been to a dog's birthday party before," she said.

"What?" Sawyer asked in mock surprise. "The woman who milked snakes has never been to something as pedestrian as a canine celebration?"

"Smart-ass." Ignoring the dirty look and lazy growl from Vito, she popped the fry into her mouth. "I don't think he likes me."

"Maybe because he is a she." Sawyer slung his arm over the back of the booth and twisted a strand of her hair around his fingers.

Without thinking about it she relaxed back into his embrace, feeling like she belonged there in a way she didn't want to delve too deeply into. In a few weeks she'd be on her way to Australia to help the endangered Rock Wallabies and he'd be off changing Singapore's skyline. Their paths couldn't be any more different. This was a fun diversion, a mini-adventure, nothing more—so analyzing it instead of just enjoying the moment while it lasted wouldn't do a damn bit of good.

Vito picked that moment to emit another half-hearted growl.

"A girl, huh? That would explain it," Clover said.

"What?" he asked.

"Even Vito is a candidate to be the next Mrs. Carlyle." She stole another fry. "God help you if your mom finds out."

"If I buy you an extra-large pineapple shake and an order of your own fries, will you keep your mouth shut about it?" he asked before feeding her a fry.

"*Bahaya*," she mumbled.

Vito cocked her head to one side.

Sawyer chuckled. "What does that mean?"

It meant danger because that's the exact zone she was flying into without a parachute, but she wasn't about to admit that.

So she lied. "Consider me bribed."

The fry in her mouth turned to sawdust.

• • •

"You'd better not be eating all the popcorn," Sawyer demanded two days later as he walked into the living room with two cold beers after successfully hiding another pair of hiking boots. If he didn't learn to control that urge, he was going to end up paying for a dozen pairs that were stuffed into one secret place or another in his penthouse.

Clover froze, a handful of popcorn halfway to her mouth. "The bowl was extra full, it would have spilled everywhere and ruined your couch."

"Likely story," he said, sitting down next to her. He put the beers on the coffee table and grabbed the remote before she picked something horrible for movie night.

She snuggled up next to him, moving into the same position they ended up in whenever they were in one of her HGTV marathons. "So you're really not willing to play rock, paper, scissors for the right to pick the movie?"

"Hell no." Clover was hot. She rocked his world. But he could not take another mini-marathon of *Flea Market Flip*. "You've suckered me into fixing up that stupid bar cart."

She snorted. "Talk all you want, I know you had fun."

"It was total misery, which is why I get to pick the movie."

"Whatever you say, Mr. Stuffikins."

Like a smart man, he kept his mouth shut and flipped

through the list of streaming movies. Truth was, he'd had fun renovating the cart. She'd made it fun, teasing him about how someone whose company built skyscrapers had never used a paint spray gun before. The finished cart was in the living room, a bright red splash of color in his otherwise black and metallic room, drawing his attention the same way as the woman in his arms had started to do.

Per usual, the listed movies picked because of his watching history fell into two distinct categories: shit blows up and RomComs. He was about to swap over to the explosion side of things when one of his favorites popped on the screen.

"We could watch this. There's fencing, fighting, torture, revenge, giants, monsters, chases, escapes, true love, and miracles."

She twisted around and looked up at him, her eyes wide. "Did you just quote *The Princess Bride*?"

Well, there was no use denying it now, but the expected embarrassment didn't hit. Like almost everything else when it came to Clover, that reaction was unexpected. He hit play on the movie. "I have a thing."

"Oh no way, I want all the dirty details." She picked up both beers, kept one and handed him the other.

As the opening credits played on the movie, he took a long drink. "Do I get to take you home tonight even after I spill my secrets and you know I love watching old RomComs?"

Her answer was a quick brush of her lips against his. "If you don't, there'll be hell to pay."

That soft kiss turned into another and another and another until the man in black was climbing the Cliffs of Insanity before Clover pulled away and grabbed the popcorn and then settled back down snuggled against him.

"We're gonna miss the movie," she said.

"Life is pain. Anyone who says differently is selling

something," he paraphrased another of his favorite lines.

But the thing was, since Clover had walked into his office and become his personal buffer, his life had lost that black tinge of pain that he hadn't even realized had been there. The question was, would it come back when their contract was up, and did he even want to find out?

Chapter Fourteen

Normally, a brunch trip to Grounded Coffee with Daphne meant Clover rushed to claim the seat at their regular table that would give her the perfect view of the coffee house's amazingly hot in-house pastry chef as he made the chocolate-filled croissants and other goodies destined to go straight to her ass. This time, though, she didn't even realize she was sitting with her back to the large window dividing the kitchen from the seating area until Daphne slid into prime viewing seat number one and dug into her food.

"Oh my God." Daphne gasped, her forkful of bacon and spinach quiche stopping halfway between her plate and her mouth. "It really must be love."

Trying not the burn with guilt, Clover finished the bite of taste-free and chalky croissant. Okay, it probably tasted wonderful but not to her at the moment. The evil eye her conscience was giving her pretty much killed any good the delectable could do for her taste buds.

"What are you talking about?" she asked, sounding as convincingly innocent as she had when she'd been eight and had gotten caught with the last crumbs of an entire plate's worth of Christmas cookies.

"Hot chef," Daphne responded. "You didn't even look before you plopped down."

Buying time by stuffing another bite of flaky, buttery chalk dust into her mouth, she forced herself to make eye contact with her best friend. Daphne had her elbows on their table and her chin propped up on one hand, her brown eyes wide with interest.

"I'm just keeping the mystery alive for our friendship." *Oh yeah, Clover. That doesn't sound like bullshit at all.* "What fun would it be if you knew everything about me?"

"Like that game is even necessary," Daphne argued and popped another bite of quiche into her mouth. "I've barely heard from you lately and this is the first time I've laid eyes on you in weeks."

"It's been a little busy." In a hot, sweaty sex against the wall, in the shower, and occasionally on the bed kind of way.

Daphne arched an eyebrow. "All that wedding planning, huh?"

What once had probably been a perfectly good croissant transformed into a lead weight in the pit of her stomach. God, she hated lying. This was why she'd been dodging her bestie *and* her mom. It was easier to forget what a total asshole she was being to the people she loved if she wasn't eye to eye with them. The truth danced on the tip of her tongue before pounding against her clamped shut lips. But instead of letting the words out, she forced herself to walk the Sawyer Carlyle personal buffer company line.

"Exactly." She nodded and slammed back the remains of her espresso cup, kind of for real hoping it would make her spontaneously combust on the spot.

It didn't. Instead, she just gave her insides third degree burns.

"That is bullshit," Daphne said.

Clover jerked to attention, torn away from her own pity party.

Daphne rolled her eyes and continued. "I know you're not getting married."

"According to the paper I am." Mostly true. Heart rate? Autobahn fast.

"Where's the ring?" Daphne asked.

"I don't have one." Her palms started to sweat.

"Does he dress left or right?" her best friend asked in

a rush and a wicked little grin.

"Left." Totally true. Also, her lying-induced anxiety was making her stomach cramp up.

"Middle name?"

She gulped. "Charles." It *could* be Charles. It also just happened to be the name of the guy who'd taken their brunch order.

"Favorite breakfast food?"

"Waffles." At least that's what Sawyer loved to pop in the toaster for post-coital refreshment—a mental image she didn't need when her pulse was already jackhammering in her ears.

Daphne took a sip of coffee and looking bored all of a sudden asked, "When are you leaving for Australia?"

"Two and a half weeks." Finally, one she didn't have to mislead about.

"Called it!" Daphne raised her arm and pumped her fist. "The whole engagement is bullshit. So what's the real story?"

Oh crap. If she was getting married, there would be no Australia.

Figuratively cornered by Daphne's eyes and the power of long-term friendship, her cheeks blazed, her heart slammed against her ribs, and the words rushed out—along with some very unfortunately timed stress tears.

"Just because I'm still going to Australia doesn't mean the engagement is fake or that I'm dodging my mom's calls because I hate lying to her or that I've been making myself stay away from you guys because I knew you'd figure out the truth." Breaths coming in short gasps, she looked down at the napkin she'd shredded without realizing it and grabbed a fresh one from the dispenser on the table to dry her cheeks and wipe her runny nose. Damn. She did not mean for all of that to come out. Maybe it hadn't. If she prayed hard enough maybe it had only happened in her head. She glanced up at Daphne, and she was staring at her with mouth agape. Nope. She'd definitely said it out loud. "*Tae.*"

"I don't know what that last word was," Daphne said, "and I'm still processing the rest."

"It means shit in Tagalog." Which was the best possible word for what she'd just said because there would be no stopping the interrogation that was going to happen next.

"Okay, let me get this straight." Her friend took a quick sip of coffee. "You're not engaged?"

Clover shook her head. "No."

"Thank God," she said and sank back against her seat. "I thought you'd lost your fucking mind or had joined a cult."

"None of the above." She reached for her espresso with hands that didn't shake for the first time since she'd arrived at Grounded Coffee. "I'm Sawyer's personal buffer."

"You're a fluffer?" Daphne asked in a stage whisper. "Like in porn?"

"No!" Clover said, perhaps a bit too forcefully considering the looks they got from some of the people sitting near their table. "*Mierda.*"

Great. Let's just add making a public fool of yourself to everything else.

She offered the strangers a smile—a perfectly polite response if she'd been in small town Sparksville, but one that only elicited confused and wary reactions from the good people of Harbor City who learned from birth not to acknowledge each other. The only benefit of that being that they all very quickly turned back to their own tables.

Daphne leaned in close and lowered her voice, "You're having sex with him, though."

"What makes you say that?" And there went what little remained of her napkin.

"Because if you weren't you would have just straight denied it," she said, bold as brass. "Face it, Clover, you can't keep shit from me—obviously, since it took about ten minutes to break you. Don't ever turn to a life of crime. You'd suck at it."

And didn't she know it. "Noted."

"So what's the real deal?"

Glancing over at the other tables to make sure no one was listening, Clover scooted her chair closer, relief at finally being able to talk to someone loosening the tension tying her guts in a knot. "You can't tell anyone. Ever."

"Goodie. That means this is gonna be good." Daphne held out her hand to the middle of the table and held out her pinkie. "I solemnly swear I'll keep my big mouth shut. Spill."

Clover couldn't help but grin. It was a sign of unity they'd developed one night years ago in their freshman dorm after half a dozen too many cheap beers. Still, the silly action represented them and their unrelenting loyalty. So she held her hand aloft, finger pointing, and touched her pinkie to Daphne's. Then, she told her everything—minus all the glorious naked details. By the time she got to the end, Daphne had been rendered silent.

"So in a few weeks, we break off the engagement, he finalizes some big deal and gets his mom to cool her matchmaking efforts, and I jet off to Australia fifteen grand richer," Clover said. "We both walk away happy."

She relaxed back against her seat, able to enjoy hanging out with Daphne without any weird I'm-lying-my-face-off guilt eating away at her. A lightness filled her, happy and content. All was right with the world. However, judging by the expression on Daphne's face, she wasn't feeling the same.

Finally, Daphne spoke up, "But you're sleeping with him."

Okay, this was an obvious misunderstanding, but Clover had this one down. "It's not like I'm an employee, and he's not paying me for that. It's just for fun."

One of her eyebrows popped up practically to her blond hairline. "Uh-huh."

Clover stiffened, indignation zapping up her spine. "What's that mean?"

"Well…" Daphne paused, pushing the broken pieces of crust from her quiche around her plate. "You're not exactly a casual sex kinda girl even with your obsession with new experiences."

"I'm not a prude." And why was she having to defend herself? It was her life.

"You can take the girl out of Sparksville," Daphne said. "But you can't take Sparksville out of the girl."

Her chest tightened and Clover pressed her lips together before she said something she'd regret later. Daphne was her friend. Her *best* friend. They'd disagreed before. They'd disagree again. But that didn't change the fact that they were always there for each other. It's just this time, Daphne didn't understand. Taking a deep breath, she counted to five before letting it all out in a slow exhale.

"It's just sex," she said, her voice calmer than she felt. "It's not like I'm falling in love with him. We just hang out. Did I tell you we renovated a flea market find into a bar cart?"

"He went with you to the flea market?" Daphne squeaked out the question.

Clover relaxed, thankful her attempt to change the subject worked. She could understand why. When she pictured the Sawyer Carlyle from the paparazzi photos and news clips, she had to admit it sounded ridiculous. But there was more to him than just the skyscrapers and the fancy parties—maybe more than even he realized.

"Yeah, we do all sorts of stuff together," she said. "I've been spending my days at his office helping him with his proposal for a deal in Singapore. You don't even want to know what kind of cultural missteps he was making."

"What else do you do?" Daphne asked. "Dinner out?"

"Of course, we have to make the fake engagement

look good." The fact that the past month and a half had been a complete blast had nothing to do with it. That was just gravy. Honest. "There are dinners, cocktail parties, the flea market, and movie nights in—he has a total thing for old RomComs—don't ever tell him I told you his darkest secret."

"But it's all fake," her friend said.

Ouch. That hurt. "As a three-dollar bill," Clover said with enough cheer to cover whatever was pinching her between the shoulder blades.

"And you're 100 percent positive of that?" Daphne asked, concern bleeding through so there was no doubt it wasn't judgment motivating her friend but worry.

The realization settled what was left of the apprehension stringing her tight, and she smiled at her bestie.

"Of course," she said. "I'm not morphing into my mother with dreams of a happy little life of domestic bliss where all I want is to fall in love. I have a life to lead and adventures to have."

"As long as you're sure…" Daphne let her worlds trail off.

"I am," she said with a conviction she almost felt. "Now tell me everything I've missed."

There was a beat of silence before Daphne started in on the latest shenanigans of their fuckboy neighbor down the hall and his ludicrous attempts to flirt with her. Clover listened and laughed without once wondering what Sawyer was up to—well, maybe once.

• • •

Something was missing—or to be more specific, some*one* was missing. Sawyer looked over to the conference table where Clover had left four neatly stacked rows of research on the construction market in Singapore in general and Mr. Lim's luxury apartment business specifically before going out for an early lunch with her friend. He had plenty to do, but his attention kept traveling back to the empty chair at the end of the conference table. With each look, each wondered question about what she was doing right now, he got more and more annoyed with himself. So much that the sudden appearance of his mom in his doorway filled him with a sort of twisted joy. A little mother-son battle? Oh yeah, he could make time for that today.

Helene stopped two steps into his office and glanced back over her shoulder. "Stop acting like I'm holding a gun to your head and get in here."

Sawyer's stomach roiled. His mom he was glad to see, even if she brought nothing but headaches and Irish-Catholic guilt. But a wife candidate? Yeah, he was definitely not in the mood for that. He had his mouth open ready to tell her to leave her latest eligible bachelorette cooling her heels outside when his brother walked in.

"So *this* is what this floor looks like," Hudson said, looking around the office as if it were an exotic locale. "I usually don't make it past the cafeteria level. Mrs. Esposito always saves a couple of cookies for me."

"We are not here to discuss cookies," Helene said, continuing her march forward.

"Just one in particular," Hudson said in a 40s gangster voice. "How is your bride-to-be?"

Maybe a wife candidate would be preferable to whatever these two had in mind. Sawyer bit back his groan but refused to sink back against his seat. One did not cower in front of Helene Carlyle unless one wanted to be eaten. So he steeled his spine, flexed his toes, and got ready to do the all too familiar tightrope walk of being careful of his mother's feelings while also shoving her out of his business with both hands.

He stood and walked toward the pair of leather couches arranged to admire the view of Harbor City's skyline, figuring his mother would probably be more comfortable trying to run his life from the comfort of the designer couches than the stiff-backed visitor's chair in front of his desk. "Clover is just fine."

Helene followed, sitting down with the grace and determination of a woman who knew what she wanted and knew exactly how to go about getting it. "This whole thing is ridiculous, Sawyer. Even Hudson agrees."

"I don't know," Hudson said, sitting down opposite Sawyer. "I think it's nice that the crazy kids are taking their time getting to the altar after such a dive straight into love."

Helene narrowed her eyes and cut a glare at Hudson. "You're not nearly as amusing as you think you are, young man."

"Of course I am, you're just too annoyed at my big brother to see it."

She closed her eyes and exhaled the sigh of a martyr. "Where did your father and I go wrong?"

"My therapist has a list," Hudson said with a grin for their mom and a wink for Sawyer.

He didn't know what his little brother was up to, but as long as it took the heat off of him and Clover, then Sawyer was more than willing to sit back and watch the show.

"Enough, Hudson." She held up her hand, the three-carat diamond wedding ring she still wore glinting in the sunlight streaming in through the window. "Stop trying to distract me from what we came here to do."

Damn. The woman never missed a trick.

"And what's that?" Hudson asked.

As if they both didn't know already.

"Stopping your brother before this farce goes any further," Helene said. "You can't actually marry that... that...person."

Red ate the edges of his vision away and heat shot up from his toes as his entire body tensed. It was a damn good thing he loved his mother because if he didn't, he wasn't sure what would have come out of his mouth next. Whatever it was, it wouldn't have been the kind of thing a son should say to his mom. It took a second for him to remember how to unclamp his jaw, he was holding it closed with such force.

"She. Has. A. Name."

"Fine," his mom said, not giving an inch in her steel-hard posture. "Clover. You've been holed up with her for long enough. You haven't come out to any of the charity functions or the family cocktail hour."

He let out a cold laugh. "I can't imagine why after what happened last time."

"You mean when Mom threw a couple of Mrs. Carlyle wannabes at you in front of your fiancée?" Hudson asked, his tone jovial despite the worry crinkling the corners of his eyes.

"Oh shut up, Hudson," she said, her voice unraveling around the edges. Then she took a deep breath before patting Hudson's knee in a non-verbal apology. "I'm just looking out for you, Sawyer. I only want what's best for you. After what happened with Tyler Jacobson's fiancée, Irena, I just want you to be with the kind of woman who can make you happy."

Nothing like finding your best friend's bride in her wedding lingerie in your hotel room hours before the ceremony. It seemed her true love for Tyler didn't stand a chance against her lust for Sawyer's bank account. She'd ruined her makeup crying crocodile tears and napalmed his twenty-year friendship with Tyler. A reminder of that clusterfuck was the last thing Sawyer wanted from his mom right now—well, almost the last thing.

"And you think one of your wife candidates is the way to go?" he asked, letting every ounce of distaste he had for her schemes drip into his tone.

"I was hoping it would at least get you thinking in

the right direction." Helene threw her hands up in the air. "You can't ignore the rest of the world while you focus on Carlyle Enterprises and let all the important things—the little things—escape your view."

"I'm not. I'm getting married, remember?" Not the truth, but what did that matter when it came to winning an argument?

"It's so ridiculous," she said. "What do you even know about her?"

Images flashed in his mind. The sunlight in her hair as they'd gone from booth to booth to find the perfect fixer upper at the flea market. The fact that she hogged the popcorn on movie night. That she'd graduated to extra-large shakes at Vito's. The way she'd screamed and then laughed when he'd surprised her in the shower this morning. The arch of her spine and undulation of her hips as she rode him hard. None of which were things he could share with his mother.

"I know she likes pineapple shakes and cheeseburgers with jalapeños," he blurted out. "I know she talks back to the screen during reality TV shows. I know she mutters to herself in other languages when she gets frustrated."

"But what do you know about *her*?" Helene pressed. "Who she is when it counts?"

The question stopped him dead. Over the past few weeks he'd learned a lot about what Clover liked to do, but what did he really know about the details that made her Clover and not Jane? What was it that she wasn't telling him? Sharing with him? Not that he had any right to her secrets, but the urge to know what they were called out to something inside him that he didn't recognize.

"Well then," Hudson said after the awkward pause while Sawyer's brain spun in search of answers he didn't have. "While it is always fascinating to see you two forget your mutual reluctance to talk about your feelings, I think we've all had enough of that for this decade."

Helene nodded. "I suppose you're right."

Hudson jumped up off the couch, his hand over his heart like a two-bit player in a cheap melodrama. "Someone alert the media."

It was so over the top and so typically Hudson that all the tension seeped out of the room. Helene stood and gave her youngest son an indulgent smile and a hard pat on the cheek. Then she turned to Sawyer.

"We lost your dad too young. I didn't make him stop working so much and putting in all those long hours. I should have. That's a guilt I'll feel for the rest of my life." She blinked back the wetness in her eyes. "And you're so much like him, Sawyer. You never even crawled. You just decided one day to stand up and walk to the window, planted your hands on the glass, and looked out onto the Harbor City skyline," she said, her voice shaking. "You need someone to make you slow down and appreciate the details. That person is obviously not me, but I'm hoping that whoever you marry will be the one who can do that." She paused and looked off to the left, blinking rapidly before centering her attention, once more, on him. "I can't lose you, too."

She pressed her lips tight together and inhaled a deep breath before she opened her mouth to say more. However, she must have changed her mind because instead of lecturing, she wrapped her arms around him and squeezed him close.

It wasn't like they never hugged. They weren't *that* uptight of a family, but his mom? She was a different kind of woman. Hard. Determined. Feisty, his dad had called her. Touchy feely she was not. It was one of the things they had in common. He curled his arms around her and returned the hug. They stood there like that for a minute before breaking apart. Before he could say anything, Helene— her eyes suspiciously wet again—gave him a stiff nod and strode out of his office without another word, leaving him staring after her in confusion until Hudson slapped him on the back of the head.

"If this blows up in our faces, you're going to owe me big time," Hudson said, all traces of the jester he'd been playing drained out of him. "I do not want to be on the same planet when she finds out we've been lying to her."

"She won't."

She couldn't. Losing their father had been hard on him and Hudson. Their mother had been devastated. He wouldn't be the cause of her ever feeling any pain again.

His brother walked to the door, paused on the threshold, and turned back to face him. "Just do what you always do and keep your eye on the big picture so this doesn't go sideways and fuck us both."

Guilt warred with selfishness, twisting him up inside. "When don't I?"

Hudson nodded, let out a breath, and in an instant transformed himself back into the smiling flirt he wanted everyone to think he was, then he walked out into the outer office already teasing Amara before he'd even gotten two steps away.

Without meaning to, Sawyer ended up not back at his own desk but at the end of the conference table where Clover had been working before leaving for lunch. The paper was covered in her notes, but the margins were covered in doodles of geometric shapes and a sketch of a man who looked a lot like him. The caveman inside him let out a proud and triumphant yell with plenty of chest pounding and dick waving.

It was an ego boost big enough that he forced himself to look up and focus instead on the Harbor City skyline so he could count the Carlyle buildings. Everything was falling into place. His mom was so concerned about Clover's inappropriateness that she'd halted her campaign of wife candidates. By the time Clover left, Helene would be so relieved it would be easy to persuade her to drop the marriage campaign completely. That fact should have made the amazing view from the sixty-third floor even better. It didn't. Instead of success, all he could taste in his mouth was bitter disappointment. That reaction did not fit into his ultimate vision of who he was and what he needed to do next.

They were almost to the deadline on Clover's contract, and he still hadn't gotten Mr. Lim to sign the deal for the three Singapore high-rises. Hudson was right, he couldn't afford to let this thing with Clover go sideways and add in some unexpected complications that would only fuck with his plans. Time to refocus on the big picture and stop getting distracted.

Chapter Fifteen

Back at the penthouse after work, Clover couldn't shake the feeling that something had changed between her and Sawyer. He'd been preoccupied after she'd gotten back from lunch and on the drive home he'd barely looked at her, let alone talked to her. Now, here she was in her room slipping on the pair of black heels he'd given her and a form-fitting little black dress with cap sleeves that ended right below her knees to go with him to a business event. The dress had always been her go-to when she needed a shot of confidence at a social event—or in this case a business dinner with the elusive Mr. Lim and his to-be-built high-rises. And considering how silent and broody Sawyer had been acting ever since she'd gotten back from her girls' lunch, she could use it.

"*Jangan takut*," she muttered to herself.

She didn't have time to be scared anyway. The last thing she wanted was to make them late for this dinner. She'd put too much work into putting the pieces together for a real final push for success. If everything went as planned, the deal was all but done. It was strange, she'd had a million different kinds of jobs, some that mattered but most that didn't beyond financing her next adventure. However, seeing everything come together for this deal was different. There was a sense of accomplishment that came with it, a pride of ownership. It wasn't her deal, but she was a part of making it happen—and that would stick around that top floor office in Carlyle Tower long after she'd left. And maybe, Sawyer would remember that and remember her.

Dragging her fingers through her stick-straight hair one

last time, she smoothed it down so it fell past her shoulders, grabbed the peacock purse Daphne had loaned her for that first charity event, and strode out of her bedroom hoping she looked a hell of a lot more confident than she felt.

Sawyer stood next to the table in the foyer. A pair of brand new hiking boots bearing the distinctive Dylan's Department Store tag sat in the middle of the table. The arrival of the mysteriously missing boots should have been what grabbed her attention, but it wasn't. All she could do was stare at Sawyer as he stood in his navy suit, checked shirt, and patterned tie shot through with blues and golds. His glasses were in his hand and he was pinching the bridge of his nose. She must have made a sound because he looked up and stopped dead in his tracks. The look he gave her wasn't particularly friendly, but that's not what registered with her. It was the way his suit stretched across his broad shoulders. The way the cut emphasized his muscular chest. The fact that even in a custom-made suit—or maybe because it was—the strength of his muscular thighs showed through. To top it all off, the color of his suit made the streaks of blue in mostly green and brown hazel eyes stand out and she caught her breath. Damn. It wasn't fair that one man could look so annoyed and so hot at the same time.

"Are you nervous about dinner?" she asked.

The vein in his temple pulsed as he gave her a slow once-over. "No."

Okay, that wasn't exactly convincing, and her Spidey sense was blaring a warning as if she was the Titanic and Sawyer an iceberg. "Something seems off. Is everything okay?"

"Of course."

Clover racked her brain. Had Daphne slipped? Had his mom figured it out? Was there a wife candidate who'd finally managed to catch his attention? She flinched at the thought. It wasn't a reaction she knew what to do with. So she did what she always did in these situations, she plowed ahead, heedless of the consequences, figuring it would work out in the end. Her adventures always had before.

Reaching out, she placed a hand on his forearm, the familiar zing of attraction skittering across her fingertips. "Did I do something to piss you off?"

"No." He glanced down at her hand, his jaw taut.

"Look, I don't know what's going on, but it's obvious you're annoyed." Like he might as well have a blinking neon sign overhead. He was hurting. If nothing else over the past few weeks, they'd developed a friendship, a bond. She couldn't see him like this and not try to help. "I'm not going anywhere until you tell me what's wrong."

He lifted his gaze, and the lack of any emotion in his eyes chilled her to the bone.

"Maybe that's for the best," he said in a carefully neutral tone.

She blinked in surprise, her brain spinning trying to catch up. "Are you nuts? After all the background work I've done this week about Mr. Lim? We've barely prepped you for some of the cultural intricacies."

"It's a business meeting." He slid his glasses on and then straightened his cuffs, all but dismissing her. "Mr. Lim and I have had plenty of those without you and the world hasn't blown up."

What. The. Fuck.

Heat swept up from her toes, and she let herself be carried away by it. "And you haven't closed the deal, either."

His fingers stilled on his cufflink as he slowly lifted his head, an answering frustration blazing from his eyes. Clover planted her hands on her hips and steeled herself for the onslaught. It never came. Instead, the intercom buzzed— blasting through the tense silence of the foyer.

"Mr. Carlyle," Irving the doorman said. "Your car is here."

Sawyer crossed to the elevator and pressed the talk button. "Thank you. Please let Linus know I'll be down in a minute."

He'll be down. *He'll* be down. She fought the urge to peel off one of her shoes and fling it at him. "So what's it gonna be, Sawyer? Do I stay or shall I go?"

Shoulders stiff, he jabbed his thumb into the elevator call button, not even bothering to look at her. "Why do you even want to go?"

"*Nǐ ge gǒu pì*," she snarled in Chinese because what he said *was* bullshit. "Because I've worked for this. I know you may not think much of me after you mocked my resume, but whether it's milking snakes, tasting dog food, teaching English, or working to save endangered animals, I always see things through."

"But only for the short term," he flung the truth at her like a grenade.

She took an involuntary step back before stopping herself from going any farther. Gathering her pride around her, she raised her chin and faced him head on. "Then it's a good thing we only have a few weeks to go."

The elevator doors *whooshed* open and he walked inside, each step stiff, and then turned around, his face an impassive mask. "So are you coming?"

She should tell him to fuck straight off. She should tell him that fifteen grand wasn't worth putting up with this kind of bullshit. But she didn't because she'd been telling the truth. She always saw things through to the end. Whatever the hell had happened to change him from the man she'd woken up with this morning she had no idea—anyway it didn't matter. She was here to do a job. Nothing more. Nothing less. So she was going to do it.

"How could I turn down such a gracious invitation?" Letting the angry click of her heels on the tile do any other talking for her, she marched into the elevator, making sure to keep to the opposite side of the carriage from him.

They made it down five floors in total silence before Sawyer lost whatever inner battle he'd been waging. "I'm sorry if I was rude."

Oh that was rich. "If?"

"It's just that I think we've lost sight of the big picture here," he said, his gaze on her reflection in the elevator mirror and not actually her. "And we need to take a few steps back from what we've been doing."

God save her from rich assholes who couldn't just say what they meant. "Is that your roundabout way of saying no more fucking?"

"Or flea markets or movie nights or Vito's."

So a total rejection then—of her, of their friendship. Biting down on her bottom lip she fought back the sudden wetness threatening her mascara. "So you're breaking the contract?"

"Renegotiating," he said without heat. After all, for him it was just business. "In a few days, I'm leaving for a short trip to Singapore for a final push with Mr. Lim anyway, so it really won't matter. By the time I get back, we'll only have a little time left in our agreement."

"And then I'll leave for Australia." And for once the idea of getting on that airplane and flying far, far away from anything that even remotely reminded her of how she'd grown up in Sparksville lost its appeal. When had that changed? Fuck if she knew. But it had. "After all, who wants to get stuck in one place?"

"Not you," he said.

Her gaze caught his in the mirrored doors and for a second she thought she saw something there, but then it faded back into nothing. The elevator doors opened and he offered her his arm. She tucked her hand into the crook of his elbow and they crossed the lobby to the car waiting outside. The zing from Sawyer's touch was still there, but it was tempered by something bittersweet that she couldn't identify, not that it would do her any good anyway. He was right. She was a short-term commitment girl who didn't believe in being tied down to any place or anything or anyone—and that's exactly how she liked it.

• • •

Just when Sawyer thought his night couldn't get any shittier, he and Clover arrived at their table at the restaurant to find Mr. Lim deep in conversation with Tyler Jacobson. Following the maître d through the hushed chatter of The Passport Club, Harbor City's latest "it" restaurant, his mind spun wondering what play Tyler was making. The man was as smart as he was vindictive. A shitty combination when you were on his bad side, and Sawyer very much had been for the past two years.

Clover let out a little gasp, and he knew she'd spotted the man determined to make his life as difficult as possible sitting with the one person who had the power to approve one of the biggest deals ever for Carlyle Enterprises.

"*An zua*. What's he doing here?" Clover asked.

"Fucking with my life in some new and clever way."

It wasn't the first time since the wedding fiasco that Tyler had acted like a grudge-holding ass. Up until now it had been stupid things, stealing his restaurant reservations, poaching a date, letting slip an embarrassing story. He hadn't messed with Sawyer's business. Until now. The maître d stopped in front of the table, and Mr. Lim stood up to greet them. Tyler stayed in his seat, as arrogant as ever.

"Mr. Carlyle, it is so good to see you again," Mr. Lim said as he shook Sawyer's hand.

"Always a pleasure," Sawyer said, still trying to work out the best way to handle Tyler. "May I introduce my fiancée, Miss Clover Lee."

"Miss Lee." Mr. Lim offered her his hand to shake.

"Selamat Petang," Clover said, shaking Mr. Lim's hand as she bowed slightly. *"Apa kabar?"*

"Baik," Mr. Lim said, his smile genuine. "You've been to Singapore, Miss Lee?"

"Yes, I was lucky enough to spend six months there recently."

"You will have to visit us again soon. Perhaps when Mr. Carlyle comes in a few days?"

"I would love that but, unfortunately, my schedule won't permit it," she said, her body language stiffening just the slightest bit.

Of course, Tyler picked that moment to slide out from the semi-circle booth and kiss Clover's cheek as if they were old friends. "Wedding planning keeping you busy?"

"Exactly," she said, giving Tyler a curious look. "It's good to see you again, Tyler."

"Forgive me for not informing you earlier that Mr. Jacobson will be joining us," Mr. Lim said. "He's recently become a strategic advisor for my company's dealings in America."

Fuck. That explained why this deal hadn't been signed yet. All this time Sawyer had been looking at the big picture for what it was missing and hadn't noticed that something rotten had been added.

"Not to worry, Sawyer and I go way back. Don't we?" Tyler said, holding out his hand with a smile that was as genuine as the Rolexes being sold on the corner of Eighty-Sixth Street to the tourists.

"Jacobson." He shook his former best friend's hand, squeezing it hard enough that the other man's knuckles rubbed together in a silent warning to watch his step.

"Wonderful," Mr. Lim said and gestured toward the table. "Shall we sit?"

All of the tables at The Passport Club were semi-circular booths looking out onto a small stage. Tonight, the red velvet stage curtain was closed. He ended up on the end across from Mr. Lim with Tyler sitting between Sawyer and Clover. It hadn't been an accident. Tyler had excelled at chess and had learned to use those skills in the real world. Most of the time it went to building the client base for his multimillion dollar consulting business. Tonight, the bastard was obviously using it to fuck with Sawyer.

For their part, Clover and Mr. Lim seemed oblivious as they looked over the menu, talked in Malay, and picked out the dishes for the table.

"She's quite beautiful." Tyler took a sip of his scotch.

Fury, hot and sudden, swept up his body and his hands were fisted before he knew it. If Tyler even looked at Clover funny, he'd— He took a deep breath, forcing his mind to still and relaxed his hands. "Stay away from her."

The other man's mouth curled into a wicked grin, the first genuine emotion he'd shown that night. "What kind of man would I be if I poached another man's fiancée?"

"You know that was all Irena and not me," Sawyer said, keeping his voice low and his tone pleasant so neither Clover nor Mr. Lim would realize what was happening.

"Of course." Tyler raised his glass in a toast and then downed it in one large gulp. Then he held up his glass and two fingers, catching the eye of a nearby waiter who nodded and hustled toward the bar. "Someone of your stature would never do something so crass as break up a man's marriage before it even started. Even a dumb scholarship kid like me realizes that."

Tyler may have been a scholarship kid to Atlantic Prep, but he'd never been dumb—except when it came to Irena. Even Sawyer had seen that she was nothing more than a gold digger looking for a big enough pot. Tyler hadn't realized until it was too late and that painful failure was obviously all he could see now.

"I won't apologize for something I didn't do." Again.

And again. And *again*. He'd been down that road too many times with shit results. He'd moved on. It was beyond time that the other man should, too.

Tyler chuckled and patted him on the shoulder, making it look to the rest of the world as if they were still friends. "I wouldn't dream of asking you to."

No. He'd just hold a grudge for the rest of his life.

"So how did you manage this?" Sawyer asked.

"Advising Mr. Lim? We happened to run into each other a few months ago, and I've been offering my insight."

No doubt about all the ways in which Carlyle Enterprise was a bad choice to build the trio of high-rises on Pulau Ujong.

Before he could press him, though, the waiter arrived with two scotches, one of which he placed in front of Tyler and the other in front of Sawyer, and then he took their order from Clover and Mr. Lim. After that, it was the kind of surface, getting-to-know-you chitchat he fucking hated but was the way of business dinners in Singapore. It took years to develop relationships in Singapore, and Sawyer had been nurturing this one for three. Carlyle Enterprises couldn't allow Tyler to sink it, they had too much time and planning invested already.

By the time the food arrived in large family-style dishes that everyone shared, Sawyer was on edge. The warning siren that had whistled when he'd spotted Tyler at the table was blaring in his ear now. So he did what he almost never did, he turned on the charm, asking Mr. Lim about his family and life in Singapore, his abysmal golf game, and his killer tennis game. Of course, that meant that Tyler had all of Clover's attention and that burned a hole right through Sawyer's stomach lining. It shouldn't. What did he care? She had a part to play, that was all. But just like it had been since Clover had come into his life, he couldn't help but turn his attention to her with every soft giggle and smile.

Tyler, for his part, was really playing it up. He didn't cross any lines, but he walked right up on them—tucking a stray hair behind her ear, leaning in to whisper conspiratorially, making her laugh when all Sawyer had done tonight was piss her off. By the time Mr. Lim had begun another story about a golf ball sailing into a sand trap, Sawyer was only half listening because the sound of blood rushing through his ears was too damn loud to catch more than every third word.

"It is good to see a man who is so taken with his bride," Mr. Lim said, the change in subject jerking Sawyer's full attention back to him.

This is exactly why he shouldn't have brought Clover tonight. Hudson was right. She was a distraction he didn't need right now. "I'm sorry."

"Do not apologize." Mr. Lim offered an indulgent smile. "I am the same way when I am around my own wife. Perhaps you can come over for dinner when you are in Singapore? I'm sure she would love to meet you."

"I would be honored."

"Then it is a deal."

"Hopefully not the only one." He'd have to take advantage of having Mr. Lim separated from Tyler to seal the deal. This trip just might be his final shot.

"We shall see after your final site visit." Mr. Lim nodded. "I'm anxious to see your proposal after that."

"You're going to love his proposal," Clover said, her smile open and engaging as she looked away from Tyler. "I took a sneak peek and it is really going to fit in with the eclectic nature of Singapore's skyline."

"What was your favorite building in Singapore?" Mr. Lim asked.

"Honestly, I couldn't say, I was enjoying the people," she looked down at the plate in front of her "and the food too much."

Mr. Lim chuckled and nodded. "We have that much

in common."

And there, just like that Clover had intrigued the other man and set him at ease. Sawyer couldn't get over it. The woman was a whirlwind.

The rest of dinner was more stories about golf and family from Mr. Lim while Sawyer fought not to drag Tyler out of the booth so he could smack the flirting asshole around. Not that Clover was helping. She laughed at all of the other man's jokes and ignored Sawyer completely. The first time she even looked at him since they'd sat down was when he slid in next to her in the Town Car's backseat. She looked over at him, her posture ramrod straight, that luscious mouth that had smiled at every stupid joke from Tyler was a flat line and the friendliness in her eyes she'd shown to Mr. Lim had grown cold.

He waited for her to say something, *anything,* but she didn't. Instead she fastened her seatbelt, clasped her hands in her lap, and looked out the window as they drove through the busy streets of Harbor City. By the time they were back in the elevator on their way up to his penthouse, frustration and anger—at himself? her? who knew—was a ball of fire eating him up inside, and it needed to go somewhere or he'd go up in flames.

"What in the hell was that?" he asked, his voice as cold as he was hot.

"It *would* have been a wonderful dinner if you hadn't been giving me the evil eye the whole time." Clover narrowed her eyes at him as a pink flush of anger rushed into her cheeks. "I know details aren't your thing, but if you want the world to believe we're getting married, then acting like an asshole to me isn't the way to get it done."

"I shouldn't have brought you. It was a distraction."

She let out a frustrated growl. "Blur like *sotong.*"

That was weird enough to cool his temper a few degrees while his brain tried—and failed—to decode it. "What does that even mean?"

"That you're clueless like a cuttlefish, a little something I picked up teaching English in Singapore," she said, turning her attention back to the buttons next to the doors lighting up with each floor they passed. "The point being that you shouldn't blame your lack of focus on me."

"Oh really, so that little show with Tyler wasn't your way of getting back at me for earlier?" The memory had his temper roaring back to lava levels.

"Believe it or not, the world does not revolve around you."

"So you were flirting with him for fun?" The question exploded in the elevator carriage. "Were you just keeping your options open for your next adventure after you come back from Australia?"

He saw with exacting, slow motion detail the moment the barb burrowed underneath her skin. Her brown eyes, dark with a furious passion, went wide with shock. Her red lips parted with a gasp. Her chin trembled…once…twice before going hard when she clenched her jaw.

"You prick," she said. The faintest hint of wetness in her eyes disappeared with a blink, but it was still there in her voice.

This is when he should apologize, take back what he'd said only because he'd known it would hurt her. But any good sense he had was burning in the flames of his frustrated anger. He didn't understand what had happened, but something had. Clover had begun to crowd into the corners of his big vision, changing it in subtle ways that threw the rest of it off. He found himself thinking about her at strange times in the day, counting down the hours until they were alone again, becoming desperate to touch her soft skin. Even now, when he was so mad he could barely think, he wanted her like he'd never wanted anyone else. He couldn't—wouldn't—have that. His life was orderly. Predetermined. His. No one, not even the woman who could manage not only to drag him to a flea market but make it fun, was going to change that—no matter how much he needed to feel her under him and hear her soft moans of satisfaction as she came.

So instead of saying sorry, he doubled down on his attack. "My prick has been your favorite part about me."

She rolled her eyes. "Yeah, I like it when you use it, not when you act like it. There's a difference—one you obviously can't grasp."

The elevator doors opened and she strode out, her heels clicking angrily on the tile floor of his foyer as she marched toward the hallway leading to her bedroom—a room she hadn't slept in since that first night. Even the idea of not sleeping with her hit him like a sucker punch to the kidney.

"Where do you think you're going?" Sawyer rushed out of the elevator, following. "I'm not done talking to you."

"Yeah?" Clover kept walking. "Well, I'm done with you."

Maybe it was because he couldn't let her have the last word. Maybe it was because he couldn't stand to see her go. It didn't matter because he was striding after her before he even realized he was moving. He reached a hand out but she stopped and whirled around faster than he could touch her. Her cheeks were flush and her breath came in fast inhales through her parted lips, the obvious signs of just how angry she was with him at the moment. But it wasn't just mad. Her nipples had pebbled against the tight fit of her black dress, and her pupils had dilated with desire.

"I don't like you very much right now." She tugged her bottom lip between her teeth, pulling it taut.

His cock thickened against his thigh as his frustration made a hairpin turn into something else. "The feeling's mutual."

"So why do I want to fuck you so bad my panties are

soaked?" Her words didn't come with a flirty look or a sexy turn. It didn't take a genius to figure out that she was as pissed as he was that this *thing* between them wasn't so easily shoved aside.

Not tonight anyway.

He took a step forward, not touching her but close enough that the air around them snapped, crackled, popped. "Attraction isn't logical."

"That's the first thing you've said all night that makes sense." She grabbed his tie and yanked him lower until her mouth was on his in a hard, demanding kiss.

Chapter Sixteen

Kissing Sawyer after what an ass he'd been all night was the last thing Clover should be doing, but it was also the only thing she wanted. Going back to her room and taking care of the need building inside her by herself wasn't going to do it. She needed more. Damn it, she needed him.

She broke the kiss and dropped her hands to his belt. "I don't want slow." She yanked the leather free from the buckle and moved on to the button and zipper holding his pants closed. "I don't want easy." She shoved his pants down his hips along with his boxers. "I don't want foreplay or sweet nothings or teasing out our orgasms until we're both about to break." She wrapped her hand tight around his hard, warm cock and felt it jerk in response to her touch. "I want to fuck you out of my system so that I can stop thinking of you all the damn time."

"Take off your panties and pull up your skirt." He toed off his shoes.

Her fingers froze in the middle of pushing his pants the rest of the way down. "What?"

"You heard me." His mouth came down on hers in a rough kiss that left her mouth bruised and wanting more when he pulled away. "You want a good, hard fuck? Get rid of your panties before I rip them off you."

Why did such a glorious dick have to be attached to such a pompous asshole? "You're not in charge here."

Something flashed in his eyes a half second before he grabbed her by the waist, spun her around, and jerked up her skirt so it was around her waist. He locked an arm around her waist and pulled her back against his chest so she could feel the outline of his dick against her ass. "I'd say the question of who's in charge is up for interpretation." He hooked a finger in the band of her panties and ripped them free.

The scrap of black lace drifted to the floor, followed a second later by the thunk of her purse after she dropped it. Spinning in his hold, she turned to face him—the added height of her heels bringing her almost eye to eye with him. Good. Tonight she was going to see every reaction, every emotion, every response before he had time to hide them from her. Tonight, those little details would be hers.

She pressed both palms to his chest and shoved. "Control isn't up for negotiation."

Pants and underwear twisted around his ankles, he stumbled back a step and took her down to the floor with him. They ended up in a tangle of limbs with her sitting astride him, the stiff length of him pressed against her slick folds. She rocked against him, sliding up and down the underside of his cock, the tip of him bumping against her clit on every return trip, making her core clench. *Jesus.* She closed her eyes and threw back her head, concentrating on the pleasure because she couldn't let herself connect the overwhelming sensation to the man or she might just lose herself to it and to him.

He brought his hands to her hips, his fingers squeezing her flesh and slowing the rhythm. Following his lead was a temptation she couldn't surrender to. He'd take her, make her want more, make her want *him*. Looking down, she gazed at his still buttoned up shirt straining against his wide chest, the loosened tie wrinkled from where she'd grabbed it, and the glasses that sat askew on his face that did nothing to hide the desire turning his hazel eyes dark and almost gave in despite knowing what a mistake it would be.

Stilling on top of him, she pulled back from the edge. "Hands above your head."

"Are you fucking kidding?"

Part of her was asking the same thing. "Not in the least."

"What?" He snorted. "You want me to just lie here and be your breathing dildo?"

Like what she *really* wanted was something she wanted to figure out right now. "Sounds like a beautiful plan to me."

They stared are each other, neither moving. The pang of discomfort made itself known in her knees where they pressed against the hard tile floor. Tomorrow, there might be bruises. She didn't care. The really important thing was winning this negotiation. Discomfort was beginning to build to a throb when he lifted his finger from her hip, then another, and another. Only once both of his arms were raised above his head, one hand laying on top of the other, did she reach over, grab her purse off the floor and dump out the contents. There in the pile of lipstick, emergency eyeliner, her wallet, and her phone was the one item she wanted right now—a condom. She picked it up and tore it open with her teeth.

Watching him, his jaw as hard as the rest of him, she lifted her hips and rolled the condom over him. He closed his eyes and took in a shaky breath, and her heart shifted. God, even in a pseudo-submissive posture like this he was dangerous. Damn it, she could not go there. Not with him. She hadn't been lying. She needed him out of her system before it was too late. A month, that's all the time it had been and yet it felt like so much longer. Forget dangerous, he was fucking deadly.

"No kissing," she said, desperate for rules, for boundaries.

He opened his eyes, and one eyebrow arched over the edge of his cock-eyed glasses. "Whatever you say, *boss*."

The little reminder of the true nature of their relationship and the fifteen-thousand-dollar check waiting for her at the end of it slapped a piece of reality into the middle of her lust-fogged brain. Yeah, that was the other part of the equation. Four weeks had passed. Only two weeks and a few days to go and then she'd be gone. Before the implications could settle in, she lowered herself down on him, going against her own proffered directions and taking it slow, inch by inch until he filled her completely.

Sawyer fisted his hands and squeezed his eyes shut, but otherwise didn't move. For a second, she couldn't. All she could take in was the feeling of having him inside her. Biting down on her bottom lip so she'd keep her mouth shut and stick to the script she'd written herself, she undulated her hips as she lifted herself up and down on him. Pleasure slid through her with every rub of his cock against her G-spot and she made her moves languid and smooth despite her intentions. Sawyer lay beneath her taking it, letting her set the pace, make the demands. If he wanted, he could flip them both over and change the power dynamic, but for whatever reason he didn't. Instead, he watched her and answered her every downward glide with an unhurried upward thrust of his own, making sure he reached every part of her he could in his position.

The lace of her bra scratched against her hard nipples, but there was nothing she could do to relieve the ache in her breasts. Like Sawyer, she was still fully dressed from the waist up. Hell, she still had her shoes on. It was supposed to make the whole thing between them less personal, more of an uncomplicated need being met than any kind of meaningful connection, but all the addition of clothing did was make it even more obvious that she wanted him. The fact that she was leaving in a few weeks didn't matter, she'd started to fall for him. It was like a rock had been pushed off a cliff, it was rolling downhill and nothing—not time or the reality of the situation—was going to stop it. All she could do was hope it didn't obliterate her when it hit.

Sawyer let out a half tortured, half blissed-out moan.

"You go any slower and you'll break your own rules."

"Is that a complaint?" she asked, coming down hard and leaning forward so her mouth was right above his, the temptation to break another of her rules drawing her there.

"I'd never do that while buried inside you." He brought his head up an inch or two off the floor, obviously expecting her to meet him halfway.

The last vestiges of her survival instincts flared to life. He could expect all he wanted. "Then shut up."

Unfazed, he smirked. "You got it, Clover."

The use of her name snapped something. She could feel the tears building along with her orgasm, which one came first was up to her and she wasn't about to let it be the tears. So she arched her spine and leaned back, bracing her hands against his muscular thighs, digging her fingernails into him, and rode him hard and fast. His hands came down from above his head and he cupped her ass, driving her against him until they were a blur of motion and the sounds of their bodies coming together filled the hallway. It started in her core, as the head of his cock repeatedly rubbed against the bundle of nerves inside her opening with each stroke and grew outward until her entire body vibrated with sensation almost too pleasurable to be good. Right when she was at the edge of too much, it exploded and her orgasm electrified her, locking up her muscles and making her body one unyielding line.

Sawyer's fingers bit into her and he slammed her body down onto his one last time before coming with a harsh groan. They stayed like that for a moment, breathing hard with their bodies intertwined as if what had been before and what would come after didn't matter—only now did.

The buzz of her phone vibrating against the tile floor in the middle of the mess of her spilled purse brought her out of that bit of fantasy. Glancing down at it as she climbed off Sawyer; it took a second for the words of the text on her screen to make sense.

> Mom: *At the hospital with your dad. We think it's his heart again. Please call home.*

She felt dizzy, the blood draining from her face.

"Clover, what's wrong?" Sawyer asked, concern etched in his voice.

Panic pinched her lungs until she could barely take in a breath as she read the text a second and third time with disbelieving eyes. When the last ghost of denial faded away, she fought to keep the floor beneath her. Her hands shook as she grabbed the phone and it took two tries before she hit the right name on her contacts list. Listening to it ring and ring, she pulled her skirt down and shoved everything back into her purse.

"Hey there," her mom's voicemail greeting started. "Sorry I missed your call, leave a message and I'll get back to you as soon as I can."

"Mom, it's Jane. I just got your message. I'm on my way to the hospital now. Call me as soon as you can and let me know what's going on." She hit the end call button and hurried to her room.

"Clover, what's happened?" Sawyer asked again, chasing after her and pulling up his pants as he shuffled down the hall.

She stopped in her doorway, fingers curled around the frame to anchor her to the here and now while worry ate away at her self-control. Telling Sawyer, involving him in her life further, was the last thing she should do under the circumstances, but the words poured out of her. "My dad. He's in the hospital. I need to get an Uber to the train station."

"You don't have to do that, I'll drive you to Sparksville." He pulled her into a reassuring hug. "It'll be faster."

It was a horrible idea. They weren't engaged for real and not thirty minutes ago they'd been at each other's throats. But he was right. The train would take twice as long as the drive. If they pushed the speed limit, they could be in Sparksville in an hour and a half. The train, with all its stops, would be three hours minimum. God knew what could happen to her dad in that span of time.

"Okay, let me just change and throw some clothes in a bag." She pushed out of his embrace. "I just need five minutes to get myself together."

"Take your time. I'll be waiting at the elevator when you're ready." He turned and took a step away but paused and pivoted. "Everything will be okay. Whatever it takes, we'll make sure of it."

"Thanks, Sawyer."

He nodded and headed back down the hall to his rooms.

It was an empty vow, but it was just the kind of promise she needed right now because for as much as she had spent her life up until now running away from her family and Sparksville, she'd never really expected for anything bad to happen, for it to change.

Please God, let Dad be okay.

And with that silent prayer, she hustled into her room and began stuffing clothes into her overnight bag.

Chapter Seventeen

Clover had given up her overnight bag to Sawyer as soon as they got in the elevator. Normally, it would have been something she'd have argued about—she hated that whole "weak woman" thing—but at the moment, so many worries were running through her brain like negative vipers that she couldn't find the energy to put up a fuss. When they stepped out of the elevator, Irving was waiting by the door, holding it open.

"Everything's arranged just like you asked, Mr. Carlyle," he said. "Miss Lee, I'm sorry about your news."

"Thank you, Irving," she said as she hurried toward him.

"Yes, ma'am." He tipped his cap, sympathy in his eyes, and held open the door. "I'll be praying for your father."

The small kindness brought tears to her eyes and she bit the inside of her cheek to stop them from spilling over.

"Thank you," she said, giving him the best smile she could manage as she rushed through the door, Sawyer right behind her.

They hurried out to the waiting Town Car and got in the backseat. Linus was already behind the wheel and pulled into traffic as soon as they had their seatbelts fastened.

"The fastest way is to take Thirteenth to the Grambas Bridge," she said, already mentally plotting out the fastest route. "After that we can—"

"We're not going that way," Sawyer interrupted. "We're taking a helicopter."

She blinked in surprise. "What?"

"It'll take us an hour to get to Sparksville instead of two." His phone beeped and he checked the message.

"Amara already arranged to have a car waiting for us at the airport so we can go straight to the hospital."

Helicopter. We. Hospital. She was hearing the words just fine, but in her rattled state they weren't making sense. The bags at Sawyer's feet snagged her attention. Her bag was bright yellow with frayed handles. The other bag was black, in impeccable shape, and so expensive looking it practically smelled like money. With everything that was going on, of course her brain grabbed ahold of the least important detail and wouldn't let it go.

"Why do you have a bag?"

"Because I'm coming with you." He nudged it closer to her bag. "I won't leave you alone at a time like this."

It was a weird thing to say considering only an hour before he'd been counting down the hours until he could end their fake engagement. "I won't be alone. I'll be with my family."

He stared at her with a rush of emotions warring in his eyes that she couldn't decipher. "If we get there and you want me gone, I'll leave. Fair enough?"

What should she say? He'd packed up and was out the door with her in a matter of minutes, had arranged for a helicopter so they could make the trip in half the time, and already had a car waiting for them at the airport. When minutes counted, he'd made sure to get the most out of every one.

Stuffing away her hurt feelings from earlier, she nodded. "Thank you."

"Then let this officially establish that I'm a dick, not an asshole—which I obviously proved tonight. I'm sorry." He smiled and draped an arm around her shoulders, pulling her close and brushing a kiss across the top of her head. "Everything's gonna be okay."

God, she hoped so.

Linus made the drive to Carlyle Tower in less time than

she thought possible. They scrambled out of the car and took the express elevator to the roof where the helicopter was waiting. Her stomach shimmied and shook at takeoff but settled as they flew west away from Harbor City. She and Sawyer had earphones and a mic so they could talk over the roar, but he didn't push conversation. Instead, he held her hand as memories of her father washed over her. The time they'd gone fishing and she'd rolled the canoe, getting both of them good and soaked. The afternoons he'd spent teaching the intricacies of football and the beauty that was a baseball stat sheet. The fact that when she'd declared she wanted to live in Harbor City and go on adventures around the globe for a few years after graduation, he'd supported her even as her mom tried everything in the book to get Clover to change her mind.

Her dad had always been there for her. And what had she done in return? Left town. Rarely visited. Limited phone calls to once a week. All because she was afraid that Sparksville would suck her back in and she'd never make it out again. She'd end up like her mom, pregnant unexpectedly and married soon after. No adventure. Just day after day of packing school lunches, the PTA, and eating chicken pot pie every Thursday night because it was her husband's favorite. Guilt, regret, and fear slashed at her like knives, cutting her up from the inside out.

Her roiling stomach let her know they'd started their descent before she noticed the water tower with the Sparksville High School bulldog painted on it. The municipal airport wasn't big, but there was plenty of space for the helicopter to land. She and Sawyer got out, making sure to duck low to avoid the rotating chopper blades, and hurried over to a nondescript sedan parked on the tarmac.

Sawyer threw their bags in the trunk while she got in the passenger seat, too jittery to handle driving. She'd just clicked her seatbelt shut when he slid behind the wheel and started up the car. The dashboard navigation unit lit up, showing the step-by-step direction to the hospital that the rental employee had programed in before leaving the keys in the visor.

The drive to the hospital was a blur. Before she knew it, she and Sawyer were rushing through the automatic doors into an emergency room that resembled a library more than even a slow night at Harbor City General. There was a teenager feeding the candy machine a dollar, but no one else was in the small room packed with chairs.

"Jane?" a woman called out.

Heart hammering against her ribs as she prepared for the worst, Clover turned and spotted Mrs. Hermitage, one of her mom's best friends, behind the intake desk on the opposite side of the room. Squeezing Sawyer's hand tight in a moment of pure panic, she forced herself to take a deep breath. If her family wasn't in the waiting room, that was a good sign. Right? Her mind said yes, but her feet wouldn't move. With a gentle tug, Sawyer led her over to the intake desk.

"Oh, honey, I thought that was you." The other woman stood up and leaned over the desk to give her a quick hug before sitting back down. "I haven't seen you in forever."

And now was *not* the time to catch up. "My dad, is he back there?" she asked, gesturing to the sliding doors with No ADMITTANCE WITHOUT AUTHORIZATION painted on it.

Mrs. Hermitage shook her head. "They've taken him up to a room for a night of observation. It wasn't a heart attack, just a nasty case of angina. I can't give you any more specifics, but your mom asked me to send you right up if I spotted you. She dropped her phone in her coffee and the darn thing went on the fritz. Nobody knows anybody's actual phone number anymore."

All the stress and fear from the last few hours drained out of her along with the adrenaline that had kept her functioning. She stumbled back, but Sawyer was there to catch her. He wrapped an arm around her and pulled her in close, and she let him. The relief overwhelming the inner voice warning her of danger ahead.

"Do you know the room number?" Sawyer asked as he herded Clover toward the elevators.

"He's in room 405."

"Thank you, ma'am," he said as the elevator doors closed.

Clover pulled herself together as they went up, taking in deep breaths and managing to mostly block out the sandalwood and cashmere scent of Sawyer's cologne but not the comfort of his arms or the reassurance of his steady heartbeat against her cheek. All of her emotions were twisted and confused, but one thing rose above it all.

Okay. Her dad was going to be okay.

That's all that mattered. Whatever happened with Sawyer, she'd figure out a way to make it through mostly intact. After all, not all adventures had happy endings. It was past time she grew up and accepted that.

The elevator doors *whooshed* open and they walked out onto the fourth floor.

The door to her dad's room was open and her mom's voice wafted out. "Phillip Lee, I can't believe you snuck out for a cigarette. I thought you quit three years ago."

"I had for the most part," her dad shot back. "Anyway it was a stressful game, and I needed a moment."

"If you weren't hooked up to a machine right now…"

"Hi, Mom," Clover said from the doorway.

Her mom turned away from where her dad lay in the hospital bed. Her mascara had run a bit and she looked exhausted, but the smile on her face was as big as Clover had ever seen it. She opened up her arms and Clover walked into them, reaching down to hold her father's hand while her mother hugged her like a woman who'd almost lost her whole world that night—which she kinda almost had.

"So everything's okay?" Clover asked, her voice a little high from how hard her mom was squeezing her.

Her mom let her go with a final pat on her back. "Except for the fact that I might have to kill your father." She shot a dirty look at the man she'd been married to for twenty-six years. "A cigarette. Can you believe that?"

Phillip rolled his eyes. "I have one every few months under times of great duress."

"You mean whenever you're watching a game and it's not going your team's way," her mom said with an exasperated huff.

"Pretty much." Her dad winked at Clover. "Hey, pumpkin."

She sniffled despite knowing tears were the last thing he'd want to see right now. "Hi, Dad."

"I'd get up and give you a hug, but I'm afraid your mom would crack me upside the head for moving any more than necessary."

"Good Lord, Phillip." Her mom threw up her hands in frustration. "I thought you were having a heart attack. You do have a history you know."

He gave a little shrug. "It's just angina."

"Which means no more sneaking cigarettes, and you're gonna start eating better so your blood pressure doesn't go out of whack again," her mom said. "And if you can't calm down, no more games on TV."

"Jesus, just take away all the things worth living for, why don't you?" her dad groused, but the deep worry lines between his eyes showed that he'd been almost as scared as her mom.

"I'll still be here," her mom snapped.

Phillip glanced over at his wife and any trace of anxiety slid away. "As long as that's the case, I guess I can suffer through without the rest."

"Well you'd better because I can't live without you."
Her mom wiped away another black-tinged tear and gave
her dad a quick kiss on the cheek before straightening
and looking back at Sawyer who was hanging back in the
doorway. "And is that your mystery fiancé hiding in the
doorway? Come on in. I know we're not at our best right
now, but we promise not to bite you."

"I'd get that in writing, if I were you," her dad said
with a grin.

Sawyer walked over, and there was a manly handshake
from her dad—well, as manly as he could make it considering
he was lying in a hospital bed wearing a gown that didn't
close all the way in the back—and a hug from her mom.
That's when her younger brother Bobby came in, a coffee
cup in one hand and a half-eaten bag of Corn Nuts in the
other. She'd barely had time to introduce him to Sawyer
when a nurse came in, announced visiting hours were over,
and hustled them out of the room and into the hall.

"Well, we might as well head home," her mom said as
they rode the elevator down. "You two will be staying with
us, of course. Now we can finally have that family lunch that
hasn't fit into your busy schedules."

Clover's conscience jabbed her right in the heart. If
they left without staying for lunch, it would hurt everyone.
If they stayed and she had to lie to her family's face about
the non-existent wedding planning, it would hurt everyone.
Jesus. It was just supposed to be a fun adventure that would
get her some financial freedom. It wasn't supposed to get
so damn complicated.

"Family lunch?" Sawyer asked while she stood there
silent like an idiot.

"Oh yes, it's a family tradition, and I won't take no
for an answer," her mom said. "Plus, if you're there, it will
distract Phillip from the fact that I'm hiding the remote to
the TV as soon as we get home."

Oh God. There was no getting out of this for her, but she couldn't force Sawyer to go through with it. He'd already done enough. The smart thing was to get him out of Sparksville before her family got attached and walking away from him became even more complicated.

• • •

Sawyer kept a car and a half's distance between the rental and Mrs. Lee's back bumper as he followed her through downtown Sparksville. After years of having Linus drive him around, it was nice to get behind the wheel again and feel the motor purr—even if it was an anemic four cylinder. In the passenger seat, Clover was twisting the hem of her Keep It Weird hoodie around her fingers and gnawing her bottom lip. He wished like hell that he knew what to do right now, but he hadn't planned out past getting her here. The details—as usual—were lost to him.

They made it through the second stoplight and past The Sugar Palace Donut House before she broke the silence. "I really appreciate everything, but you don't have to stay. We can tell my mom a work emergency came up."

"Is that what you've been doing when they've invited us to the family lunch?" He left the part about her not even bothering to ask him to himself because he couldn't understand why that bugged him. It just did.

Her cheeks turned pink enough to be visible in the light coming in from the street lamps. "Yes."

"Why?" There it was. That twisted squeeze of his lungs, the annoyance bubbling up. Not that he cared. After all, their relationship was just a sham. It wasn't real. Whether he met her family or not didn't matter.

Keep telling yourself that, Carlyle.

"Lying to them on the phone is one thing," she said, a slight tremble coming through in her voice. "Doing it face-to-face is something else, especially after what just happened with my dad."

"I understand." In half a breath, he was back in the hospital room with his father; the beeping of the heart monitor had been so loud before it went silent. "When my dad died three years ago, it was a massive heart attack that came right out of the blue. It's why sidetracking my mom's campaign to marry me off has been so difficult. She took my dad's death hard. I mean we all did, but Mom lost herself for a while. I guess Hudson and I got used to dealing with her with kid gloves."

Clover reached out and put her hand on his leg. "I'm so sorry."

They'd taken turns talking her into going out to lunch, into seeing her friends again, and into rejoining the events and charities she'd always been a part of. She'd fought. The woman was as stubborn as anyone he'd ever known, but she'd made it to the other side so it had been worth it. She was definitely back to her old fighting weight.

"Thanks, but since you've met Helene Carlyle you know she's a tough old bird—don't you ever tell her that I called her that. What happened to your dad, it's made me realize just how far she's come from the dark days. It's probably past time that Hudson and I reined in the whole treat her like she's made of glass thing."

She withdrew her hand and turned so she faced the window instead of him. "You're going to tell her the truth about us and the whole Marry Off Sawyer campaign?"

He followed Clover's mom's car onto Caller Court, concentrating on the road instead of the way his lungs had tightened or the fact that he could still feel the imprint of her fingers on his leg. "It's probably past time, don't you think?"

"Yeah." She nodded, but kept her face averted. "So let's go with a business emergency cover story. You can head back to Harbor City, and I'll figure out how to tell them the truth in the morning."

Gut tight, he turned into the driveway of number forty-three Caller Court while Clover's mom pulled into the garage.

He should be relieved. It was an uncomplicated solution to a messy problem. All he needed to do was say thank you, but that's not what came out. "I can stay, have your back when you tell them the truth."

This time she did turn to face him. The porch light shining in through the window highlighted the gold of her hair. One side of her mouth was curled up in a semblance of a smile but not quite making it, as if she just couldn't fake it anymore tonight. The lies had taken a toll.

"I appreciate that," she said, "but you're not the only one who's facing up to the realization that how you've been handling family up until now may not have been the best option."

Neither of them said anything as they got out of the car. He went around to the trunk and got her bag, leaving his own on top of the spare tire. Then he followed her inside to the Lees' warm, yellow kitchen decorated with wildflowers and photos of coffee mugs. Bobby said good night and headed up the stairs. Sawyer placed Clover's bag on the kitchen island while her mom started a fresh pot of coffee despite the fact that it was ten o'clock at night. Clover had gone over to a framed family photo on the counter and picked it up. If he hadn't known any better, he would have thought it was the first time she'd ever seen it.

Earlier today his mom had asked him what he really knew about Clover. The truth was, not a lot. He knew what she liked to do, how she liked her hamburgers, that she dipped her fries in vinegar, and that she laughed at all the same places he did in movies. That wasn't the same, though, as actually knowing her and what made her tick. Now he wouldn't. She'd come back to the penthouse in a couple of days and get her stuff. He'd cut her a check for the full amount. She wasn't the one who'd decided to end things early, after all. And then she'd be off to Australia and he'd go back to his life the way it was before she'd shown up at Carlyle Towers, answering an ad for a personal buffer that he'd never placed.

The fact that he felt like he'd swallowed glass just meant that it was better to get out of here sooner rather than later. "Mrs. Lee—"

"Laura, I insist. We're going to be family after all," she interrupted. "Don't worry, I'm making decaf. Do you want some?"

Clover sat down the photo and crossed over to stand by him. "Mom, Sawyer has to head back to Harbor City."

"Really?" Laura said, her eyes wide with surprise.

"Yes." He nodded, playing his part. "There's been an emergency at the office."

"Uh-huh." Laura looked from Clover to him and back again, her gaze cool and assessing. "Well, we'll just move family lunch up to family brunch so you can head back to the city tomorrow afternoon. Even a busy man like yourself needs a morning off every once in a while."

"Mom, it doesn't really work like tha—"

"I'll stay." The moment the words were out of his mouth, the tightness in his shoulders released, and he realized it was exactly the answer he'd wanted to give the whole time.

"You will?" Both women asked at the same time. One was pleased while the other was not in the least.

"You're right," he said. "It's Friday night. The office will still be there on Monday."

"Wonderful!" Laura clapped. "I'll get you set up in the guest room. Jane, you'll be in your old room. I know, I know you're grown adults, but this is my house and my rules—and I have a lot of them or so my children tell me."

He was beginning to see why Clover had learned the importance of good negotiation. "Yes, ma'am."

"Laura—or Mom. You two *are* engaged after all." She let out a little whoop of excitement, put one arm around him and another around Clover before pulling them in for a tight hug.

Looking over the top of Laura's head, there was no missing the dirty look Clover was giving him. He was a selfish bastard. He knew. But his time with Clover was up the minute they got back to Harbor City and if he could delay that for another twelve hours, he'd take it. Tomorrow would be soon enough to own up to the truth. Until then, he'd take all the distraction he could get.

Chapter Eighteen

An hour of tossing and turning later, Clover rolled over in the lumpy twin-size bed she'd grown up sleeping in and grabbed her cell phone. Squinting at the screen that seemed abnormally bright in the pitch dark of her room, she started thumb typing.

Clover: *We need to talk.*

That was one way to put it. It sounded so much nicer than *I need to smack you upside the head for complicating an already fucked up situation.* The fact that part of her was thrilled he was staying—even after the bullshit at dinner tonight—told her just how much she needed him out of her life. Daphne had been right. She wasn't a casual sex kind of girl and if she didn't get out soon, she'd pay the price.

Her phone vibrated in her hand.

Sawyer: *Honey, I know you're mad.*

A flutter of anticipation made her catch her breath. It wasn't fair. He only called her that when they were either naked or damn close to getting there. Snapping her legs shut, she let her fingers do a whole other kind of talking.

Clover: *Don't call me that.*

Sawyer: *???*

Clover: *You know exactly what name I'm talking about.*

Sawyer: *You've always liked it when I called you that before…and what we were doing when I called you that.*

Bastard. He may not be a great flirt, but he was definitely getting better. Or maybe it was just that he knew her well enough to know exactly how to get her off track. Well, it wasn't going to work.

Clover: *Not my amused face —>*

Sawyer: *I can fix that.*

Her nipples peaked at the suggestion. *Down girls, we're mad at him.*

Clover: *How? By sneaking out in the middle of the night and going back to Harbor City?*

Sawyer: *And break your mom's heart? No way.*

Clover: *Your ego is out of control. I'm serious. This is my family.*

Sawyer: *I know. Look, can we do this in person?*

She could barely do this by text. Meeting him in person was not a good idea. He'd screwed her over when he'd changed his mind and decided to stay for family brunch tomorrow. Still, she wanted to see him. *Anda el diablo.* There was no winning. She chickened out and stayed in her room and would be miserable. She snuck out of the house and took him down the dock so they could talk without fear of being overheard and she would be miserable.

But with one option you actually get to see him. You won't be able to do that after tomorrow.

She swallowed past the rock that had formed in her

throat and typed with trembling fingers, unsure of anything except the fact that this was more than likely a mistake — one she had to make.

> Clover: *Meet me at the back gate. You'll have to go out the window—>garage roof—>shed roof—>ground.*

> Sawyer: *What am I, 16? And how often did you sneak out?*

> Clover: *None of your business. And my mom's a super light sleeper, if she hears you walking around she'll want to be a good hostess and see what you need then she'll never get any sleep and she needs it tonight.*

> Sawyer: *So out the window I go.*

Clover slipped on her jeans and grabbed a sweatshirt to pull over her tank top if it got cold. Shoving her cell in her back pocket, she tiptoed up the staircase from her basement room — sticking to the right side to avoid the squeaky sections — and hustled out the kitchen door that led out to her mom's garden on the side of the house. The strawberries were out in full force along with spinach, tomatoes, and bell peppers among other things — along with an entire army of bizarre garden gnomes. From lumberjacks to bakers to evil witches to half gnome/half animal hybrids, her mom's collection had doubled from when Clover still lived at home. It was weird but at least it made finding a birthday gift easy.

She walked around the corner of the house and over to the back gate where Sawyer stood in the light of the full moon staring at the gnome-shaped gate handle.

"Your mom has a weird thing for gnomes," he said.

"You have no idea." She opened the gate, intertwined

her fingers with his, and walked through. "Come on."

The line of trees between the backyard and Lake Earhart had been her first playground for adventure filled with hollowed out trees that served as fairy kingdoms, pirates that lived in the branches overhead, and—of course—an entire village of gnomes plotting worldwide domination. When she got older, it was where she'd gone to escape and plan. Now, holding Sawyer's hand, she looked up at the thick green leaves overhead and the bright wildflowers at her feet and realized that she couldn't remember a day when she wasn't running away from the white picket existence she'd been born into. However, instead of running to the trees or the lake beyond them, she went around the globe.

It only took a minute of traipsing through the trees before they got to the small clearing around the lake and her family's dock that led out into it. Her dad's boat was moored at the marina at the other end of the lake, but the summer storage box sat at the end of the dock. She hurried over to it and pulled out a blanket so they wouldn't get splinters in their ass while they sat and figured out how to get through tomorrow without giving her dad a heart attack for real. Then after a few days, she'd break the news to her family from the safety of Harbor City. Chicken? Her? Absolutely.

She sat down facing the lake, it's waters smooth and inky blue. "We need to come up with the details that will make tomorrow work—and it can't be the truth because I really don't want to welcome dad home by giving him a heart attack for real."

"We already did, remember?" He sat down next to her, close enough that their hips and thighs touched, sending a jolt of electricity dancing along her skin. "The napkin?"

"No." She shook her head. "That's not gonna fly with my family. My mom is like a laser-guided missile when it comes to the truth. Nothing gets past her."

He shrugged and lay back on the blanket, his arms

folded so his hands were behind his head. In a plain white T-shirt and a pair of dark indigo jeans that clung to his hips, he looked like he belonged here in the world she'd grown up in. She shouldn't be surprised. He'd been as at ease in his office at the top of Carlyle Tower as he'd been at the flea market haggling over the metal medical cart they'd renovated. Unlike her inability to fit into his world, he'd done just fine finding a place for himself in hers.

"So we stick to the truth without elaborating," he said, bringing her back to the reality of the here and now.

She snorted, just trying to picture her mom *not* digging for details. "How's *that* story go?"

Out in the lake, a fish cleared the surface with a pop and dove back in with a soft splash.

"You fascinated me from the moment I met you and after that we were inseparable."

"Fascinated you?" It sounded ridiculous. He was a multibillionaire with model-like wife candidates everywhere he turned and *she* fascinated him. More like was different enough to stoke his curiosity for a few weeks. "Is that what we're going with?"

"It seems close enough to the truth to work."

"And after we get back tomorrow night?" Her chest tightened, and she looked down at where her hands were clenched in her lap, letting her hair fall over her face. Damn it. She hated it when Daphne was right. Forget falling for him, she was already halfway there.

"We'll think of something in the car."

"No helicopter this time?" she teased, trying to regain some of the emotional high ground from that part of herself that was starting to crumble.

He laughed and rolled onto his side facing her, propping up his head in his hand. "You don't want to know what kind of favor I'm going to owe Hudson for borrowing that."

"I thought you and your brother were close."

"We are, but he's…well, he's Hudson."

Grasping ahold of the conversational lifeline that didn't have anything to do with lying or saying good-bye, she settled back onto the blanket, echoing his position on his side. "What does that mean?"

"That he's a guy who seems like he doesn't have anything on his mind except for ways to burn through his trust fund as quickly as possible, but that's not really him. He just does a damn good job of hiding who he really is."

"Why?"

"You'd have to ask him. We don't have deep introspective chats about our feelings. Do you with your brother?"

"Bobby?" She laughed out loud. Even the idea of a heart-to-heart with her brother was too weird to be able to form a mental picture of what it would be like. "No. If it doesn't happen in his lab, Bobby isn't very interested. He's got all of his attention glued to whatever experiments he's working on. He graduated from college at the top of his class while I was still in high school, and he's two years younger than me."

Sawyer reached out and tucked a stray hair behind her ear, his fingers grazing the shell of her ear and sending a delicious shiver down her spine. "But he came home when he got the call about your dad."

"It's family." Unable to stop herself, she turned her head so that her face brushed against his warm palm. "It's what you do."

"You obviously care, so why do you spend all your time avoiding them?" he asked, gliding his thumb across her cheek.

"Are you my shrink all of the sudden?" She pulled away, cutting off the touch she craved so much, and rolled onto her back because if she didn't she might not be able to later—and that scared her right down to her pink toenails.

"Or is this like spilling my guts to the stranger at the bar because I know I'll never see him again?"

"Sure." He slipped off his glasses and sat them on the storage box beside them. "Now that the world is a little bit fuzzy, I can be your stranger at the bar. Tell me everything."

It was both exactly what she wanted to hear and just the words to shred her up a little bit more. Looking up at him—at this man she wouldn't see again after tomorrow—the knot in her belly unwound, and she knew exactly what she needed to do next. The first rule of adventuring was to enjoy the experience while you could and that was exactly what she was going to do tonight with Sawyer.

• • •

Sawyer lay on his back on the blanket, looking up at the stars—a true big-picture view—and held his breath. When Clover had brought him out to the lake, he'd half expected her to push him in and try to drown him after the stunt he'd pulled. But she hadn't. Instead, here they were with one last night together—and he wasn't about to waste it.

"When I was eleven, I overheard my parents arguing," she said softly, a ribbon of vulnerability threaded through her voice as she sat up, bent her legs, and wrapped her arms around her knees. "Mom wanted to go on a cruise and dad said he couldn't imagine being stuck on a boat for a week with a bunch of drunk strangers. She said something about how she'd had plans to travel the world but everything had changed when she'd gotten pregnant. All she wanted was one week. He agreed. It wasn't until later that night that I did the math. I was born seven months after they got married."

The lost look on her face gutted him. He rolled up into a sitting position, wrapped an arm around her shoulders, and pulled her close, the urge to comfort her overriding everything else. "They seem happy, though."

"They are." Clover sighed and turned her face so her

cheek rested in the pocket of his shoulder. The light from the full moon making her blond hair look like it glowed. "That's the part I've never understood."

"Business or love, every relationship is compromise."

She looked up at him, one eyebrow raised in sardonic disbelief. "Tell me more, Dr. Sawyer, of the lessons in love you learned from old chick flicks?"

He grinned down at her and tweaked the button tip of her nose. "Low blow."

"Just an accurate one," she shot back. "Look, you're no more well-adjusted than I am. Look at your family dynamic."

She pulled back from him and lay back on the blanket, and he followed suit.

From an outsider's perspective, he could understand why she saw it that way, but there was more to the story that he hadn't ever talked about with anyone—until now. "You never saw us before my dad died."

"What was it like?"

"It was…" Words failed him. God, how could he explain it? Staring up at the star-filled night unlike any he ever saw in Harbor City, an achy soreness started in the middle of his chest and spread outward. "Everything it's not now. My dad's death was completely unexpected. We didn't have time to prepare, to think, to plan. It was just like all of the sudden the world had changed. I had to take over Carlyle Enterprises. Hudson and I had to take care of our mom. The international building market softened. Everything was…different."

"Too many new details," she said, understanding thick in her voice as she reached out and intertwined her fingers with his and squeezed.

"And they were never my specialty."

Fuck, now that was an understatement. Still, when he was with Clover all he could notice were the details. The silk of her hair. The smoothness of her skin. The soft smile she gave him first thing in the morning before she woke up. But that wasn't everything. It was all the little things from her quick mind to her smart mouth to her craving for adventure that made her so damned irresistible—and dangerous to him.

He should get up now. Walk back to the house. Go to bed. Wake up and fake his way through a brunch with a family he'd never see again. But he didn't move a muscle.

Maybe Hudson was right and all of those RomComs had fucked up his head because sitting here with Clover he couldn't think of any place he'd rather be. Or maybe it was that being with Clover had begun to feel right, something that if he said out loud would probably send her sprinting toward her next adventure like a world record–holding track-and-field star.

She shifted beside him, turning so she faced him. Echoing her movements, he did the same. They were so close, mouths only inches apart, but neither of them made a move as anticipation began as a buzz in the back of his head and moved south.

Her pink tongue darted out and glided across her plump bottom lip. "I'm not ready to go in yet."

"And I'm not going anywhere without you." Dipping his head, he closed the distance between them and claimed the woman he had no right to.

Chapter Nineteen

This is what Clover wanted—needed—a night that didn't have a tomorrow, just a now. Tomorrow could take care of itself because tonight she had Sawyer.

Breaking the kiss, she nudged him onto his back, following so she ended up straddling his hips. God, he was sexy as hell, all square jaw, muscles, and hard planes. She leaned forward and traced her lips across his stubble-covered jaw and down his corded neck as she fisted his T-shirt, yanking it higher.

"Off. Now."

"You are so fucking demanding," he said with half a laugh.

"Like you aren't." She glided her fingertips over the ridges of his abs like a topographical map of heaven, and he sucked in a breath through his teeth. No one was laughing now.

"I'm the one on my back and totally at your mercy," he said, but the predatory look in his eyes said he was anything but vulnerable.

"As if that's ever the case."

His hand went to the small of her back and he rolled her, putting her underneath him. "I guess you're right."

Heart racing, she stared up at him, trying to remember to breathe because basic bodily functions seemed amazingly difficult when all she wanted was to take all he was offering. Damn. It shouldn't be so easy for him to turn her into a boneless mass of want and hunger, but he did. So she fought against it, marshaling all her effort into maintaining at least a sheen of indifference.

Looking up at him through her eyelashes, she gave him her best sex kitten look. "Say it again."

"Why? Does being right get you hot and wet and needy for me?" Now his fingers were the ones doing the walking, caressing her skin over the thin material of her tank top and sending little jolts of electricity across her skin.

"You do that just by breathing," she answered, desire making her voice breathy.

Standing up, he reached behind his head and stripped off his shirt and dropped it onto the dock. His pants and boxers followed. Hands on his hips, the moonlight at his back, he stared down at her—more confident and sure of himself than any man she'd ever known. If there was one moment in this adventure she'd never forget, it was this.

"*Oh Dios mío,*" she sighed.

One side of his mouth quirked up. "I know I'm either doing something right or something wrong when you start talking in another language."

"Right. You are doing something very, very right." Except, of course, for the fact that he wasn't touching her. Not that she'd sit around waiting for that.

Rolling up into a sitting position, she looked her fill— as if that was possible—before moving onto her knees in front of him so that his hard cock was only inches from her mouth. She curled her hand around his girth, her middle finger almost but not quite touching her thumb when she encircled him.

He let out a soft groan as he stared at her hand. "All I had to do was get naked?"

"And stand there looking like the Greek god of moonlight and sexy times."

"If I agree, then that's when you say my ego is out of control."

She licked her lips. "Looks like you'll have to find a way to shut me up, then."

"You're definitely giving me ideas."

Judging by the gravelly tone in his voice, just the right kind of ideas. She tightened her grip on his cock, stroking it from the base to the head as pre-come pooled on the tip. It wasn't an invitation she was going to decline. Keeping her tongue flat and wide, she lapped it up as she watched him let his head drop back as he groaned again.

"You can't stop there," he said, not a plea but not quite an order.

Tormenting him at a time like this was just the sort of thing she loved to do and he got off on. "Are we negotiating?"

"No." One word. One order.

Her core clenched. "Good."

She curled her fingers around his thick forearms and moved them so his hands cupped either side of her head then opened her mouth, wrapped her lips around his swollen head, and took him in as far as she could before retreating. His groan echoed in her ears as she reached behind and cupped his hard ass. That sound, the one that said he was already lost in the moment. God, she was going to miss it, but if she thought about that then she'd miss these last few hours with him and she wasn't willing to give that up. She'd have the rest of her life to remember.

"You're killing me." His fingers tangled in her hair, pulling in some places, and he joined her efforts and slid his cock through her parted lips. "And you're still wearing all your clothes."

She wouldn't be for long, but she was enjoying this too much to stop now so she sucked him deeper until he filled her mouth completely and the head of his cock dipped down into her throat. Relishing the way his ass tightened under her fingers, she kept it up, taking him in and letting him go, until he held her head firm and withdrew from her mouth with an audible pop.

"I'm beginning to think you're an exhibitionist," she

teased.

"All I'm thinking is that you have too many clothes on," he said, his voice as hard as the rest of him. "Take 'em off."

If she was a more patient woman, she'd make him wait—or have him tear them off of her like he'd done to her panties. But that time was passed. She wasn't about to deny either of them what they really wanted, not tonight. She slid her jeans and panties down over her hips and then took off her tank top as she stepped out of the material around her ankles.

• • •

Watching Clover strip was like watching the sun rise after the longest, coldest night of the year. It made the whole world a better place. It made time stand still, and it made him want to be a better man so he'd be worthy of touching even a single inch of her soft skin.

"Jesus, you're beautiful."

"I hope you're not planning to just look," she said, feathering her fingers across her tits.

"Only for a little bit longer."

If this was their last night together—and despite what he knew was the right thing to do, he wasn't willing to agree to that right now—he was going to look his fill, put it to memory. The way her blond hair fell to her shoulders, not long enough to reach the rosy tips of her hard nipples. The flare of her hip as her body curved out from the pinch of her waist. The line of six freckles on the back of her thigh pointing up to her perfect ass. All of that was amazing, but it wasn't what he really saw when he looked at her standing tall and proud in front of him, daring him to look his fill. It was what he'd seen of her before. The way she'd laughed so loud at one of the flea market dealer's corny jokes that everyone around them turned to look. The ease with which she jumped into new situations without the slightest hesitation. The tired smile she gave him and the soft, satisfied sigh she made after they were both wrecked from brain-depleting orgasms that made him want to do it all over again just to see and hear it again.

Hudson had warned him about getting distracted, but Sawyer knew he was way past that for all the absolutely no good it did him. She had adventures to go on that didn't involve him or his big-picture vision, and while part of him—that selfish, shitty part of him—wanted to keep her with him, he couldn't do it because his brother was right. It *would* cost him too much, just not in the way Hudson meant or Sawyer wanted to admit—even to himself.

"Enough lookie-loo time," she said, closing the distance between them.

Her fingertips gliding down the middle of his chest broke him out of his daze.

He grabbed her wrist before she could get to his happy trail and he lost the will to set some ground rules. "This will be slow." He lowered her arm to her side and let go. "There will be foreplay." He dragged the pad of his thumb across her full bottom lip. "There will be kissing." He dipped his head lower, stopping just shy of her mouth. "There will be no negotiating."

Of course, he never said it would be gentle or sweet, so when he kissed her he did it like a man staking a claim because tonight Clover was his. Her lips parted and he swept his tongue inside, tasting her and teasing her until she sank against him, and he wrapped his arms around her. Fuck, she was soft in all the places he was hard and aching. His hands roamed over her smooth skin, imprinting on her in an invisible script that said all the things he could not.

Her hands were everywhere—sliding down his spine, squeezing his ass, and roaming across any inch of skin she could reach—as they kissed, taking everything from each other they could and giving back just as much. It wasn't enough. He needed to feel her everywhere so he loosened his hold on her and they slid to the blanket. He broke the kiss, tracing his lips across the line of her jaw and down the long column of her throat.

"Sawyer." Her plea.

"Yes." His answering promise.

He cupped her tits, brought them higher and lowered his mouth to them and circled his tongue around her pebbled nipples, first one and then the other. Answering her moan, he grazed his teeth across one nipple before drawing it into his mouth and sucking hard. She cried out, her fingers gripping his hair. So he did it again and again until she'd wrapped her legs around one of his and rubbed her wet folds against his thigh in search of relief.

"What do you want, Clover?"

"Touch me."

"Where?"

"Everywhere."

"Here?" He slid his fingers down her side, following the dip and expanse of her waist and hip.

She may have meant her frustrated groan to hurry him along, but it did the opposite. They both might be cursing later but he planned on drawing this out as long as he could stand it, which judging by the tingling ache in his balls would definitely not be as long as he wanted. Still, he caressed the gentle curve of her belly, going low enough for her to let out a whimper of gratitude before traveling upward and rolling one hard nipple.

"Touch me."

"Where?"

"Please. I'm so wet. I need you."

It was such a desperate appeal, to deny her would just be cruel. He glided his fingers down her stomach—slowly, after all he was still a prick—while she writhed underneath him until he parted her slick lips and circled her swollen clit.

Her legs parted, her spine bowed, and the words that left her mouth could have been English or another language, he couldn't tell because he was concentrating too hard on not giving in to every instinct screaming at him to put his hard cock where his fingers were. But just touching her like this wasn't enough.

He rocked back on his haunches. "Spread your legs."

She did without hesitation, her core glistening in the moonlight, and all thoughts of taking it slow left him. He had to have more of her. Now. He leaned down, his hands circling her thighs and then going underneath her to cup her ass, lifted her hips, and tasted her. She was so wet, so soft and ready for him as her rolled his tongue over her clit.

Her fingers dug into his scalp as her hips bucked upward, pressing herself more firmly against him. "Make me come."

His girl wasn't fooling around anymore. She'd played his game and was obviously now done. Who was he to tell her no? Adding his fingers to the tongue action, he pushed her closer and closer to the edge as her sucked, licked, and rolled her most sensitive spot until he felt her thighs tremble on either side of his face.

"Sawyer," she cried out as her orgasm hit.

Her heels dug into his back as she rode the wave, and he continued to lap at her core with an ever-softer touch as she began to come down. By the time he sat up, she had that hazy, satisfied look on her face of a woman—his woman—who'd had her world thoroughly rocked. She sighed and gave him that tired smile of hers that brought out the chest-pounding caveman inside him.

"You can mark foreplay off the list for tonight," he said, brushing a wet kiss across the belly button.

"Thank God," she said, chuckling as she slapped her hand around the messy mounds of their clothes until she hit his jeans. Without waiting for him to say anything, she grabbed his wallet out of the back pocket and pulled out a condom. "I'm ready for the main event."

"That makes two of us."

"I should say so." Her gaze dropped to his cock and she flipped the condom over to him.

He ripped it open in a rush, rolled it on, and sat back on his ass. "Come here."

• • •

Clover's thighs were still a jiggly mess, her brain drowning in a lust-induced fog, but she managed to make it over to Sawyer. Bracing her hands on his shoulders with her feet on either side of his hips, she watched his face as she lowered herself down onto him inch by inch until he filled her completely. His jaw tightened and the vein in his temple throbbed as he waited for her to adjust to his size. No rushing for him, not even now when they were both so desperate for it. Then, when her muscles relaxed enough from the massive climax she'd just had to let him inside, she wrapped her legs around his back and kept her gaze on his face as she undulated her hips, angling her body so her clit rubbed up against him with every wave.

"God, you feel so good," he said, his voice rough with desire.

If she could have formed words she would have told him ditto, but his hands were on her back, sliding down to her ass and pushing her down harder on him, and the part of her brain in charge of speech didn't work anymore. She dug her fingers into the thick muscles of his shoulders, grounding herself to the moment and to him, and lowered her mouth to his. It wasn't a gentle kiss. It was hard and yearning and needy. It was a demand she couldn't voice and a question she couldn't ask. It was everything in the world that mattered.

Forward and back she rocked against him, taking him deep within her before letting him go. Over and over he buried himself in her, thrusting and retreating until a light sheen of sweat covered them, making it hard for her to hold on to him but she wouldn't let go. She couldn't. Her thighs ached. Again and again her core squeezed him every time she raised her hips and took him until he filled her completely, until all her body knew was the sensations of desire and pleasure pouring over her.

Sawyer shifted beneath her, changing the angle of his thrust so that it hit the bundle of nerves inside her opening and she gasped, breaking the kiss. Good didn't begin to describe it. Mind-blowing was close but still not close enough.

"Fuck."

"Couldn't have said it better myself," he said, sliding one hand between their bodies and pressing his thumb to one side of her clit.

A jolt of sensation rocketed through her. "Yes."

He lessened the pressure then reapplied it over and over as she rocked against him, taking his cock in as deep as she could. "That's it, ride me until you come again."

As if the mere mention of it was enough to trigger her, the second orgasm hit without warning, turning the night Technicolor and blocking out the rest of the world except for Sawyer.

"God, I love watching that," he said, each word coming in time with his thrusts as he gripped her hips and moved her up and down. "I'm not—" His climax hit before he could finish the sentence and her name fell from his lips.

By the time he came back to himself, she'd half convinced herself that she'd memorized every line on his face, every strand of his hair, every line of muscle.

"I think you killed me," he mumbled.

She brushed her lips across his. "Only a little."

Rolling off Sawyer and laying down on her back, Clover ignored the little voice telling her to be careful—to remember the clock was ticking down the minutes until all of this was over. Being naked next to Sawyer with the stars spread out like a blanket above them and the sound of the water lapping at the shore in time with his breaths, she gave in to the lazy, bone-melting satisfaction that only an amazing orgasm could deliver. She felt too good to listen to the invisible asshole of a naysayer on her shoulder.

Sawyer let out a happy sigh and lay back onto the blanket. "Five minutes and we head in."

God, he was optimistic. "Make it ten and I'm in."

"Are you ever *not* negotiating?"

"I do sleep occasionally."

He reached out and intertwined his fingers with hers. "Smart-ass."

"You know me so well."

"I'm beginning to." He squeezed her hand.

And a beginning was all they'd get, the little jerk on her shoulder whispered, yanking her out of her post-coital happy haze and throwing her right back down into hard reality. It was for the best, really. Body protesting, she sat up and reached for her panties—and froze. The sticky slickness on her upper thighs didn't come from her. Confusion. Understanding. Panic. They swept through her one right after the other like a ninety-miles-per-hour wind gust, leaving her heart racing and her lungs heaving.

"What's wrong?" Sawyer asked, the question sharp and jolting.

"The condom." She couldn't look at him, only the red and green plaid pattern of the blanket. "Is it okay?"

"What do you… Shit."

She was up and to the edge of the dock before reality sank in. Jumping in wouldn't do her a damn bit of good. No use crying over spilled semen and all that. *Oh yes there fucking was.* Her throat constricted as she turned around.

Sawyer stood in the middle of the blanket, the

moonlight illuminating the wing tattoos on his chest and the shocked expression on his face.

"Okay, is there a twenty-four-hour pharmacy here?" he asked, calm even in the face of disaster. "We can go get the morning after pill and—"

"I can't. I'm allergic." There were three inactive ingredients in the pill and one of them made her react like someone with a peanut allergy in a nut factory.

"You can't take it?" Now there was that icy panic in his voice that she felt in her veins.

She shook her head. "Nope."

"Okay, so…"

"We wait to see if I'm pregnant or not. It's the only thing we can do." She yanked on her jeans and pulled on her tank top, her stomach roiling and her mind going eight directions at the speed of light all at once. "No offense, but can we not have this talk right now? I just want to go inside."

Once there, she'd shut the door to her childhood bedroom and stare at the water stain on her ceiling until she stopped feeling like she was going to puke or pass out.

Sawyer nodded, his eyes brighter behind the glasses he'd put back on. "Sure."

He got dressed quickly, she rolled up the blanket and tucked it under her arm, and they left the lake behind them. The walk through the woods back to the house was filled with shadows and silence. By the time they got to the gate with its cheery gnome handle, Clover was cold inside and out.

Sawyer stopped her before she could walk through the gate. "It's gonna be okay. We'll figure it out."

The words were pretty, but she knew the truth. Whatever else the past few weeks had been for Sawyer and her, they weren't a prelude to something permanent. He was an industry titan from a wealthy family with a big-picture plan for everything. She was a working-class girl from Sparksville who'd never met a job she couldn't quit or an adventure she could turn down. They weren't a forever couple. They weren't even a for now couple. Fake engagement, real maybe baby. She glanced up at the house behind the white picket fence. Despite her best efforts, she might just turn into her mother anyway. Her gut cramped.

"Let's just keep this between us until we know if I'm even pregnant. That's *not* negotiable."

"Agreed." But it didn't sound like he liked it.

She nodded her head, unable to do much more than mutter a quiet, "Good night."

He didn't stop her as she walked through the gate, around the corner of the house, and in through the kitchen door to her childhood home, the one she'd sworn she'd never come back to or build one like it for herself.

Chapter Twenty

The sun was up and Clover could hear voices coming down the hall from the kitchen. She smoothed her shirt over her flat belly and ran a brush through her hair. The bed was made. The bathroom connected to her bedroom put back to how it had been before. Her overnighter had been repacked and zipped closed. She'd delayed as long as she could. Time to put a smile on and pretend that everything hadn't just changed. More than that, she had to do it all while lying to her family about the man she wasn't about to marry and wouldn't be seeing after today.

Still, she didn't move toward her closed bedroom door.

A baby. Maybe.

Her period was due in about a week. Until then, there was nothing she could do but wait and worry and…ignore the small bubble of excitement surrounding the boulder of anxiety in her stomach and the dream she'd had last night of a baby with her hair and Sawyer's hazel eyes. That wasn't the life for her. She was about new places and new experiences, not a static life behind a white picket fence.

Hustling out of the room before that mental image could take hold, she walked down the hallway toward the kitchen, the telltale smell of smoke announcing that her mother was in the kitchen. God love the woman, but she could burn water, which is why her dad did most of the cooking.

"You're gonna burn the place down, Laura," her dad's voice filtered out of the kitchen, along with the haze of burned bacon–scented air.

"You just got back from the hospital. Don't make me

send you back there, Phillip," her mom retorted. "Now, go sit in the living room like I told you until everything's ready."

The smoke detector let out a long squawk before being silenced as Clover approached the kitchen, listening to the banter that had been a part of her parents' marriage for as long as she could remember. She hesitated in the doorway. Her brother was at the table, a book open on the table and oblivious to the goings-on around him. Her mom looked harried but happy as she stood in front of the stove waving a tea towel to push the smoke from the pan toward the open back door. Her dad, a little paler than normal with a tired pinch to his eyes, leaned against the half-wall dividing the kitchen from the living room.

"Good thing I didn't marry you for your cooking," Phillip said, shaking his head.

Her mom tossed the towel across one shoulder and marched over to her dad. "Nope, you married me because, and I quote, you couldn't imagine your life without the most beautiful woman you ever met."

"More like the most maddening," he said, beaming down at her.

"And you love it." Laura went up on her toes and kissed Phillip's cheek. "Now get out of here. Sawyer and I can handle brunch."

Sawyer?

At that moment, the man in question came strolling out of the walk-in pantry his arms filled with pancake mix, syrup, chocolate chips, and powdered sugar. Some of the sugar must have poofed up from the bag because there was a fine dusting of white across one of his glass lenses. He looked totally out of place and completely ridiculous, and her heart skipped anyway. Damn it. Not the reaction she needed to be having right now.

He spotted her and stopped. Every nerve ending in her body came alive when he looked at her and the bubble of hope that had no right to be inside her expanded just a little.

A baby. Maybe.

Don't do it, Clover girl.

They didn't make sense together and a maybe baby wasn't going to change that. The best thing she could do for her own sanity was remember that this wasn't a real engagement. It was a job. One that would pay for her trip to Australia and more adventures after that. To imagine anything else would just lead to heartbreak. Even if there was a baby, that couldn't be the cornerstone to a lasting relationship. She may have spent her life fighting against going down the same path as her mom, but there was no denying that her mom and dad loved each other. *Really* loved each other. She wouldn't settle for anything less and she wasn't cruel enough to raise a child in an environment where its mom and dad didn't have that.

"Morning," Sawyer said, crossing to the kitchen island and setting everything down on it. "Please tell me your dad taught you how to make pancakes."

Despite her black mood, she laughed. "He did."

"Thank God." Sawyer winked at her as he started measuring out pancake mix according to the directions on the box. "I was gonna feel really bad if I helped your mom burn down the house."

Some of the tension ebbed out of her shoulders. Whatever else happened, Sawyer wasn't going to let this be awkward—at least not at her parents' house. Later they'd deal with it, but for now they were just two people pretending that everything was as it seemed. She plugged in the large griddle on the island and grabbed a spatula from a drawer. If he could do this, so could she. Together, they just might carry it off.

"Morning, pumpkin," her dad said, ambling over for a hug and a surreptitious look at the ingredients Sawyer had gathered and how he was mixing them together.

She squeezed her dad as tight as she dared. "I thought we were picking you up in an hour?"

"Well I—"

"Bullied the doctor into letting him out first thing this morning," Laura cut in. "The damn fool took a taxi home."

"Don't listen to a word she says," her dad said, looking every bit like someone caught with his hand in the cookie jar but denying it anyway. "Dr. Thornson was totally on board with the plan."

Leaning into his arms, she inhaled the familiar scent of his aftershave and offered up a silent prayer of thanks for some things that didn't change. "I'm so glad you're okay, Dad."

"Me, too, pumpkin." He gave her a kiss on the top of her head and then wandered out of the kitchen to the worn chair in the living room that he refused to let her mom take to the county landfill.

And so things settled into a comfortable silence with her dad reading the paper while her mom set the table and she and Sawyer made the pancakes. It was the kind of domestic scene that would normally make her feet itch, but today it didn't—and she refused to question why.

Half an hour later, the syrup had barely been poured on top of her pancakes before her mom went into inquisition mode.

"So this all happened pretty fast," her mom said, not touching the three pancakes, hash browns, Canadian bacon, regular bacon, and berry assortment on her plate. "I gotta tell you, Clover, your dad and I were very surprised when we heard *secondhand* about the engagement and then you've been avoiding my calls since then and it has us worried."

Subtle, her mom was not.

"I know, Mom, and I'm sorry about not saying anything but…" She got to the end of her words before her brain had time to think up anything.

"It was my fault," Sawyer picked up the slack. "I talked her into surprising you, but word snuck out before we had a chance."

"Uh-huh," her mom didn't sound convinced.

"So why the big rush to an engagement? It's not like you two have known each other for that long," her dad asked, his mouth half full of pancakes.

Her gut clenched and, reflexively, she put a hand on her belly. "It just sort of happened."

"It freaked me way out. You see, I'm a big-picture person and marriage has never figured into the plan." Sawyer picked up the coffee pot and gestured toward her mom's half-empty cup. "Refill?" After waiting for her mom to nod, he went on. "But my mom had it in her head that it was past time I got married."

"That sounds familiar," Bobby muttered, his eyes glued to the science journal laying by his plate. "The parental unit actually thought I was a better hope for grandkids than Jane."

"You're in the lab too much," her mom said with a sigh.

Her dad nodded. "Yeah, we want to make sure you have kids early before one of your experiments turns you into a superhero."

Clover perked up. This was news. Her family had given up on her doing the whole marriage and kids thing? Okay, maybe her dad had, but mom had never stopped with her little reminders. Sawyer must have sensed the tension stiffening her spine because he reached under the table and took her hand in his before continuing.

"Well, my mom was on a formal campaign and my brother thought it would be funny to put out an ad for someone to act as a buffer between my mom and me," he said, obviously omitting the timing of that occurrence.

"What?" her mom gasped.

"No, not like that," Sawyer said in a rush. "Like a

personal assistant who could dissuade my mom from trying to twist my arm to go on dates with her wife candidates."

"Please God, don't ever let our parents meet," Bobby said, shaking his head. "Can you two elope or something?"

Sawyer raised his coffee mug in a commiserating salute. "Clover turned out to be the perfect fit and not just for the job. We connected right away. A few pineapple shakes and trips to the flea market later, and I was hooked."

Her dad's fork fell with a clank onto his plate, his eyes wide. His face had lost what little color it had. Fear twisting her lungs tight, Clover was out of her seat in seconds rushing to his side. She and her mom got there at the same time.

"Stop your fussing," he said, waving them off as an embarrassed flush filled his cheeks. "I'm fine."

Clover's pulse pounded in her ears as she took a hard look at her dad, but he looked annoyed, not like he was about to have a heart attack for real. She let out a deep breath and slid back into her chair.

"I've gotta get this straight. You voluntarily went to the flea market? With Jane? On one of her DIY hell trips?" her dad said, his tone a mix of awe and horror. "And you didn't run screaming?"

Sawyer nodded, just the right amount of bemused wonder on his face.

"Laura, darling, call off the dogs," her dad said with a chuckle, sneaking a sip of his wife's coffee before she could swipe the cup from his grip. "This man's a goner."

• • •

Was he a goner? Almost two hours into the drive back to Harbor City and Sawyer couldn't shake the question.

He wasn't, of course. That would be ridiculous. It was an unusual situation, and add to that the fact that the condom broke last night and of course it could appear that way, even if someone didn't know all of the relevant facts. Like that the whole farce of an engagement was just another fun adventure for her and an efficient way for him to submarine Operation Marry Off Sawyer. Well, not the condom breaking part. That was just the bit of reality to smack both of them upside the heads.

Could she be pregnant? Yeah. Was she? Highly doubtful. It was just the once.

Said every high school-aged parent ever.

Okay, he was *not* going there.

Back to something he could control: this fake engagement/very real and very hot no-strings affair. Had Clover become a distraction? He snuck a peek at her out of the corner of his eye. She was winding a strand of hair around her finger while she gnawed her bottom lip raw and stared out the window at the outer suburbs of Harbor City. Her sunglasses were on, which kept him from seeing the look in her brown eyes, but he didn't need that to know. She'd been curled up in the passenger seat the entire trip as if she could make herself small enough to disappear. The urge to reach out to her, take her hand at the very least, made him grip the steering wheel tighter because with every mile closer they got to home, the slower he drove. It was beginning to get obvious—especially considering the number of cars whipping around him in their rush to get to the city. He had a deal to prep, a trip to Singapore to get ready for, and yet here he was cruising down the highway at a brisk fifty-five miles per hour.

Was he distracted? Hell yes.

Which is *exactly* why they'd decided to end the fake engagement early. It made sense, it fit with his big-picture plan for Carlyle Enterprises and for him—it was the only thing that mattered. And the only reason why he was driving five miles under the speed limit instead of his regular fifteen over was because he was in a shitty rental that shook anytime he took it over sixty.

Really.

It sure as hell wasn't because the conversation was so stellar. Neither of them had said much of anything since piling into the rental and waving good-bye to her parents. Scanning the highway for something to start a conversation, his gaze hit a minivan with more stick figure kids than he could imagine on the back window, a cop pulling over someone going the opposite direction, and a billboard for a discount bridal shop. Yeah, a whole lotta nothing there. Still, he had to try something. They couldn't end things like this, so he opened his mouth and let go with the first words that popped into his head.

"We could get married."

He almost swerved off the road, correcting right as the wheels went over the rumble strips on the side of the highway. *Where in the hell had that statement come from?*

Clover smacked a palm down on the dashboard to brace herself and snorted. "Yeah right."

"Why not?" he asked, returning the middle finger salute from the driver in the next lane.

She didn't even turn to look at him, just curled her knees tighter to her chest. "You're you and I'm me."

"What does that mean?" His frustration made the question louder than he meant.

Now she did look at him, twisting in her seat and revealing the hard set to her jaw and the swollen redness of her bottom lip. "Tell me what you envision for our married life together."

His mind went blank. He hadn't been telling her parents a story at brunch. He'd never planned on getting married. Hudson was the ladies' man. He was the boring Carlyle brother. The one who went to work. The one who focused on growing Carlyle Enterprises. The one who had absolutely no identity outside of the company—nor had he ever wanted one.

Her lips curled into a tight smile and she returned to her original position, staring out the passenger window. "That's what I thought."

Gripping the steering wheel tight enough that his knuckles turned white, he counted to twenty. Another set of cars passed them as his lungs tightened and his pulse began to race. "You might be pregnant."

"And you think that is the proper foundation for building a life together?" she asked, her voice barely loud enough to be heard over the lawn mower engine making the car go. "A broken condom?"

Fuck. That was the core of it, wasn't it? He could lie and say yes, but she'd see through him in an instant. And in that moment, he hated himself for it. This wasn't how his world worked. It wasn't how this was supposed to go. But the thing was, for the first time in his life since his dad died, he had no fucking clue what happened next and it ate away at him right down to the bone.

"If you are pregnant," he said, pressing the gas pedal down because he needed to do something—*anything*—at that moment. "I won't be a missing part of my child's life."

Clover let out a weary sigh and rested her temple against the passenger window. "I'd never want you to be. If I'm pregnant—and that's a big if—we'll figure it out from there."

"Fine," he ground out as he passed a minivan. "But until we know one way or another we go ahead with the engagement as if it was real."

"Why?"

He grabbed ahold of the first reason that came to mind. "Because I have you under contract for another two weeks, and I'm not agreeing to early separation. That's not up for negotiation."

"The contract, of course." Maybe she was just tired, but her voice sounded thicker than before. "So we go on pretending to be engaged until we know one way or another in a week or two. But no matter how it turns out, remember that I'm not a white picket fence kind of girl and you sure aren't the kind of guy to clock out of the office at five every day to go home to your wife and kids."

Was she wrong? No. They were who they were. Those differences were no big deal when it was all about hot sex and fun, but twenty years down the line? He had no plan for that. Still, he couldn't stop himself from pushing.

"Look, I'm not saying it would be a perfect marriage, but…" The words died out as some emotion he couldn't— didn't want—to identify jacked up his thinking. "Just consider it."

God knew he would. As Harbor City's skyline, dotted with Carlyle Enterprises buildings, took shape in the near distance, the idea was already taking root in his head in ways that all of his mother's schemes to find him the perfect Harbor City socialite wife never had.

Chapter Twenty-One

Two awkward, silence-filled days later, Clover shuffled through the front door of the apartment she shared with Daphne, her shoulders aching and her body weary. The setting sun streamed through the living room windows, landing on the bowl of popcorn, open bottle of wine, and two plastic glasses sitting in the middle of the reclaimed steamer trunk they'd converted into a coffee table. Judging from the amount of noise coming from the kitchen, though, Daphne was in there singing and putting the finishing touches on the double plate of cookies they always had on movie night.

Standing in the open doorway, she hesitated, not sure whether to move forward or slink back and text her that something had come up. Being around people—especially someone who knew her well—didn't seem like a great plan right now. The dense emotional fog that had been swirling around her since that night by the lake thickened, making it hard to breathe, to think, to do just about anything. She never should have said yes to movie night this week.

"*Lupakan ia*," she said and turned toward the door.

But before she could make tracks, Daphne walked out of the kitchen carrying a plate of cookies.

"Clover!" she hollered in a singsong voice. "When you didn't answer my text, I was afraid you were ditching me to keep no-strings-attached banging your fake fiancé before time ran out and you had to leave for Australia."

That one teasing statement cut through the haze around Clover. No strings. Banging. Sawyer. Maybe baby. Australia. Too late. All of it came at her in a rush like a cold, stinging burst of wind that cut right through her, bone deep and breath stealing. Her throat tightened, her lungs pinched, and the hot tears that had been lurking behind that numbing fog spilled down her cheeks.

Daphne squawked in concern, put down the plate she was holding, and rushed over to her, wrapping her arms around her in a hug and squeezing tight. It didn't stop the tears, but it relieved the pressure of the ache that had built up over the last few days. She wasn't alone in this *whatever* it was. It took several deep breaths, but she finally managed to stop crying and Daphne let her go.

Daphne took Clover by the shoulders and gave her a long, hard look. "Oh, honey, what happened?" Then she handed Clover a double chocolate cookie and a glass of red wine that was twice the size of a normal pour.

The wine was tempting—so fucking tempting—but she set it down on the entry table and took a bite of the cookie instead. It didn't taste like much but if she couldn't have wine, the magical and medicinal properties of chocolate were going to have to do all the work.

Daphne herded her into the living room. "I can call my cousin to kick his ass."

Looking at her best friend so ready to go to bat for her without even knowing why, she almost started crying again. Chin trembling, she sat down on the couch and took in a long breath through her nose and braced herself for saying the words that had been screaming inside her head out loud.

"The condom broke."

Daphne stilled, her brown eyes wide.

"What did he say?"

"He asked me to marry him." There, that sounded almost neutral and not at all like she was about to start bawling again.

"What did you say?"

"Nothing. What could I say?" The memory of the resigned look in Sawyer's eyes when he'd asked her to think about it was like picking at a scab right over her heart. "Oh yeah, so I may or may not be pregnant but we have phenomenal sex. Let's see how the whole tying yourself to one person forever works out because you know the one thing I've dreamed about since I was a little girl was being barefoot, pregnant, and handcuffed to a vacuum cleaner."

Daphne rolled her eyes. "I don't think that's really how marriages work these days." Then she draped an arm around Clover's shoulders and gave her a solid squeeze. "What can I do?"

Was doing some sort of spell to make her period come asking too much? "Not make me watch a horrible movie and let me eat all the chocolate chip cookies I can stuff in my face."

"Done." Daphne picked up the chocolate chip cookie plate and handed it over. "So what are you going to do? Do you want kids?"

"I didn't think so but…" She rubbed her palm in a circle on her belly, the motion calming her even if it didn't lessen any of the uncertainty in her life right now. Sawyer didn't want to marry her, not really. He just wanted to force the unexpected event to fit into the plan he already had worked out for his life. "It's hard to explain."

"Try," Daphne said.

Clover took in a deep breath and tried to organize the thoughts whirling around in her head. The truth of it was she hadn't tried to put everything into words before. All she knew was that everything hurt and she couldn't pinpoint exactly why. So she started with the point she was most certain of and started talking.

"I love my mom, but that's not the life I ever wanted for myself," she said. "She eats apple pie every Sunday even though she hates it and that's just one example of how she stuffs away what she wants for someone else. Plus, she never gets to go anywhere. Sparksville and my dad are her whole world—along with Bobby and me, of course. I didn't want that. I wanted to live. I wanted to experience every new thing out there. I didn't want to miss out on a single experience when she missed out on a million because she was tied down by her family. I never questioned it." Her heart hammered against her ribs and she took a second to swallow past the emotion blocking her throat. "But now I look around and realize that I'm twenty-six years old, have never held a job for longer than a few months, have been all over the globe, and I'm not any closer to feeling like I have it all than I was when I was in my old bedroom in high school writing in my diary that I'd never end up like my mother." This was it, that thing looming in the dark shadows of her head, the ones she never bothered to shine a light on—not until she answered that ad for a personal buffer. "Then I met Sawyer and I started to like being in one place. Being with him wasn't boring or stifling or a chore. It was…thrilling and fun and a little bit scary, but in a good way." Her pulse sped up as all sorts of things she'd been afraid to consider started clicking into place. "I was still trying new things and new experiences—it was just a pineapple shake at a diner instead of a drink most people couldn't pronounce in a country I'd never been to before. And when the condom broke, I freaked out but not all the way. Part of me was… hopeful and excited about the possibility of a baby and of having a life with Sawyer." The realization was freeing even as she acknowledged the bittersweet futility of it all. "But when he asked me to marry him out of obligation it was like watching all the things I didn't even realize I was starting to want get blown out of the water."

"Oh God," Daphne said with a soft groan as she leaned forward and gave Clover a sympathetic hug. "You fell in love."

"I think I did." And there went the waterworks with the very glamorous addition of a runny nose because this was what her formerly very happy life had come to.

Her best friend grabbed a napkin from the stack next to the popcorn bowl and handed it to her. "It's not the worst thing to have happen, Clover."

Her hands shaky and her breath coming in tortured gasps, Clover wiped her cheeks dry and blew her nose and yanked back control over her tear ducts. "I won't marry him because he feels responsible for a baby that may not even exist, but I can't seem to walk away from him, either."

"So you wait and see if you're pregnant."

Clover stuffed half a cookie in her mouth because if these weren't the kind of emotions that needed to be eaten away, she didn't know what kind were. "And then?"

"Then I'll be here for you like I've always been, and I'll support you in whatever you choose," Daphne said and held out her pinky. "Promise."

Barely managing not to start sniffling again, Clover straightened out her pinkie finger and touched it to Daphne's. A pinky promise was about as good as it was going to get for her right about now and she knew it, but sometimes that was good enough—and right now it had to be because she was still fake engaged to a man she loved for real who didn't love her back.

• • •

The next morning with his suitcase in hand, Sawyer took a last look at Clover's closed bedroom door, clamped his jaws together tight enough to rattle his teeth, and stepped into the elevator. He kept his gaze on the buttons lighting up one after the other rather than his own reflection in the mirrored doors. He didn't need to look to see the dark circles under his eyes that were minimized if not eliminated by his glasses. Three days of near silence between him and Clover—with most of their talking being at the office about the Singapore deal—had left him feeling like shit.

Neither of them had mentioned the possible baby or his marriage proposal. Was he a chicken shit for letting it lay? Probably. But he'd promised himself to give her space and so that's what he was going to do. His phone vibrated against his chest and he withdrew it from his inside jacket pocket.

Mom: *We need to talk.*

That was definitely not going to happen.

Sawyer: *Headed off to airport for a quick trip to Singapore. Talk when I get back?*

He stared at his phone, half believing it might just explode at any moment.

Mom: *Of course.*

He let out the breath he'd been holding right as the elevator doors opened. He nodded at Irving on his way through the lobby and made it almost to the doors when his phone vibrated in his hand.

Mom: *Is Clover going with you?*

His gut clenched and his steps faltered just enough as he walked through the Carlyle Towers front doors that Linus gave him a funny look as he held open the Town Car's door. Sawyer recovered his stride and got into the car's back seat. He stared at the empty seat beside him before answering his mom's question.

Sawyer: *No.*

Mom: *Have a safe trip. Good luck with Mr. Lim.*

Finally nailing this Singapore deal should be all he was thinking about right now, but it wasn't. Instead, all he could think about during the drive to the airport, the walk through security, and checking into the elite class VIP lounge was Clover. What was she doing right now? Was she feeling okay? Was she scared? Was she excited? Did she hate his guts? Was she going to say yes? Was he a complete and total fucking whiny wimp?

Survey says yes. Man up, asshole.

Sawyer grabbed a bag of chips and sat down in one of the lounge's empty seats. The airport version of the news was playing on a big screen TV and an older man was reading a newspaper in the next seat. A row over, a toddler dressed in a T-shirt with a cartoon pig on it and a tutu skirt wandered from one end of the chairs to another under the watchful gaze of her parents. The kid sang some nonsense song as she patted her hands three times on the chair before moving on to the next one. Whatever game she was playing, it had her entertained.

"How many do you have at home?" the older man sitting nearby asked him as he folded his newspaper shut.

"None," Sawyer said, his attention still focused on the girl who had hair almost the same shade of blond as Clover's. "Not yet."

"You sound hopeful, that's good." The old man turned his face and watched the little girl who had added a spin move to her routine "They change your lives, those little ones, and mostly for the better once you get past the sleepless beginning."

"How many kids do you have?"

The man smiled, pride filling his eyes. "Five. All grown now."

"That's a lot of sleepless nights."

"Well, with the right woman, you barely notice it." He reached into his pocket and brought out his wallet, flipped it open, and tapped on a photo of a much younger version of the man and a woman in a wedding dress. "You gotta make sure to get that part right first because the kids all eventually leave the nest and then you're left with yourselves for the rest of forever."

Sawyer's vision of forever hadn't involved Clover or kids or marriage or anything else, and then he'd walked out of his office one day and there she was. He was an idiot for not realizing sooner. He was just relaxing back against his seat when a voice over the intercom announced Sawyer's flight was boarding.

"That's my flight," he said, nodding his good-bye to the older man.

"Have a good trip and good luck finding the right woman."

Forever with Clover. It had a nice ring to it. "I think I might have."

The old man snorted. "Youth is wasted on the young. If it was me, you can be sure I wouldn't be lazing around *thinking* I had the right woman. I'd make damn sure and then do whatever it took to make sure she thought the same, too."

The old man was onto something. Getting Clover to see the advantages of his proposal would be a challenge. He had to make sure it didn't sound like he was locking her into the very life she most feared.

"I'll keep that in mind," Sawyer said with a laugh and hurried to the gate for his flight, confident that by the time he got back to Harbor City in three days he'd have the perfect negotiation plan ready to go.

• • •

Two days after Sawyer had left for Singapore, Clover was wandering the empty penthouse, still no closer to knowing if she was pregnant or what in the hell she was going to do after he got back when the intercom by the elevator buzzed.

"Ma'am," Irving said through the intercom. "You're…

um… Mrs. Carlyle is on her way up."

Colillas de mono. She gulped, her silent worry about what *might* happen suddenly superseded by what was about to happen. "Now?"

"Yes, ma'am."

Glancing around the foyer for a hole that would swallow her up, she threw out the first thought that made its way through her freaked-out brain. "But Sawyer isn't here."

"Yes, ma'am."

When her miracle getaway hole failed to appear, she took a deep breath and tried not to give into the panic. "Are you giving me a heads up so I don't have a heart attack when she pops out of the elevator like the Wicked Witch of the West?"

Irving made what sounded like a strangled laugh that transformed into a coughing fit. "I can't comment on that, ma'am."

Of course not. *He* wasn't the one about to be interrogated by Helene Carlyle. "Thanks, Irving."

"Yes ma'am."

Clover pressed a fist to her belly and wished she'd paid more attention during the meditation breathing course Daphne had dragged her to a few months ago. Instead of deep cleansing breaths, all she was able to accomplish at the moment was borderline hyperventilating. Great. Helene Carlyle, terrorizer of doormen and procurer of socially-acceptable wife candidates was—the elevator dinged and Clover's stomach did a droopy loop and her shoulders sagged—here.

Helene swept out of the elevator, looking every inch like the queen of Harbor City's elite from her perfectly understated and yet enormously expensive wrap dress to the simple pearl studs in her ears. She gave Clover a slow up and down from the hem of her skinny jeans to the straps of her loose chiffon tank top and gave a weary sigh.

Biting back a caustic comment, Clover hit the elevator down button because the faster it got all the way back up here the faster her fake mother-in-law to be could leave. "Sorry, but Sawyer's not here."

"I'm not here for him," Helene said, brushing an invisible piece of lint from her dress — as if lint would *dare* to land on her. "We're going shopping."

Oh. That sounded about as much fun as a world without chocolate. "Why?"

"I have a gala in two days and while Sawyer is many things, he is still a man with horrible sense for women's fashion."

"I can pick out my own dress." Plus, it was highly doubtful she'd be going to the gala. Her period was due any minute, and she'd even worn white jeans and her favorite pair of panties today to hurry it along. Everyone knew Aunt Flo loved to fuck up anything white and/or pretty.

"Your ability to pick an item of clothing is not in question," Helene said, her tone making a mockery of her words. "However, your ability to pick one that is appropriate for your first appearance at a major event as Sawyer's fiancée is."

"*Tolong*," she muttered under her breath, although she doubted even if anyone could hear they'd answer her call for help, and as long as she had to continue with the fake engagement farce, telling Helene to buzz off was not a possible option. "I appreciate the offer, but I'm going to have to say no."

Helene ground her teeth together and the vein popped out in her temple, reminiscent of her son. "I'm not good at apologizing."

"*That* was an apology?" Not actually laughing out loud was hard. Still, she managed it.

"It's a habit my son got from me, I'll just warn you of that now," she said, regaining her imperial air. "Also, having trouble finding a happy middle ground seems to be a family trait. That's why Sawyer is so focused on the company and only the company—until you came along. I'd like the opportunity to get to know the woman who was able to get him to focus on something other than the family business a little better before the wedding."

"I'm not sure I'm the reason for any change." In fact, she was pretty damn sure she wasn't.

"You may not be sure, but I am. Trust me. I tried everything I could think of to get him to slow down before going the nuclear route and pushing possible wives at him. By then I was out of options, and I couldn't stand losing my son to an early death from overwork like I had my husband."

Ooof. That hit her right in the hormonal feels. God, she couldn't do this. "Helene…" The rest of what she was going to say vanished out of her head at the superior look the other woman gave her when she used her first name. "Mrs. Carlyle?"

"You can call me Helene, we're going to be family after all."

The elevator dinged its arrival and the doors *whooshed* open. Helene strode inside, obviously confident that Clover was going to follow behind—and she might have, if she could move her feet. The mention of family had all the guilt and anxiety rushing back to the surface, overwhelming everything except her ability to remember to breathe.

Helene gave her a hard look and pressed down the door open button. "Please don't make that face. Let's just go find you the perfect dress…and a last-minute appointment with my hair stylist."

The little dig, subtle and yet perfectly aimed, was just the thing to break Clover out of her icy trance. Helene and Sawyer might not be carbon copies, but there were plenty of similarities between the two and as with the son, there was no way she was going to get Helene out of the penthouse without letting her think she won. So they'd go through the shopping farce and Clover could return whatever dress she ended up getting at the first opportunity. It's not like she was ever going to need a ball gown after her she walked out of the penthouse for the last time.

"If I say yes to the dress, will you back off my hair?" she asked.

Helene gave her a skeptical look. "You'll try on whatever I suggest?"

"Yes, but that doesn't mean I'll get it."

"But I'm buying," Helene said, waving off the objection as if laying out thousands on a dress was no big deal, which for her it probably wasn't.

"I couldn't accept." The last thing she wanted was to walk away from Sawyer owing his family.

"You don't have a choice. Those are my terms"—she paused as if considering an option that was slightly less distasteful than Clover picking out her own dress—"but I'll let you pay for lunch."

The woman wasn't going without her. That much was obvious. With reluctant admiration and half looking forward to the distraction from waiting for her period, Clover grabbed her purse from the entryway table and got in the elevator. "You negotiate better than Sawyer."

"Darling," Helene said with a satisfied grin, "tell me something I don't know. Come on, if I'm lucky I'll have the opportunity to scare Irving again."

As the elevator doors closed, Clover didn't have a single doubt that Helene Carlyle could accomplish that with only minimal effort.

Three hours later, Clover found herself under the heat hood at Helene's salon. She wasn't sure how she'd gotten there, but the woman had outmaneuvered her at every turn. She really was a force to be reckoned with. So while Clover sat there with tinfoil in her hair, Helene sipped tea from a delicate china cup.

After setting her cup down on the saucer, Helene gave her an assessing once-over. "Sawyer's very set in his ways, you know."

"You don't have to tell me." No, she'd lived through the experience of learning that all on her own. Her hand automatically went to her belly.

"I suppose I don't," Helene said. "He's just never had any other interests than Carlyle Enterprises, not from the time he was old enough to ride to work with his father. As a little boy, he was just the same as he is now. Simply shorter and with a more limited vocabulary."

"That doesn't surprise me." Clover chuckled despite everything going on between her and Sawyer because the mental image of him as a toddler in a suit was too funny not to. "Although I was surprised by how obsessed he is with the business that he's never built anything with his own hands. I guess that's why it was so much fun to renovate the bar cart together."

One perfectly waxed and shaped dark brown eyebrow went up, and Helene leaned forward. "Explain renovate."

What was it with this family? Didn't they ever have craft time? Growing up, her mom had always made sure there was plenty of glitter, glue, odds and ends, construction paper, and other things so she and Bobby could invent and renovate. Her first project had been her three-drawer dresser that her mom had let her go to town on with a glue gun and a jar of old buttons. Really, that had been the beginning of her obsession.

"Sawyer and I got this old medical cart from the 50s at a flea market and then stripped it, sanded it, repainted it, and added a few bits and bobs to make it unique."

"And he helped you with that manual labor?" Helene asked before taking another sip of tea.

"Uh-huh." Clover nodded. "I know, he wasn't into it at

first, either, but he came around eventually. I've even gotten him to take some time off on his work-at-home Fridays to watch *Flea Market Flip* so we can get ideas for the next day's trip to the flea market. We're on the lookout for an old sewing table but haven't found one we like quite yet."

It took a few seconds for the bubbles of excitement about hitting the flea market with Sawyer to settle and then for reality to take a pin to each one so it popped. Once her period came, they'd never go hunting for a sewing table again. She swallowed past the emotion suddenly clogging her throat because it wasn't the flea market she'd really miss but going there with Sawyer. And that just sucked.

Helene didn't seem to be experiencing the same bittersweet realization. Instead, the older woman just looked at Clover and smiled. "I'm impressed, dear."

She was just about to ask why when the stylist appeared at her side and declared it was time to rinse. And with a small smile at her former nemesis, Clover followed the stylist. After all, finally making headway with Helene didn't matter in the big picture because she'd be gone forever in just a few days.

Chapter Twenty-Two

Sawyer paced the foyer in his penthouse. Still a little jet lagged from his return trip from Singapore, the last thing he wanted was to put on a tux and attend one of the Kenning Fund Galas his mom had organized, but if it meant spending time with Clover, then it was a sacrifice he was more than willing to take. His plane had been delayed and he'd barely made it home in time to change for the evening.

Nerves needing an outlet, he fiddled with the box containing the heirloom emerald and diamond ring he'd gotten out of the bank vault on the drive home from the airport. He'd spent most of the flight home thinking about how to do this before settling on a plan. The details were sketchy—shocker—but he had the big picture clear in his head. Since the limo ride would be their only opportunity to be alone, he'd do it there. He couldn't wait until after the gala. It was past time to close the deal.

The door to her room opened and Clover walked out. He almost swallowed his tongue.

She wore a silver, gold, and black gown that hugged her curves and caught the light as she moved. Her hair was pulled up—not in a messy knot like he'd seen before but some sort of complicated hairstyle that twisted as it wound around her head, ending up in a loosely braided bun in the back. Loose tendrils in different shades of blond fell around her face, tempting him to reach out and touch their smooth curls.

"You look beautiful."

"Thank you." She smoothed her hand down her skirt. "I went shopping yesterday with your mom."

He started to laugh, figuring that she was kidding. However, when she didn't crack a smile he realized she actually *had* gone shopping with his mom. "How did that happen?"

One side of her mouth twisted upward. "Let's just say that I now understand why you find it so hard to tell your mother no."

Now *that* was something he understood all too well. "Welcome to the family."

Her lips fell into a straight line, and she pressed them together hard enough that a little white line appeared around them.

Shit. He had no fucking clue what he'd done wrong, but obviously something. Then it hit him. Family. Baby. *Fuck.* He was a moron.

Push forward, numb nuts.

Taking his own advice, he held out his arm to her and kept the word count to a minimum. "Shall we?"

Awkward didn't begin to cover the elevator ride. Never in his life had he ever wished he'd gotten some of the skill to charm people that had gone to Hudson. Hell, right now he'd settle for not being a complete asshole. He clasped his hands together to hide their slight shake. He should not have had the second double espresso on the tail end of the twenty-four-hour flight. Not only was he jittery, his brain was a jet-lagged mess.

"So is there any news?" he asked. He'd been gone for three days after all.

Clover's chin went up. Never a good sign. "You mean have I gotten my period?"

He hadn't, but it was too late to rephrase his question now so he nodded.

"No," she said and walked out of the elevator and through the lobby, the sway of her hips a thing of mesmerizing beauty as she strode across the sidewalk and slipped into the back of the Town Car as Linus held open the door.

He managed to wait through two stoplights before the box in his pocket began to feel like a ticking bomb. He needed to do it before they got to the gala. He couldn't explain why it had to work that way, but he couldn't shake the feeling that his time was just about up. It was probably just the nerves and caffeine talking, but once the idea had settled into the back of his brain it was all he could think about.

The city lights illuminated Clover's profile as they drove down Fifty-Seventh Street, highlighting the curve of her full lips and the delicate beauty of her face. The sight robbed him of everything but the need to let the rest of the world know that she was his. Marriage may not have been part of his big-picture plan in the beginning, but it was now. And all because of Clover.

With the Bayview Hotel looming only a few blocks ahead, he reached in his pocket and pulled out the ring box, opened it, and held it out to Clover. "I got this for you."

She took one look at the emerald and diamond engagement ring inside and gasped before glancing up at him.

Steeling himself, Sawyer knew he had one shot. He had to do this right, play up that she wouldn't be giving up her independence or her dreams. Fuck it up and he'd risk hearing a two instead of a three-letter answer.

"I know this isn't exactly the way either of us expected things to work out, but I think it's for the best," he said, his heart in his throat. "I spent a lot of time thinking while I was traveling—about you, about me, and about the two of us together. We work well together. You were amazing on the Singapore deal and you would have so much more opportunities to travel as part of Carlyle Enterprises. So even if there's not a baby, I think we should make our fake engagement real. We make a good team."

A charged silence stretched between them as the Town Car pulled up to the curb in front of the hotel. The prickly cactus that settled in his stomach whenever he missed some little detail scratched against his stomach lining.

Finally, she turned toward him completely, her face carefully neutral. "I'm a good teammate?"

Okay, that wasn't exactly the response he was expecting. He opened his mouth to fix whatever it was that he'd fucked up but Linus picked that moment to open the door.

Knowing time was up but desperate to fix things, he took her hand and slipped on the engagement ring his grandfather had made for his grandmother. "I know I keep saying this but… just think about it."

Clover stared at the ring as she tugged her bottom lip between her teeth but kept the rest of her body completely still. Then, after a moment, she closed her eyes, clenched her teeth together tight enough to square her jaw, and let out a shaky breath. When she opened her eyes again, he couldn't miss the glimmer of wetness in them or the bittersweet acceptance.

"We'd better get inside," she said before taking Linus's outstretched hand to exit the limo.

Sawyer got out after her and slid his hand across the small of her back, the familiar spike of lust rushing through him at the slightest feel of her, but he couldn't shake the itching suspicion that he'd missed some detail and that while Clover might be wearing his ring, he hadn't yet sealed the deal.

• • •

The ring felt weird on Clover's hand—heavy, pokey, awkward—but zeroing in on that gave her something to focus on besides the stone-cold realization that she couldn't do this any longer. Baby or no baby, tonight was it. She just wished she had it in her to at least enjoy the last few hours with him. Even if he didn't love her, she could still have one last fantasy night pretending that he wanted her for more than a teammate.

Teammate.

"*Quelle merde,*" she said under her breath, the first inklings of indignation rising up through the hurt and disappointment.

She grabbed the anger with both hands and held tight, relishing having something crystal clear to understand after days of emotional confusion. As far as marriage proposals went, Sawyer's second was even worse than his first. Did he want her to be his wife or an employee with benefits? She shouldn't be surprised, though. That's how she fit into the big-picture plan he had of his life. It wasn't about her—or the maybe baby—at all. Yet here she was with his hand at the small of her back and a smile pasted on her face as they made their way through the crowded ballroom at the Bayview Hotel to the table where Helene Carlyle was holding court.

"Sawyer, welcome home." Helene stood up and gave her son a hug before turning to Clover. "Doesn't your bride-to-be look beautiful?"

"She always does," Sawyer said, sounding genuine.

Her heart cramped because of course he was. She didn't doubt the attraction between them, only what it meant outside of the bedroom.

"Agreed." Hudson leaned toward her and lowered his voice to a conspiratorial level, "May I have this dance before my mom gets her claws into you to get all the latest wedding details?"

She laughed at the absurdity of it all, the sound coming out harsh even to her own ears. "A perfect idea."

The dance floor was crowded but Hudson navigated through the couples to a less crowded corner as if he'd been doing it his whole life, which he probably had. As he led them into a turn, she took a hard look at him. He was just as handsome as Sawyer only light where his brother was dark. But behind the flirtatious blue eyes and reputation as one of Harbor City's most active players, something else was lurking. Not that it mattered. She wouldn't be around to tease the truth out of him. Anyway, judging by the way his mouth tightened every time he glanced at the table where Sawyer and Helene sat, he had something to say.

"You might as well get it out now," Clover said.

"Direct." He gave her a curious look. "Good. That'll help."

Oh. It was going to be that kind of talk. "It always helps to speed the process along."

"Agreed." He nodded and moved them on a smooth path around the other dancing couples. "Is this all still fake between you two?"

Her steps faltered, but she recovered quickly. "What do you mean?"

"The engagement, you two as a couple?"

Acid gurgled in her stomach. Not trusting herself to say anything without having an emotional breakdown of a sort, she just nodded.

"Shit." Hudson grimaced. "And I thought I'd had it all right." He must have seen the confusion on her face because he went on. "The job ad. I was the one who pulled your resume out of the pile. Here you were, someone who seemed flighty on the outside, but every trip you took wasn't about just having fun. You were teaching English, helping to build businesses, and saving endangered animals. Underneath all of that adventurous spirit was a woman who wanted to do good in the world, she just needed to find her purpose. It seemed to me like you'd be the perfect match for my brother who seems all fucked up in the head about his purpose because it's not Carlyle Enterprises—or at least that shouldn't be the sum total of it."

If he'd just told her that he was actually an alien here on an undercover mission, she wouldn't have been more surprised. "You're part of the Marry Off Sawyer campaign?"

"On the down low." He grinned and spun her a little bit farther away from the other couples on the dance floor. "I couldn't let my mom know I was helping. It would ruin my image. Didn't you ever wonder why all of the other job applicants were bodyguard-types except for you?"

The mental image of squashing into the only open seat between two huge guys in suits and dead-eyed expressions flashed in her mind. "I thought I was in the wrong place."

"And I would have put big money on the belief that you were exactly where you belonged." Hudson sighed and shook his head. "It doesn't matter now, though. You've got to put a stop to this fake engagement before it goes any further. I know it all started out as a simple thing until the Singapore deal closed, but now it's a problem."

He wasn't wrong. The truth of it shouldn't hurt, but it did. "You mean *I'm* a problem."

Hudson offered her a kind smile. "Yes. I know my mom took you out shopping the other day. It may not seem like it at first, but she's a woman who gets attached to people and after what happened when we lost my father…" his voice trailed off for a second. "You seem like a nice person and I hate to be such a cold bastard, but I need to put my family first. You have to break it off with Sawyer sooner rather than later."

"It's…" She searched for the right word to describe the complete mess of a situation she found herself in, "complicated."

"And it's only going to get more so."

He wasn't wrong. Whether she was pregnant or not, she couldn't settle for being Sawyer's teammate. She knew it. She'd *always* known it, she just hadn't wanted to admit it—even to herself. "Your mom and Sawyer think they're the steel will in the family, but they're wrong, aren't they?"

Hudson raised his broad shoulders in a noncommittal shrug as the music ended, and he began walking her back toward the table.

Three steps in and an all-too-familiar ache started in her pelvis. Realization made her stomach drop. "If you'll excuse me," she said and started walking toward the bathroom just outside the ballroom doors.

By the time she walked out ten minutes later, knowing for sure she wasn't pregnant and unable to decide whether to be happy or sad, she wasn't surprised to find Sawyer waiting for her in the hall. Of course, that didn't make seeing him hurt any less. The Bayview Hotel in the middle of a gala probably wasn't the place to do this. No. It definitely wasn't the place to do this, but if she went back to the penthouse with him, she wasn't sure she'd be able to walk away tonight. Or any other night. Love was a real asshole that way. It had to be now or never.

"We need to talk—in private," she said.

His body tensed, but to his credit he didn't try to pull the truth out of her right away. Instead he took her hand—the frisson of desire his touch ignited was almost a cruelty—and led her down the hall until they found an unlocked supply closet. Once inside, she shut the door and leaned against it, needing the support it offered.

"I'm not pregnant." She should be relieved—and she was…kind of.

His shoulders sank. "You're not?"

"No."

Sawyer started pacing in the small room. "It doesn't change anything." Three steps to the shelves holding toiletries. "We'd still make a great team. We can still make this work." He turned and took three steps in the other direction to the shelves stacked high with towels. "It just gives me more time to work kids into—"

"Your big vision?" She finished the sentence for him, amazed that her heartbreak didn't send her to her knees.

"Yes." He stopped pacing and couldn't have looked any more satisfied if he tried.

God, it devastated her, but she had to give him every chance to tell her she was wrong—that he wanted to stay together because he loved her. "Because we make a good team."

The first hint of doubt crept into his hazel eyes even as he nodded.

She bit the inside of her cheek hard enough to keep the tears at bay if not the misery eating her up. "I don't want to get married because I'm half of a good team. I want more than that, and so should you."

"But you wouldn't have to give up traveling or adventures or feel like you're trapped behind a white picket fence," he said, his words coming out fast with a tinge of desperation. "The penthouse doesn't even *have* a fence."

God she hurt, all the way down to her bone marrow. She loved him. He didn't love her. It wasn't enough—for either of them. Gritting her teeth to stop herself from crying, she slipped off the engagement ring and held it out to him.

But instead of taking it, he just stood there staring as anger began to seep into his eyes. "So you're just gonna walk away and that's it? We're done?"

"Yes." It was as much as she could say at the moment without worrying she'd break down.

She couldn't do a damn thing to comfort him, so she laid the ring on a low stack of towels and went back to the door—every motion as deliberate and painful as if she was walking through a frozen ocean.

"Fine. Go," he snarled. "The whole fake engagement was just a stupid fucking bullshit story anyway."

No. It wasn't bullshit. It was heartache and pain and

the best time of her life. Now she had to do the right thing for both of them even though it shredded up her insides until she was a bloody mess. They both deserved more. So she went.

She managed to walk through the hotel and catch a cab to the penthouse where she crammed all of her stuff back into her suitcase. She left behind the fancy dresses, the expensive shoes, and the one pair of hiking boots that had actually been delivered. Australia wasn't in the picture anymore and she couldn't care less. Hudson was right. With all of her adventures, she'd been looking for her purpose. She still hadn't found it, but at least now she knew she wasn't going to do so by traveling halfway around the globe. She was done running—from her fears, from her expectations, from herself.

The numb bubble surrounding Clover didn't pop until she was standing outside the apartment she shared with Daphne. She tried her key but her hands shook too much to get it in the lock, so she finally gave up and rang the bell. By the time the door opened, she had a river of mascara streaming down her face.

"Oh, honey," Daphne said wrapping her arms around her and bringing her inside. "It's gonna be okay."

But Clover knew deep in that part of her soul that couldn't lie that it wasn't going to be, not even close.

• • •

Three hours and three double whiskeys later, Sawyer stumbled around his penthouse ready for battle with an opponent who had already vacated the premises. Staring at the bare hangers in her closet next to the cocktail dresses he'd bought for her, the shoes he'd fucked her in, and the one pair of hiking boots for her trip to Australia that he hadn't managed to hide away before she saw them, he realized that Clover's abandonment must have been what Irving had wanted to warn him about when he brushed the man off and rushed into the elevator. A bitter taste coated his tongue as he slammed the closet door shut and stormed out of her room. Of course it wasn't her room—not anymore.

He took a beer from the fridge and tipped back the bottle as he tore off his bow tie and shrugged out of his jacket. Fucking monkey suit was choking him. That's the reason why he couldn't get a decent amount of air into his lungs to alleviate the vice grip squeezing them tight. The beer was gone by the time he lowered the bottle. Another. That would help him get rid of the pounding in his head and wipe away the memory of Clover's face when she'd tried to hand him the engagement ring.

He swiped another beer from the fridge and his arm protested. *Fuck.* Moving hurt. Breathing hurt. Thinking hurt. The only thing to do in this situation was to sit down, turn on the television, and get as drunk as possible as fast as possible until he couldn't see the sly smirk she made when she was winning a negotiation or hear her soft moan as she came or remember the smooth silk of her skin under his fingers.

Listing toward the living room, he grabbed a bottle of whiskey from Clover's flea market bar cart on the way and settled onto the couch in a haze. He clicked the remote and an episode of *Flea Market Flip* appeared on his TV. His finger hovered over the button to change the channel but he couldn't push it. They'd seen this one together. The older women kicked their husbands' asses. The remote slipped from his hand and landed on the coffee table with a hard thunk.

Watching this horrible show was like pouring rock salt into a gaping wound, but he couldn't stop because what all the alcohol in his system couldn't dull was the fact that Clover was gone and it was his fault. He'd missed some detail that really mattered. He'd fucked up. Now he'd pay the price.

Chapter Twenty-Three

Someone had taken a tire iron to Sawyer's head. It was the only explanation for the pounding that was loud enough to rattle his teeth. He opened his eyes and sat up. That was a mistake. His stomach pitched and the room spun just enough to make him squeeze his eyes shut, white knuckle the couch, and promise to whomever was listening that he would never *ever* do whatever it was that he'd done to get that way ever again.

The intercom buzzed and the sound vibrated down his spine.

Okay, it wasn't a tire iron, but Irving's buzzer finger that was trying to kill him. Girding himself, he took a breath and then stood up and staggered toward the intercom box by the elevator.

He pressed his hand to the talk button and leaned his sweaty forehead against the cool elevator doors. "Irving."

"This is not Irving," his mother said, her normally strident tone had an extra robotic quality thanks to the crappy intercom speaker and his whiskey-soaked brain. "Undo the override lock on your elevator."

When had he locked the elevator? Last night? No yesterday morning. It was coming back now. Clover had punched through his rib cage to rip out his still beating heart, he'd gotten very, *very* drunk for several days, and after that it got gray—or was that amber-colored—and foggy. Whatever color his world was, it required solitude to really soak up all of the self-pity. It was definitely not the place for his mother—especially not when he was so foul after almost two days in the same tuxedo pants and undershirt that he could smell himself.

"Mom, I'm not really—"

"Do not even bother," she interrupted. "Your brother has told me everything about the idiotic fake engagement you two cooked up."

Well, he didn't have to worry about puking anymore because his stomach had dropped down three floors. "Shit."

"That's a succinct way of putting it. Now undo the elevator override lock."

"I'm not really feeling well." Or sane. Or remotely human.

"Just imagine how you'll be feeling when your sixty-one-year-old mother has to climb dozens of sets of stairs just to give you a piece of her mind. Unlock the elevator immediately, Sawyer Anthony Carlyle."

His middle name. It didn't matter that he was a grown man, it was still parental fucking kryptonite. Knowing he was going to regret it but that he didn't have a choice, he entered his security code into the touchscreen menu and unlocked the elevator. Then, while the touchscreen displayed the floor numbers as the elevator passed them on its way up to the penthouse, he ambled back to the living room and the chaos that awaited him there. Yet another do-it-yourself show was on the TV. About a dozen empty beer bottles, a mostly empty bottle of whiskey, and a half-eaten bag of sriracha-flavored chips littered the coffee table. He was contemplating cleaning the mess up when the elevator doors opened. His mom and Hudson got off.

"Oh look," Sawyer said, his voice a rusty unused sound, "you brought Brutus with you."

"Hudson didn't betray you. He's trying to help you." Helene gave Sawyer a long, disgusted up and down look before grimacing. "Are you still drunk?"

"What makes you think I'm drunk?" he asked from the safety of his non-moving couch because the rest of the room was starting to tilt on its axis.

"You're still in your tux and the gala was two days ago," his mom said, keeping her distance—no doubt to avoid the smell.

Hudson, on the other hand, leaned forward and took a deep and dramatic whiff. "And you smell like a dive bar floor after they turn on the lights."

"Good thing neither of you need to be here anyway, so go away." He grabbed the bottle of whiskey more for show than anything since the contents of his stomach echoed the slosh of the amber liquid in the bottle.

Hudson swiped it out of his hands and set it down on the bright red bar cart. "You've had enough."

Sawyer couldn't look away from the cart. He and Clover had refinished it out on the balcony and staring at it was like dragging barbwire across his skin. So he kept staring at it as a punishment for her leaving and a reminder that she'd been here at all. He got up and stumbled toward it. "I'll say when I've had enough."

"No, you'll listen," his mom said, stopping him in his tracks.

The change in momentum was more than his fragile sense of balance could take. He flung his arm out to keep from tipping over, connecting with a chair and sliding down into it.

Holding on to his anger since his dignity had disappeared, he glared at his mom and brother. "You obviously want to say whatever it is that you've got on your mind, so say it and leave."

"You're a moron," Hudson said.

"Maybe," Sawyer said, sounding every bit like an asshole but unable to stop himself. "But I'm still smarter than you."

Helene walked in between them, stopping the argument before it even got started, and halted in front of Sawyer's chair. Arms crossed and her expression grim, she shook her head in dismay. Then she got down to giving him the talking to she'd obviously come here for.

"For the past year, I have been so afraid that you'd go through life without having what your father and I had— love," she said. "You're so busy with Carlyle Enterprises and your blasted big-picture vision that you miss all the little things that make life important. The small moments that combine to make something great. After what happened with your father, I couldn't let you make the same mistakes he did. And I couldn't fail you the way I failed him by not finding a way to make you see that there's more to life than your damned big-picture plan. So I began pushing wife candidate after wife candidate at you and you barely even noticed."

"Oh I noticed," he grumbled.

"Not until Clover came around," she shot back.

Having her memory imprinted on his brain was bad enough. Hearing her name was unbearable. "If you're here to talk about her, you can just leave now because she's gone."

"We're all aware of that," Hudson said. "Irving is a fountain of information."

To everyone but him it seemed.

Helene went on as if neither of her children had said a word. "When your brother told me about this juvenile little plan you came up with to have Clover pose as your fiancée, I was utterly annoyed."

He swore he could smell smoke as the creaky gears in his head jammed to a halt. Eyes narrowed, he turned to Hudson. "I can't believe you told her."

"When you didn't show up to work for the first time in your entire life yesterday, Mom broke out the pliers and battery jumper cables." Hudson shrugged. "She broke me."

Sawyer sank back into the chair, defeat weighing his shoulder down. "Thanks a lot."

Still ignoring her children's sniping, Helene continued, "And then when Linus told me about your absolutely horrible proposal—"

Jesus. Humiliation heated his face to wildfire levels. "Is there anyone who can keep their mouth shut around you?"

"No," Helene said. "Not even your fake fiancée who told me all about your dates to the flea market. I've never met anyone who could get you out of the all-business-all-the-time mindset. But she did. And looking at how you're handling the fact that she left, I can only come to one conclusion. You are as in love with Clover as she is with you."

If he'd had it in him, he would have laughed. It would have been a bitter, mean little laugh but a laugh all the same. Instead, he just sat there like a man who'd been slugged one too many times by a heavyweight boxer.

"Try again," he managed to get out. "She said no."

"To being your *teammate*?" Helene snorted, a sound he'd never heard her make before in his entire life. "Color me shocked."

Why did the women in his life keep getting stuck on that word? Correction. Not women. Woman. Clover was gone. Out of his life. It was just woman now. And that woman was his mom. That wasn't fucking pathetic at all.

"It wasn't like that," he said, the pit of his stomach filling with the kind of dread that only happened when he'd fucked up. "I didn't want her to think that marriage meant the end of her autonomy, her sense of adventure. I didn't want her to feel trapped."

"So instead you made her feel unloved," Helene said. "Well done. Add to that your brother brilliantly interfering by telling her to break it off with you."

"You what?" He bounded out of the chair toward Hudson, swinging.

His brother easily avoided his wild punch before connecting a jab to Sawyer's jaw. Sawyer's head snapped back and pain vibrated through his already aching head. Not that it mattered. His brother—the one he'd always trusted to have his back—had pushed Clover away. Red leaked into Sawyer's vision and he struck out with everything he had. Unfortunately, after almost two days of only alcohol and sriracha-flavored chips, that wasn't much. Hudson bobbed and weaved, then shoved Sawyer hard until he landed back in the chair he'd jumped out of.

"Oh, stop it." Helene glared at both of them. "Sawyer, you'd already mucked it all up before your brother opened his big mouth anyway. No one wants to get married because their future spouse thinks they make a good teammate. Everyone wants to be—and deserves to be—noticed and loved for the little things that make them who they are, the details that make them special. If you love her, those are the reasons why you do and you have to tell her every one."

What bullshit.

All the frustration that had been boiling inside him spilled over. "I do notice all of those details about Clover," he yelled, loud enough that the words reverberated in his head. "The way she chews her lip when she's nervous. The way the sunlight catches her hair and brings out the red you don't see otherwise. The way her brain moves so quick in negotiations. The way she owns a room the moment she walks into it."

His mother lifted an eyebrow but otherwise didn't react to his outburst. "Then I suggest you find a way to tell her that."

All the fight leaked out of him as the realization hit of just how much he'd fucked everything up. If he didn't feel like puking so much, he'd go get the bottle of whiskey from the bar cart and fall back into it.

Helene opened up her purse, reached inside, and pulled out the emerald and diamond engagement ring. "A hotel employee found this in the supply closet and the hotel notified management, who called me. Of course, I immediately recognized it as your grandmother's ring." She held it out to him. "I believe you'll be needing it."

He kept his hands fisted on his thighs and his gaze averted. He'd fucked up. Clover was gone. A ring wasn't going to bring her back. "I won't."

She harrumphed and dropped the ring onto the red bar cart. "So you say."

Obviously deciding that she'd driven the sword in deep enough, Helene motioned to Hudson and they both walked to the elevator and disappeared inside, leaving him alone to stew in his own misery and stink. From where he sat, he could see the ring glimmering as the light streaming in from the balcony landed on the bar cart. He should throw both items over the balcony railing. The thing squeezing his chest tight loosened. He'd never had a better idea. Get rid of them and anything else that she'd ever touched. Then, he could create a new big-picture plan on the clean slate that would be left.

Energized for the first time since he'd left the Bayview Hotel, Sawyer leaped out of his chair and strode over to the closet where he had hidden all of the stupid hiking boots she'd ordered. He piled them high on the bar cart. He reached out to grab it by the handles ready to toss the whole lot overboard and— He couldn't do it. Maybe later, after a shower. That would clear his head, and afterward he'd get rid of anything that even remotely reminded him of Clover. Now that was a big-picture plan.

• • •

Achy but cried out, Clover cuddled deeper under her covers and pressed "Next Episode" on her tablet. So what if she was now three episodes deep in a superhero show about a woman who drank too much and did her best to act like she didn't give a shit about anyone except her best friend.

Perfect for someone who was in a fuck-the-world kind of mood. It wasn't like Clover had anywhere to go or anything to do. She was unemployed. Australia was officially a pipe dream. And she had a hole in her chest where her heart used to be. Plus she couldn't get Hudson's words out of her head about how she'd been looking for her purpose. What was the point of it all? What good was having all of the adventures in the world and helping people if she didn't have anyone to share those experiences with?

Take, for example, her mom. For most of Clover's life, if she'd had to nail down a purpose and a point, it would be to make sure she didn't turn out shackled to a white picket fence like her mom. But after what happened with her dad, she'd seen her parents' life in a new light. They were happy together. It wasn't perfect. It wasn't all sunshine and rainbows. But it was real, it was good, and—she suddenly realized—it was an experience, an adventure, she wanted to have, too.

The credits on her show had just started to run when her tablet screen froze and her mom's face popped up as if she'd conjured her by thought alone, and Clover clicked accept. "Hi, Mom."

"Are you sick honey?" her mom asked. "You don't look so hot."

Thanks for the confirmation, Mom. "No, just considering never getting out of bed again."

Concern put a little *V* between her mom's eyes. "What happened?"

Oh Dios mío, where did she start? Really, there was only one place she could. So, she told her mom about the weirdest temp job ad she'd ever read for a personal buffer then continued on to telling off Sawyer's mom without realizing, landing the job, and then ending up with a fake fiancé. By then she was on a roll and naturally went on to explain how pineapple shakes led to flea market finds and then, finally, to a maybe baby and the world's worst proposal from the man she loved who didn't love her back.

And because the fates were bitches, she was crying again by the time she got to the end of it. "I couldn't say yes."

"Even though you love him," her mom said, her voice soft with sympathy.

"Especially because of that." She hiccupped and wiped her nose with one of the last tissues in the box by her bed.

Her mom sighed, her own bottom lip trembling. "Oh, honey, I'm so sorry."

"It's my fault." She wiped a tear away with the back of her hand and took a deep breath. "I was just so worried about getting trapped in some kind of domestic prison that I never realized I was falling in love with Sawyer until it was too late."

Her mom cocked her head. "Domestic prison?"

"Mom, I've been a complete ass to you." A choked sob had her shoulders shaking as tears streamed unchecked down her face. "You gave up so much when you got pregnant with me and had to marry Dad—"

Clover's voice broke, the need to finally tell her mom everything overweighing any hesitation to peel back the polite covering and finally say what had been eating away at her for all these years. "I never wanted to be like you, Mom. That's why I kept leaving." There. She'd finally said it, but she didn't feel better. She felt worse. Worse than a complete ass, if that was possible. She swiped at her wet face, trying to clear her vision enough to gauge how much those words had hurt her mom.

"I know, honey," her mom said. "It's okay. I know to you I always seemed to have given up everything to be with your father."

"But you did, Mom! No more trips for you. No more adventures. No more excitement. You sacrificed everything and still ended up eating apple pie, which you hate, on a weekly basis just because dad likes apple pie for Sunday brunch. I swore to myself that I'd never end up like that." The tears started falling again in earnest as she realized how she'd short-changed her mom for her entire life. She was the worst daughter ever. "All I could see was all you'd given up, not what you gained, too."

"Until Sawyer."

She sniffled. "Yeah, until Sawyer."

The smile on her mom's face was the last thing Clover expected to see after laying everything out there like she had.

"It's true," her mom said with a gentle shake of her head. "I gave up a lot when I married your father, but I gained a lot more than I lost. Not to mention I didn't *have* to marry your father. I *chose* to because I loved him, and I wanted to spend the rest of my life with him—I still do. You're looking at marriage like it's a zero sum game with only one winner and loser, but it's not like that. There's middle ground. There's compromise. Your father and I have both made sacrifices, but it's worth it because we have each other."

The words hit home in a way Clover hadn't expected. *Middle ground.* That's what Helene had said Sawyer had trouble finding. Up until this moment, Clover hadn't realized she'd been missing it, too, but her mom was right. She had been living her life on an all or nothing loop.

"Do you ever regret it?" She swallowed past the emotion making her throat tight and asked the question she'd been wanting to voice ever since that overheard conversation when she was eleven. "Do you ever regret having me?"

"Never," her mom said, her voice firm. "I love your father. I love you and your brother. Would I have gone globetrotting if I hadn't married your father? Maybe. But if you spend your life just looking for the next big thing because you're so afraid of missing out, then you're bound to miss out on what you already have."

Is that what she'd been doing? Looking so far off into the horizon that she was as guilty of missing the details as Sawyer was? "So you think I should have said yes?"

"Do you love him?" her mom asked.

For all the good it did her. "Yes."

"Does he love you?"

"No," she managed to get out without crying despite the bone-deep pain ripping her up. "He said I'd be a good teammate."

Her mom gasped. "Oh, honey, I'm so sorry, but you'll get through this. You always do."

Yeah, but before she'd never realized she was running blindly. Everything had made so much more sense before Sawyer. "I should have stuck to my original plan and found a regular temp job to pay for my Australian adventure. Then, none of this would have happened."

"You can't say that. Life has a way of working out how it wants to, not necessarily how you imagined it would," her mom said. "And anyway, not all adventures are of the saving the rainforest variety, some of them involve risking your heart—and that kind are just as important."

But a hell of a lot more painful.

Still she couldn't deny her mom was onto something. "Have you always been this brilliant, Mom?"

"Pretty much." Her mom laughed. "But it's good of you to finally notice."

After bringing Clover up to speed on her dad's recovery and telling her she loved her, her mom hung up. The show Clover had been watching popped back up on the screen all dark lighting and even darker storylines. She didn't have the heart for it anymore. Instead, Clover pulled the comforter up higher, wishing she could stay buried like this forever or at least until she stopped missing her heart and the man who'd taken it.

Chapter Twenty-Four

Despite Clover's expectations the sun rose the next day. Birds sang outside her window. People laughed and talked and kissed as they walked on the sidewalk outside her building. Life went on. She could either hole up for another day in her room or start living again.

Determined that if she dressed the part of a woman who wasn't heartbroken that she'd finally start feeling like it, Clover put on her favorite sun dress. Going to the flea market was out—she just couldn't stomach it, too many memories of Sawyer—but the Harbor City Farmer's Market this afternoon was a possibility. She could probably talk Daphne into going with her, maybe they could stop at Grounded Coffee for pastries. And if she was lucky, she'd even make it three minutes without thinking of Sawyer. Then, she'd start working on the next three minutes.

As if the best friend mind meld was in effect, Daphne knocked on her open bedroom door.

"I have a surprise for you," Daphne said, holding something behind her back.

"Is it more chocolate?" she asked jokingly—or as close to it as she could get right now.

Fake it until you make it, girl.

Daphne's smile was strained as she walked in. "Maybe."

Her bestie couldn't make eye contact and looked totally guilty. Whatever she was up to, it didn't have anything to do with chocolate.

"You've had a rough time, so, I got you a ticket," Daphne said, her voice like an announcer telling someone they'd just won a new car.

Okay, she hadn't known what to expect, but that was definitely *not* on the list. "I'm scared to ask, but for what?"

"A trip to Iceland." Daphne held out a printed piece of paper with a picture of the Northern Lights at the top. "It's not Australia and it's only for a week, but it would be a new adventure."

"And I got a ticket to go, too," she continued. "So it'll be a girls' adventure. It's not for six months, but I thought now would be a good time to give it to you."

Clover accepted the paper, her hands shaking just the slightest bit, too emotional to speak. She didn't need Australia—or even Iceland—when she had her best friend. She wrapped her arms around Daphne in a solid hug that beat a pinky promise any day of the week.

"Now is the perfect time," she said, sniffling. "Thank you."

The hug was just breaking up when the doorbell rang. Daphne gave her another quick squeeze and then left to answer it.

She came back into the room a minute later. "It's him."

Clover's stomach dropped. "Who him?" she asked, even though she didn't need to.

"Sawyer," Daphne said. "Do you want to see him?"

Yes. Maybe. "No."

"Are you sure?"

Not at all, but she couldn't be sure that if she saw him now that being a teammate wouldn't start to sound like something she *could* settle for. The truth was she missed him—she *loved* him—and she hadn't stopped just because he'd broken her heart. She couldn't say all that to him or to Daphne. Not yet. So she just nodded yes as if she was sure.

"Do you want me to scare the shit out of him?" Daphne asked, a sly smile curling her lips.

Clover laughed despite it all. "Thanks for the offer, but no. Just tell him to go away."

Daphne left to go get rid of the man Clover loved as she sat on the bed with her head in her hands and tried her best to focus on the printed details of the Iceland trip through her tears. Daphne had been wrong the other night. Falling in love with Sawyer *was* the worst thing that could have happened after she'd answered that damn ad for a personal buffer.

• • •

Turned away from Clover's door, Sawyer spent the next hour in a dark haze wandering Clover's neighborhood trying to figure out what to do next. He didn't have a big-picture plan for this. He hadn't had any sort of plan when he'd gotten out of the shower this morning, passed by the bar cart he still hadn't thrown over the balcony, slipped the emerald and diamond ring into his pocket as a kind of poisoned talisman, headed out of the Carlyle High-Rise and started walking. He hadn't stopped until he got to Clover's apartment, as if it was the only destination possible.

"Slumming it, Carlyle?" a familiar voice called out.

Sawyer turned to see Tyler Jacobson sitting at one of the tables outside a cafe with a coffee and a newspaper. His former best friend kicked the empty chair across from him out and gestured for him to sit down. Sawyer hesitated but spotted the basket of pastries sitting in the middle of the table and his stomach growled. Since the likelihood of poisoning was low, he sat down and grabbed a croissant.

"Does it really matter?" he asked in between bites of pastry.

Tyler shrugged, caught the eye of the waiter across the crowded outdoor eating space, and then held up his coffee cup and one finger. By the time Sawyer was almost done demolishing the croissant, the waiter was at their table with a cup that he sat down on the table. He filled Sawyer's cup and topped off Tyler's before leaving to go help someone at another table.

"So I understand the Singapore deal is all but done," Tyler said.

Singapore? Sawyer hadn't thought about the deal that had been his three-year obsession for days. "Yeah, the trip went well."

"You don't sound as excited as I expected."

"Think about me a lot do you?" Sawyer took a drink of coffee, it was strong, hot, and just enough of a harsh jolt to get his brain back online.

"Where's that cute fiancée of yours?" Tyler asked.

Sawyer flinched and Tyler must have caught it because his eyes widened in surprise for a second before settling into a mocking superiority. "I take it you didn't manage to close that deal."

That was one way of putting it.

"I fucked it up," he said, reaching for another croissant that he ripped in half in impotent frustration.

Tyler scooted his chair closer to the table. "This I have to hear."

"Why do you fucking care?" he snarled.

"What can I say," Tyler said as he picked a raspberry Brioche out of the basket. "I'm invested in your misery."

Fuck. They'd been friends at one point, best friends. What details had he missed that could have saved it? Had he fucked up a twenty-year friendship the same way he'd ruined things with Clover? Not that it mattered. There was no going back. Life didn't give you do-overs. All he could do was step back, reconfigure all the pieces, and create a new big-picture plan. The thing was, he was having a hell of a time imagining one without Clover in it.

"You're a real asshole." But there wasn't any heat in Sawyer's words.

Tyler gave another shrug. "True, but tell me anyway."

So what had he done? How had he ruined it? The

answer was as simple as it was painful. "When I had the opportunity to tell her everything, I didn't. Now she won't talk to me."

"And by *everything* do you mean that you love her?"

"Fuck this." He shot up from his chair. Why was he even talking to Tyler? It's not like they were friends or strangers. They were enemies. "I'm not having this conversation with you of all people."

Unimpressed by the outburst, Tyler stayed sitting. "You have to make her listen. Go all out if you have to, make an idiot out of yourself—God knows I'd like a front row seat for that—but make her listen and don't fuck it up when you get that second chance."

"I'm supposed to take advice from you?"

"Do or don't." Another shrug. "I don't give a fuck."

Bullshit. This was all bullshit. Clover had made her feelings known. Twice. She didn't want him and he didn't beg. Not ever. For anyone. He'd told her that straight out in the lobby at Carlyle High-Rise. He had to get out of here. Away from Clover's neighborhood, from Tyler, from the images he couldn't get out of his head of what could have been with her. Anger and frustration obliterating everything else, Sawyer strode away from the table. He made it three steps before some urge he didn't understand stopped him.

He turned back to the table where Tyler sat with his paper and empty basket of pastries. "I'm sorry. About Irena. About all of it."

Tyler eyed him warily but didn't respond. Shit. Sawyer didn't know where all this was coming from, but it was past time they cleared the air.

"After Mr. Lim signs the paperwork, he said you'll be my liaison with the company," Sawyer continued.

Tyler nodded.

"Then let's start fresh, for old time's sake."

Cynical didn't begin to cover the look on Tyler's face as

he answered, "Are you getting sentimental on me?"

"Just too old to hold on to bullshit." And it was true. He should have realized it earlier. He should have realized a lot of things earlier.

"To new beginnings." Tyler lifted his coffee mug in a toast. "Good luck with your girl."

But she *wasn't* his and that was the problem.

With a nod, Sawyer turned and started walking. He should just go home, but he couldn't get Tyler's advice out of his head. Go all out. He had no fucking clue what that would entail. Then, he turned the corner and ended up outside a fence around a Carlyle build site for a new apartment tower. The outside was completed and a mobile hydraulic work platform was parked in front of it, its scissor legs extended so the platform was at the third-story window—the same level as Clover's apartment. He pulled out his phone and called Amara.

"I need the foreman on the Sixty-Third Street project, my lawyer, and a notary," he told her, the pieces coming together as he talked. "And a pineapple shake from Vito's." He paused to listen to her question. "No, I'm not drunk. I'm getting Clover back."

• • •

Clover taped the printout of the Iceland trip itinerary to her vanity mirror, trying to avoid seeing herself in it. The dark circles, the pale cheeks, the tired turn to her mouth. All of those would go away. She wasn't as sure of the mess inside but before she could fall into that black hole, her phone buzzed. She glanced down at where it lay on her vanity table and her breath caught.

Sawyer: *Turn around.*

Knowing she should ignore him but unable to block

him out completely, she pivoted. Sawyer stood outside her third-floor window holding a pineapple shake in one of Vito's distinctive red plastic glasses. Her stomach did that loop-de-loop thing, and her pulse sped up just at the sight of him. It wasn't fair. Maybe if she could think of him as a teammate it wouldn't be so hard. Of course, if she could do that none of this would really matter.

Promising herself that she wouldn't give in, wouldn't settle for being a teammate, she walked slowly to the window and peeked out. He was on some sort of raised platform like window washers used for the lower floors. There was a man in a suit with him who was holding a briefcase tight to his chest and sweating like he was an inch from the sun and an older woman in a dress who looked like she'd seen it all before and hadn't been impressed by any of it since 1983. On the sidewalk below, people were stopping to gawk. A police cruiser had pulled over and two cops were getting out.

She firmed her resolve, flipped the lock, and opened her window. "I'll take the shake, now go away before the cops arrest you."

Sawyer handed her the shake and laid his hand on the windowsill before she could slam it shut. "Clover, I want to introduce you to my attorney, Barry Crysling, and Delores Nars, a notary. I want to reopen negotiations."

Her heart stuttered, and her fingers tingled from where Sawyer's hand had brushed against hers, but she shoved both reactions to the back of her mind where she'd deal with them later, if at all. "Nice to meet you, Barry and Delores. I hope he pays you well for wasting your time."

She reached up and started to close the window, figuring he'd move his hand or get squashed, his choice, but this had to end. Having her heart broken twice by the same man just wasn't something she wanted to experience.

"I told you once that I wasn't a man who begged or pleaded," Sawyer said, not moving his hand or taking his gaze off her. "You'd put that in our cover story and said that I would for you. You were right. I'm begging. Please, just hear me out."

She hesitated, the window halfway down, remembering the moment in the lobby when it had all still felt like just a fun adventure before she'd gone and fallen in love. "I already have. Nothing's changed. Please don't make this harder than it is."

"Things *have* changed, thanks to several people who pointed out in great detail what a complete moron I was." He took out a napkin with the Vito's Diner logo on it. "I know you have the original, but I think we need to start over." He wrote something down on the napkin and, reaching through the partially open window, held it out to her. "These are my terms."

Her hand shook as she took the napkin and read it.

YOU.

That's all it said. Her chin started to tremble.

"That's really all I need. Just you," he rushed on. "My big-picture plan is to spend the rest of forever with you."

Clover couldn't breathe, but her heart was going a billion miles an hour as the meaning of what he was saying began to sink in.

"Yo, man on the platform," one of the cops yelled from the sidewalk but sounded like he was ten blocks away. "You got a permit for this thing?"

"That's it." Sawyer picked his hand up from the windowsill, leaving nothing to stop her from closing the window on him forever. "That's the whole thing. I can't make it happen without that, so name your terms."

Her terms? She didn't have terms. Everything they'd put on that napkin at Vito's—it was a game, a ruse, part of their fake engagement. None of it had been real. But this? God help her, she believed.

"Sir," the cop yelled again. "I'm gonna need you to

come down now."

Both of them ignored the officer as Sawyer reached in his pocket and pulled out the emerald and diamond engagement ring and went down on one knee.

"I'm not asking you to think about it, Clover. Not again. I'm asking you to marry me because I love you. I love the way you laugh at the same spots in the movies as I do. I love that you could find the secret hidden charm in a million flea market finds. I love that you turn everything into an adventure that I want to go on with you. I love the way you chew your bottom lip when you're anxious. I love that you curse in other languages. I love that you're the first person I want to see in the morning and the last one I want to touch at night. I love that even without saying a word, you've out-negotiated me. Every time. I love you, Clover Lee."

• • •

Sawyer held his breath, watching Clover as she stood behind the half-closed window. Barry was covered in flop sweat behind him, the crowd was getting bigger below him, and the cops were calling in for a ladder to bring him down. He didn't care. The only thing that mattered was the woman in front of him. He'd put it out there. He'd gone about as big as he knew how. Now it was all up to her.

And she wasn't moving. Or talking. Or doing anything but staring at him with a look on her face that he couldn't decipher.

His gut twisted and the engagement ring suddenly weighed a million pounds.

Wracking his brain for something—anything—else to say, to do, to promise he came up empty. This was it. He'd made his play and failed. He dropped his gaze to the platform floor, dropped the ring back in his pocket as he stood up, and opened his mouth to tell Barry to hit the button that would lower them down when the window began to inch open.

"Don't tell me you're going already," she said as she started to climb out of the window.

Relief swept through him as he took her hand and helped her out onto the platform. "I'll stay for as long as it takes."

"And if that means forever?" she asked looking up at him.

"Then forever it is." In fact, nothing had ever sounded better to him.

She sniffled and wiped away a tear from her cheek. "You broke my heart."

He gathered her close, offering up a silent pledge to do whatever it took to make it up to her. "I'm sorry."

"Don't ever let it happen again."

He hooked a finger under her chin and tilted it up so she could look at him and know he meant every word. "Not in all the forevers."

"I love you, Clover Lee."

"I love you more," she said, rising up on her tiptoes and wrapping her arms around his neck.

"I think that's something we'll be debating forever, honey." Dipping his head lower, he kissed her and thanked the fates and God and anyone else who was up there for getting him here because the big picture he'd been looking at all these years had been only a narrow glimpse of the possibilities of what could be. With Clover, he saw so much more.

Epilogue

Three Years Later…

The crowd at the Carlyle family cocktail party had changed. Instead of unmarried socialites and champagne glasses, it was family and…champagne—it was still the Carlyles after all.

Sawyer looked around, unable to stop noticing all the details that made his life so much more than it had been before. Clover stood next to him, her hair shining in the setting sun. Laura Lee and Phillip were laughing at something Hudson said while his fiancée rolled her eyes and chuckled. He'd always known his brother was hiding something, he'd never have guessed just what it was because he'd never looked close enough. Big brother fail for sure. Details mattered and thanks to the woman by his side he wouldn't be missing those any more. Clover's best friend Daphne was there, too, still looking a little jet-lagged after the girl's trip to Nepal they'd taken. And then there was Helene who was chasing little Michael with his chubby toddler legs around the grand piano. Mikey, as they called him to differentiate Sawyer's son from Sawyer's father who Mikey was named after, had a handful of birthday cake mashed in his right hand and was running full speed ahead, just like he had from the day he took his first step. Like his father, there was no walking for that kid.

"You know, I think if my dad had lived to see this he would have changed his favorite view," Sawyer said, curling an arm around Clover's waist and drawing her in close. "I know I have."

She smiled up at him. "There's nothing quite like seeing your mom with apple crumb cake handprints on her Dior skirt."

"I don't think she's even noticed." The woman who'd spent her adult life scaring most of Harbor City's society had become putty in the hands of her grandchild.

"Well, if she didn't notice that I'm wearing these," Clover lifted her hiking boot clad foot "then we can definitely say she's baby crazy."

"Maybe we should take advantage of that by letting her watch Mikey while we take a trip to South America," he said, the plan already coming together in his head. "There's a group in Peru that's setting up a women's business collective. I hear they need a negotiator to work out a deal with some international distributors."

"Let's do that next month," she said, her eyes sparkling with that something that had sucker punched him the first time he'd set eyes on her.

"I know that look. That's usually one that has me agreeing to things I never thought I'd say yes to."

She shrugged nonchalantly. "I think we need to work on a project to keep Mikey from getting lonely."

"You want to take him with us?" He wasn't against it, but he couldn't shake the feeling that wasn't what she meant at all.

"Nope."

Understanding dawned. "Number two?"

She winked at him. "Let's make that happen."

"But what about all the travel I promised you before we got married? You've only gone through one of the seven pairs of hiking boots I'd hidden away."

"There will be plenty of time for that." She raised herself up on her tiptoes, bringing her face within kissing distance of his. "A whole lifetime."

How could he say no to that? "Deal."

He dipped his head and kissed her, knowing he'd been out-negotiated again and not caring at all because he'd still won. They both had.

Acknowledgments

Where to begin? Well, I have to start with the bucket of paint provided by Liz Pelletier, who if she doesn't already regret giving me her cell number probably should. Thank you for turning what started out as a sad little conversation into a fabulous book. Of course, *The Negotiator* wouldn't have come into being without the hard work of the entire Entangled Publishing team. Huge thank yous to Erin for a gorgeous cover, Greta for amazing copy edits, Riki for marketing expertise, and the good people at Social Butterfly for helping to promote it. As always, I couldn't have done it without my partners in crime Kimberly Kincaid and Robin Covington. You two are the weirdest, most bizarre people in the world and I wouldn't have you any other way. Love ya! Then there is the Fabulous Mr. Flynn and the Flynn kids who not only help make this dream of mine a reality, they make me laugh harder than I thought possible, too. I don't deserve you, but I'm keeping you anyway. Last, but not least, a huge thank you to the readers. Without you I'm just that weird girl in the corner who makes up stories in her head. xoxo, Avery

Keep reading for a sneak peek of

69 Million Things I Hate About You,
a new standalone novel by Kira Archer.

After Kiersten wins sixty-nine million dollars in the lotto, she has more than enough money to quit working for her impossibly demanding boss. But where's the fun in that?

When billionaire Cole Harrington finds out about the office pool betting on how long it'll take him to fire his usually agreeable assistant, he decides to spice things up and see how far he can push her until she quits.

Chapter One

Kiersten Abbott jogged on her tiptoes after her boss, Marie, trying to keep her heels from clacking too loudly on the marble tile while still managing to keep up.

Moving at high speed through the office, laden down with coffee cups, coats, bags, briefcases, file folders, laptops, and any other number of items had become second nature to Kiersten. She handed off two of the three coffee cups to her besties who worked in the same office, Izzy and Cassie, who each mouthed "thank you" and quickly went back to looking busy. Marie wasn't technically their boss, but she was the first assistant to Cole Harrington, president and founder of Harrington Enterprises, the biggest think tank and development firm in Manhattan, which made her a sort of supervisor over Izzy, Cassie, and the rest of the assistants in the office. Kiersten was second assistant, which made her Marie's go-to girl. All the work, none of the credit—that went to Marie.

"Keep up," Marie said over her shoulder.

Kiersten jumped, almost spilling the remaining coffee in her hand, and hightailed it to catch up to Marie, who was marching straight for the dragon's lair.

Kiersten made it two feet inside before the sight of Mr. Harrington froze her. The man was on his treadmill, in a pair of loose sweatpants that fit low on his hips, and nothing else. And from the looks of him, he'd been on the thing a while. A few beads of sweat ran in rivulets down the hard-planed muscles of his chest and abs. And whatever the hell those amazing *V* muscles were called pointed in stark relief to what one tabloid had called "the treasure every woman in Manhattan wanted." Kiersten had scoffed when she'd read that. Seeing everything up close and personal had her rethinking her skepticism.

When one errant drop slipped beneath the band of his sweatpants, Kiersten nearly lost her grip on the coffee. Lucky little sweat drop.

Marie handed Mr. Harrington a towel and followed him to the bathroom hidden behind a cleverly disguised wooden panel in the wall. She stood outside the door, grimacing at the sound of the shower turning on. After a minute or two, she finally spoke, raising her voice to be heard over the running water.

"Mr. Harrington, I'll be out of touch this weekend, but Kiersten will be on call for you and—"

The water cut off and his voice floated through the door. "The conference is this weekend, and I'm the keynote speaker," he said. "I need you there. It'll be much easier to reschedule your thing than it would to change the conference at this late date."

"My *thing*?" Marie took a deep breath, her fists clenched at her sides. Oh shit. She was going nuclear.

Mr. Harrington came out of the bathroom, buttoning a fresh shirt. "Yes. Your thing. Whatever it is, cancel it. Change it. Move it. I don't care."

"My *thing*, as you call it, is my *wedding*," Marie shouted. "I've told you about it repeatedly. I've spent over a year planning it. It can't be rescheduled."

Kiersten's jaw dropped. No one yelled at Mr. Harrington. Hell, no one even questioned him.

"If you can't fulfill your job obligations—"

Marie flung her hands up. "Don't bother firing me. I quit!" She tossed a ring of keys and a phone onto his desk and marched out, pausing only long enough to grab her coat and purse from her own desk. "Oh my God, that felt good." She glanced at Kiersten and snorted. "Good luck."

And then she breezed out, with a spring in her step and a smile on her face.

Kiersten stood rooted to the spot. She risked a glance back at Mr. Harrington, who was slipping into his suit jacket and coming her way.

"Oh shit," she whispered under her breath.

He finally pinned his gaze on her, looking her up and down, and she prayed he hadn't heard her. Those eyes of his were startling. She'd never gotten a close enough look to really see the color, and the steel gray with a darker ring of almost black surrounding them was unexpectedly mesmerizing. He took his coat and coffee from her.

"Who are you?"

"Kiersten, sir." Her voice was barely audible, and she cleared her throat. "Your second assistant."

"Well, Kestin, you've just been promoted. Let's hope you last longer than the last three."

She opened her mouth to correct him on her name, but before she could, he was already firing orders at her as he went back to his desk and started packing up his briefcase.

"I have a meeting in twenty minutes with my project manager, and after that I should have dinner reservations at…"

He frowned and Kiersten piped up.

"Le Bernadin, sir. Your reservation is for eight o'clock."

"Thank you. Confirm that, and clear my schedule for the rest of the evening."

At least her first task was an easy one. "I confirmed it this afternoon, Mr. Harrington. You're all set."

Working with Marie had been great training. She'd pretty much been running Mr. Harrington's life anyway. Only now she had to deal with Harrington himself. The prospect sent jolts of terror and excitement zinging through her. She could finally show what she was made of and get credit for the work she was already doing. Not to mention a nice raise. Her bank account would be happy to see that. The forty-three dollars currently sitting in there would love the company. And if she had to spend her days glued to the side of her asshat of a boss, well, at least he was easy to look at.

"Wonderful," he said, turning those piercing eyes of his back on her. He stared long enough that she dropped her gaze, looking down to see if she'd spilled something on her blouse or had forgotten a button or something.

Nope, nothing wrong. She met his gaze again and this time didn't look away. Yes, the man practically made her shake in her knock-off Louboutins, but there was no reason he needed to know that.

His lips twitched with a hint of amusement. "Call me Cole."

Kiersten blinked at him. Marie had never called him by his first name. No one did.

"Mr. Harrington makes me feel old. I don't look old yet, do I?" he asked in that charming bedroom voice of his that she could swear would melt M&Ms while they were still in the bag.

Her eyes flicked over him, making his lips twitch further. "No, sir."

"No 'sirs.' Just Cole."

"Yes, sir." Damn. She couldn't stop.

He made a sound that might have been a snort and then turned back to his desk to grab his briefcase. "Here," he said, handing her the phone Marie had left. "Keep it with you at all times. I keep weird hours. Consider yourself on call. All the contacts you'll need should be in there."

He paused for a moment, his brow furrowing. "Get ahold of HR. Tell them to send over the paperwork for your new position, and we'll make everything official. I'm assuming you know where Marie kept my calendar and all the other information you'll need."

Kiersten nodded, but he wasn't really paying attention

to her as he rattled off more instructions. "Make sure you're up to date on all my pending contracts and current projects. We've got deadlines to meet, and I have no intention of missing anything because of this ridiculous upset. If you need help with passwords or anything to get into the computers, get IT up here to get everything changed around. See security on your way out for your new badge. You'll need an upgrade to have access to all the floors and offices."

He stopped and glanced back at her. "Shouldn't you be writing this down?"

"No, sir. I've got it." Thankfully, she was quick on her feet and had a memory to match. Clearly, Mr. Harrington, er...Cole, was going to keep her hopping.

"Cole. And I hope so." He went back to gathering his things, moving about his office like a mini-tornado looking for a place to land. He grabbed the ring of keys Marie had left and tossed them at her. "These should get you into the building, all the offices, my apartment, and anywhere else you might need access to. I don't know which is which, so you'll have to figure it out. My security company will need to be notified to change the passwords for the keypads at my apartment. You'll need to be there for the voice recognition and fingerprint software to be updated. There should be a list of people somewhere on Marie's desk who'll need to be notified that you're my new assistant. Make that happen. I don't want to deal with delays on anything while we argue with someone over whether or not you're authorized to have the information. Switch Marie's plane ticket and hotel reservation to your name for the conference this weekend or make your own reservations if needed. I assume you're available to go."

He gave her a look that would freeze a polar bear's balls, and she nodded. Thankfully, she had no life. She'd rather be making money than sitting at home with Ben & Jerry's.

"Good," he said. "You'll need to change her info to yours for anything else conference related. Also…" He stopped and grimaced a little. "Make sure Marie's benefits remain in place until she finds new employment, and put a reference letter on file for her. In fact, one of the firms I met with last week is looking for someone. Send them a recommendation. Also, authorize a severance package. And double the usual amount."

He gathered up the rest of his stuff and headed for the door. He paused just before he walked out. "And send her a wedding gift."

Kiersten's jaw dropped again, and this time Mr. Harrington—Cole—did give her a smile. "What? I'm not always a dick."

"Not always, but often," Mr. Larson, Cole's partner, said from the doorway where he'd apparently been waiting. He smiled and winked at Kiersten. Cole brushed by him, muttered, "Don't even think about it," and kept on going. Mr. Larson shrugged and followed him out, leaving Kiersten standing there staring after them, shell-shocked, her mind still trying to process what had just happened.

She'd been thrown into the deep end, no doubt about it. On the bright side, her salary would nearly double. Then again, she knew she'd be earning every penny of it. Cole Harrington was the dream of practically every woman in the world. Young, gorgeous, richer than God, and in many opinions more powerful. He'd developed one of the most popular dating apps around, almost before he was old enough to date himself, owned entire islands, gave generously to charities, and loved puppies and children. Everybody loved him—except the people who worked for him directly.

The phone in her hand buzzed a notification before she could even finish the thought.

"And so it begins," she muttered.

Chapter Two

"So, new assistant, huh?" Brooks Larson, Cole's longtime friend and business partner, sat across the table, nursing the dregs of a glass of wine while looking at him with that gleam in his eye he always got when he had an ulterior motive.

"Yes. And?"

Brooks shrugged. "Nothing. You just go through them pretty fast, especially for a guy who refuses to sleep with his secretary like any other self-respecting CEO."

Cole sighed and pushed away his half-eaten dinner, focusing his attention back on the files on his tablet. Brooks had been his best friend and business partner for the better part of a decade, but the man had no filter. "This isn't 1950, Brooks. She's my executive assistant, not a secretary. And she's there to *work*, not get hit on by a sleazy boss. Mixing business and pleasure is a good way to fail at both. Besides, I need my assistants focused on work, not me, or shit would never get done."

"I thought you *were* their business."

"My business is their business. My personal life is off-limits."

Brooks shrugged. "If you say so. Though I'm not sure how you get anything done with the revolving door you've got going on. What did you do to piss off Marie?"

"I needed her to work the weekend."

"And she quit over that? I thought that was part of the job description."

"It is. She had plans."

"What kind of plans?"

Cole took a sip of his water and went back to staring at his tablet, not wanting to answer. But he knew Brooks wouldn't leave it alone. "Her wedding."

Brooks stared at him like he'd grown two heads. "You expected her to cancel her own wedding so she could work?"

Cole grimaced. It sounded so much worse coming out of Brooks's mouth. "She knew I needed her at the conference. It was nonnegotiable. Why the woman would book her wedding the same weekend is beyond me."

"Did it ever occur to you she may have had the wedding booked long before the conference was set up? Women plan those things years in advance."

Cole sighed again and scrolled through the file on his tablet. "I didn't give it that much thought. At some point, she would have realized they were the same weekend and she should have changed her plans. Her job was to make my life easier. I paid her very well to be at my beck and call. It was not my job to accommodate *her*."

Brooks's brows rose, and Cole squashed the slight twinge of guilt that tried to take hold. Yeah, he'd been an ass. What else was new? Didn't change the facts. "I extended her benefits and doubled her severance package, neither of which I had to offer at all since she quit. But despite her failings, she was a decent assistant. While she lasted."

Brooks shook his head. "You sentimental devil, you."

Cole ignored that. "Don't you have work to do?"

"Always. Now, back to this assistant problem you have."

"I don't have an assistant problem. That's one of the reasons I've always got more than one."

"Right. You're the king of backups. Always have a backup for everything and you never have to worry about being without, right?"

Cole shrugged. "It's worked so far."

"Fine, so get another backup. This one is seriously hot."

"I hadn't noticed."

"Then the first thing you should do is have her schedule you an eye appointment. I thought you were busy, not dead. She has that sexy librarian thing nailed."

Cole wasn't blind. Or dead. He was lying through his teeth so he didn't have to put up with his friend giving him shit. How the hell Kiersten had been in his building without him noticing her, he'd never know. His only excuse was that Marie must have been hiding her or keeping her so busy she never managed to be in his presence. Because one glance at those big brown eyes staring up at him, her thick blond hair just begging to be released from her tight bun, had his body screaming.

Brooks was still rambling on. "Even her name—Kestin—so close to kiss—"

"Kiersten."

"What?"

"Her name is Kiersten, not Kestin."

"Then why did you call her Kestin?"

"Because I didn't catch it when she said it, and that's what I thought it was."

"She didn't correct you."

"I know."

"Why?"

Cole sighed again and flicked his finger on the tablet a little harder than necessary, sending the digital pages flying. "I don't know. You'd have to ask her."

"Hmmm, maybe I will. Maybe over dinner at—"

"No." Cole glared at him. Brooks wasn't going to get near Kiersten, even if Cole had to set her up with a full-time bodyguard.

"Jealous already?"

Cole rubbed his forehead, trying to stave off the ache that talking to Brooks often brought on. "Good assistants are hard to find. As you rightly pointed out, I have a hard time keeping them around. It's bad enough with my first assistants, but the second assistants rarely last longer than a month. But from what I can tell, Kiersten has basically been running things since she was hired. Marie had her doing everything already, so there won't be any irritating transition period to disrupt my life. I don't want you chasing her off and have to go through the trouble of training someone new, especially since I have yet to hire someone to be her backup."

"How'd you find out her real name?"

Cole held up his tablet. "Had HR send over her file."

"Anything interesting in there?"

"Yes. Now go away."

"Why? Do you have a hot date showing up?"

"I don't have time to date."

Brooks scoffed at that. "You need to start making the time. Maybe it would loosen you up a bit."

Cole ignored that. He had no trouble getting a date when he needed one for whatever function he might need to attend. But he rarely let his associations get too involved. It worked great. He had the company of a beautiful woman when he wanted it and his life to himself the rest of the time. No fuss, no future.

He'd yet to meet a woman who inspired any hint of desire to change his MO. The sudden vision of big brown eyes blinking at him sprung up. And wouldn't leave. He shook his head in irritation and did his best to shove Kiersten's image to the back of his mind.

"Dating makes women clingy," he said. "I don't do clingy. I do work."

"Yes, I've noticed," Brooks said, his voice thick with an implied eye roll. "What about that woman…Betsy or Becky or…"

"Rebecca."

"Yes, her. You dated her for a while."

Cole frowned, irritated at the reminder of his last

girlfriend. She hadn't worked out any more than the others had. "She objected to the prenup."

Brooks raised an eyebrow. "There was talk of a prenup? I didn't realize it had been that serious."

"It wasn't. But she started hinting around, so I showed her the prenup. That's usually enough to get them to lay off the wedding nonsense."

"Why? Prenups are fairly standard procedure for someone in your position."

Cole sighed. "Because my prenup isn't standard. We both agree to leave the union with what we had when we entered it and with what was individually made during."

Brooks's eyes widened. "In other words, they'd get nothing."

"Correct."

"No matter the reason for the breakup? Even if you cheat?"

"Correct."

"And if you die?"

"Then our union would be very decisively over."

"Well, obviously, but—"

"It doesn't change anything."

Brooks blew out a long breath. "Well, no wonder they don't stick around."

Cole frowned again. He knew his prenup was a bit unorthodox, but he had his reasons. He'd had it drawn up after he'd made his first hundred million...and had his heart broken by the first woman who'd been more interested in money than matrimony. It had taken several million to keep her from writing a tell-all book and selling it to the highest bidder. Now, his girlfriends signed non-disclosure agreements and anyone even hoping to be more than a girlfriend was going to get the prenup. So far, none had stuck around long enough to actually use it.

"I don't see why it's such an issue," Cole said.

Brooks laughed. "Really?"

"The woman would be marrying me, not my money. She'd get to enjoy a certain lifestyle during the marriage, of course, but if the marriage ends, I don't see why she should continue to enjoy what I worked hard to make, especially since the women I date typically make a better-than-average living on their own."

"You're never going to find someone who will agree to that."

"Someone who loved me more than my money would."

It was always the same. They all wanted to be Mrs. Harrington. Not because they loved him, but because, as his wife, they'd have better access to his fortune. A hefty settlement if it didn't work out. Widow money if they could stick it out for the long haul. Bonus money if kids were ever a part of the picture.

Hence the prenup. He'd probably never follow through with it, not that he'd admit that to Brooks. But it didn't matter, since so far no one had ever loved him enough to try it out. A document stating they got nothing was enough to make them all run.

"Well, good luck with that," Brooks said.

He finished the last swallow of wine in his glass and wiped his mouth. "I don't need luck. I just need to focus on work."

Brooks shook his head and gave him that motherly look that made Cole cringe. He glared and Brooks laughed, holding his hands up in defeat.

"All right, all right. I'll leave you to it. I've got a few late night plans to get to anyway."

Cole couldn't hold back an indulgent smile. "What a shock."

"You're just jealous," he said. He drained the last of his wine and stood to leave. "I'll see you tomorrow."

Cole watched him leave and then turned back to

his files, doing his best to ignore the now familiar twinge of regret that poked at him. His life was what it was. He occasionally wished he had someone, but they all wanted one thing, and it wasn't him. Sometimes he didn't know why he bothered. But hell, even moguls got lonely.

He sighed, gathered his things and shoved a few hundreds into the restaurant's billfold, and walked out into the night. Alone. He was better off that way. At least alone he couldn't get hurt, used.

Discover more Entangled AMARA titles...

NIGHTINGALE
a novel by Jocelyn Adams

Darcy needs to be taken seriously as a journalist, so she's set on interviewing reclusive millionaire Micah Laine. Micah proposes a deal—the bigger the secret he offers up, the bigger the cost he'll demand—a secret of her own, her wildest fantasy, a kiss. And that's just for starters.

HOT FOR THE FIREMAN
a novel by Gina L. Maxwell

When Erik Grady's chief at the fire department mandates therapy for supposed PTSD or a permanent desk job, Erik has no choice. But this doctor is not what he expected. She's curvy and hotter than a four-alarm fire. And he just happens to have firsthand experience with her curves. Of all the men to walk into psychologist Olivia Jones's office, why did it have to be her one-night stand? But she's a professional. And if he demands three dates before he'll change therapists, she'll date him, all right. It's time to see how much heat this fireman can take…

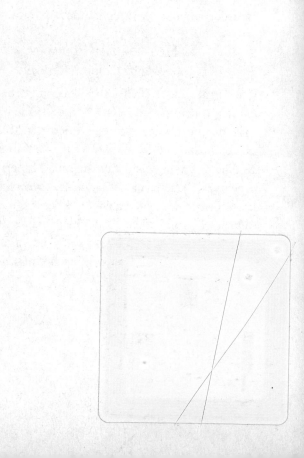